CW01390821

Gritstone

Alan Newcombe

LEAF BY LEAF

Published by Leaf by Leaf
an imprint of Cinnamon Press,
www.cinnamonpress.com

The right of Alan Newcombe to be identified as author of this work has been asserted by him in accordance with the Copyright, Designs and Patent Act, 1988. © 2024, Alan Newcombe.
Print Edition ISBN 978-1-78864-890-5

British Library Cataloguing in Publication Data. A CIP record for this book can be obtained from the British Library.

All rights reserved. No part of this publication may be reproduced, stored in a retrieval system, or in any form or by any means, electronic, mechanical, photocopying, recording or otherwise without the prior written permission of the publishers. This book may not be lent, hired out, resold or otherwise disposed of by way of trade in any form of binding or cover other than that in which it is published, without the prior consent of the publishers.

Designed and typeset in Adobe Caslon Pro by Cinnamon Press.
Cover design by Adam Craig © Adam Craig.
Cinnamon Press is represented by Inpress.

About the Author

Alan grew up in post-war London with Canadian and English parents. He witnessed the transition from the drab 1950's in a city littered with bombsites to the seismic burst of colour in the late 60's. His own memories of that era feed into the stories of his characters in his debut novel *Gritstone*.

Alan's writing encompasses a fascination with people's shared history and family heritage—but also concealment, the limits of friendship, and living outside any law.

Gritstone is set in the Calder Valley, an area Alan has known and visited for many years. The landscape lends itself to the Gothic undertow in the novel.

Alan currently does therapeutic work in schools. He plays saxophones on the free music scene in London which is now more vibrant than ever, performing with players who are pushing the envelope. He is married and has lived near Epping Forest for over forty years. He continues to lose himself there.

To Cathy

Gritstone

Napoli

October 2019

It's never too late. They say it's never too late.

The sun is disappearing. A few figures like black paper cut-outs drift along the edge of the shore. I'm lying on a recliner outside a fly-blown beach café a few miles from Naples. It's late October, the end of the season, and the locals have stopped coming. The bar is closing soon and I've ordered one more cold beer. I close my eyes and the crowded events of the past months become frozen images, stills from a film, shifting past like the shadows on the sand. I used to think I was a well-meaning person, but I'm living a life of pretence and concealment now —much more than Al ever did.

I'm on the run. I'm sixty-eight years old and I'm on the run.

It's never too late.

Gritstone House

13th May 2019

We were driving to Gritstone House in Hugh's yellow Scimitar, barrelling along past Rochdale on the final leg of the journey. The sky so dark the night seemed to have arrived hours too early—blackened clouds edged with deep purple. There had been heavy showers but the occasional sickening skid didn't deter Hugh.

I was still in the same crumpled corduroy jacket I'd been wearing three days ago when I walked out of my home and put the key through the letter box. I'd sent a final text to Siobhan, '*Going away. No plans to be back, Mike,*' before dropping my mobile into a neighbour's bin.

I had some written directions to Gritstone on my lap. Hugh didn't believe in satnavs. His fine dark grey hair was blowing back in the wind, as he drove with the window down to stay awake. We had left late and now knew we wouldn't arrive at Al's estate much before evening.

'Did you ever go to see that band Al managed?' Hugh spoke out of the side of his mouth as he veered round a plodding Morris Oxford. Neither of us had seen Al for years. Remembering his past again was mining an endless seam.

'*The Savage Boys*. Once. Seems like half a lifetime since we saw them…' I could remember that former cinema, grime ingrained into the stucco, sticky tables and tacky floors. We were submerged into a crowd of mostly guys in sagging jeans and enormous t-shirts. Siobhan and I were easily ten years older than anyone else. Apart from Al, who wore a beautifully cut black Nehru jacket. He introduced us afterwards to the bemused group staring out from under their New York Yankees baseball hats.

'He'd latched onto hip hop before it really came over the pond. The band were from Kent, weren't they?'

'Yeah.' Hugh was sliding through the gears. 'Not exactly from the 'hood …but Al was able to coach them… give them that edge. Always seemed he could turn straw into gold.'

'Rather like the Stones really.'

'Nah, they were nothing like…'

'I mean they came from Kent… well Jagger and Richards did.'

'Remember when we were young, you could only listen to either the Stones or the Beatles? Like supporting football teams. And I loved the Stones. They did some great stuff.' Hugh's blues singing of 'Lil Red Rooster' echoed past a cyclist who pulled his bike onto the hard shoulder to avoid the slipstream from the Scimitar.

'Hugh, are you at all familiar with the word *caution*?'

Hugh didn't appear to hear. 'We saw Al's group at the Corn Exchange. Lily kept asking where the drums were …I didn't know either…' The mention of Hugh's ex-wife put ten miles onto the speedometer. Hugh's car was pretty well all he had left from a former life. He'd found the Scimitar in a scrapyard. It was a time when he knew people who could save it. He still had a little money then. But when Lily finished with him, he went quiet and moved into his cabin cruiser. This was going to be the Scimitar's last ride for a while. The MOT was running out tomorrow. Hugh seemed unconcerned. He only said, 'We'll tow it to a garage when we have to.' I had a familiar sinking feeling—that Hugh expected me to come up with the money to bail him out yet again. But I was carrying hardly any cash and not sure how I'd get more.

'Al dumped them very suddenly. Always the first to end anything.' Hugh moved the conversation on from the future of the Scimitar. And I remembered seeing a large picture of the shocked faces of the boyband in a pseudo showbiz gossip-column in the *Guardian*.

'He wanted you to go to Nicaragua with him, didn't he— to fight alongside the Sandinistas?' It still rankled Al had never asked me, even though I would never have dreamed of going.

'Well, Mike, I didn't feel...' Hugh went awkward. The car slowed.

'And you didn't go...'

'I was with Lily then. She didn't want to go to a war zone.'

'No...' Lily and I never got on. She always looked drawn and tense when I was around. As if *I* was a bad influence on Hugh.

'I think Al looked down on me a bit after that.'

'He called you a poser if I remember.' I took a guilty pleasure reminding Hugh.

'Was that it? I didn't know about that.' Hugh grimaced at the road. He had somehow managed to forget Al's verdict on him.

'Al expecting to go there and fight ...well it was kind of an ask though.' I'd had a call at the time from Al to say he'd started training on a rifle range, *'I'm ready man!'*

'Asking him to stick around to pick coffee for them wasn't going to happen either.' Hugh slowed as he noticed the sign for five miles to Hebden Bridge.

'He can't have been used to rejection. In fact, I think it's the only time when he was rejected. Actually said '*No*' to.'

'But you know, Mike, Al was a sort of hero to me.'

'I know he was. But that's a long time ago.'

'Well…' There were roadworks and Hugh juddered to a halt at the temporary red light. The engine idled. 'He probably still is… you know… a hero.'

Hugh put his foot down as the light went green. 'Automatics are so tame. Without gears it's not real driving. Anyway—yeah—when he came back and decided he needed to make money, somebody like him didn't need too long to get rich.'

'It was hedge funds, wasn't it? Not that I know what a hedge fund is. But whatever, I reckon he could always smell the blood on the water.'

'That house by the sea. Did you ever go there? I only went once or twice.' Hugh tended to invite himself and then take time leaving. Al told me that persuading Hugh he'd outstayed his welcome could be like prising a limpet from a rock. I didn't tell Hugh *that*.

'I went once,' I said. That gleaming sheet of reinforced mirropane glass stretching along the front of the house looking over the beach, reflecting the incoming tide. Watching Al at work, doing all his dealing from home. An enormous screen on the living room wall, with grids and shifting figures, numbers turning from red to green. Al seemed relaxed about it all, sipping a glass of red wine. Not like those pictures you'd see of guys in the City, all strained faces holding two phones. He'd just say that in the end, it's other people's money.

'Siobhan would take Maddie there for a week in the half-term hols.'The sound of those cosy diminutives made me realise how these everyday phrases were now part of a past I had no place in. How could I explain myself to Maddie? What was Siobhan thinking of me right now? I momentarily embraced my vengeful feelings for Siobhan, in all their grubbiness. 'I want her worried. I want her to be scared shitless…' and then felt awkward and guilty.

Hugh was unaware of my introspection. He pressed down the accelerator on the empty stretch of road. 'Anyway, he hasn't told us much about his *fiancée*.'

'You keep on calling her that.'

'Well she is, isn't she? It's just the word *fiancée* and Al don't seem to inhabit the same universe. I'm slowly getting used to this alien idea. But I just imagine she'll be like all of Al's other women.'

I had a vision of an unvarying series of tall statuesque women processing past like Banquo's female descendants.

'I don't know Hugh. I mean they're both living in this community. I can't really see those other women putting up with communal living. And he's never even mentioned the possibility of marriage before. I think she'll be a bit different.'

'Founding a community. Getting married…' Hugh shook his head. 'It's weird. I can't connect any of it to Al.'

'It doesn't feel like him.'I had the nervous itch that Al might have become some unrecognisable born-again mystic. Anything seemed possible with him.

I reminded Hugh we would keep the wedding presents in the boot. We had bought two large copper-bottomed saucepans at some retail park in the Midlands. I didn't have too much cash after that. Naturally I paid for both pans.

We were nearing Hebden Bridge and I was looking for signs to Heptonstall. Once we got there, Al had said everyone knew where Gritstone House was—but he'd said it wasn't on a satnav—and the post went to a PO box. His email hadn't said much. 'They've got some funny ideas about us, but I don't care. We're doing okay and I'm making amends for my past.'

The Scimitar laboured up the steep road from Hebden Bridge and ground to a halt in a car park in the village. We wandered down the main street, past the stone-wall cottages, limestone blocks bounded by thick layers of cement. We found a small pub. It was the only place open where we could ask the way. The rain had made it a quiet night. Faced with just five regulars leaning on the bar, we looked like the interlopers we were. I felt self-conscious about my lived-in clothes. I used to be told, if people were in a kind mood, I had the build of a medieval miller. I'm thick-faced and stocky. Since that time at Gritstone I have lost weight. I'm big boned, and now I can look imposing. But that night, my belly sagged nonchalantly over the edge of my trouser belt. The tongue from my shirt dangled down my back. Hugh still looked youthful despite the lines stretching down his thin face and invading his cheeks. His squarish steel framed spectacles magnified his eyes, staring out in vague surprise as if permanently trapped in a goldfish bowl. A thick fisherman's sweater sagged over his lanky frame and skinny jeans.

We were going to need their help so I bought a round of drinks for the group by the bar. The moment we asked for Gritstone House the stories started. Up there they danced naked in the garden. A man in a dress runs over the fields playing a flute to the goats.

'Sounds like William Blake.' Hugh murmured.

'The guy—Al isn't it? He bought it cheap and gutted it. Were a farm when he took it over. We 'eard they got some posh wood-burning range cookers put in now. Used to cook with an open fire. We don't see much of 'em…well mostly we only see the guy.'

'Yeah, I wouldn't go there, mate. Last place I'd want to end up.'

'Well, we've come for Al's wedding. We're just staying for a few days.'

'Oh… he's getting married…'

There was a hesitant silence. The barman tried some verbal Polyfilla.

'So, what do you guys do?'

'Not much. Used to be a college lecturer. I'm living on my pension now… and Hugh…'

Hugh made a face.

'Hugh lives on a boat…'

'It's hardly moved for years. Just have to change the moorings from time to time.' Hugh had this self-deprecating drawl.

'And you're…' stating the obvious to me, 'You're not from round here. Can't place your accent.'

'Sort of Midlands. I've lived in a few places.'

'He's just left his home and walked out on his wife.'

'Hugh…' I spoke with more weariness than irritation. The people in the bar began staring into their glasses.

We scribbled some directions to what someone called the 'crazy house' and left quickly. It was dusk as we drove up out of the village along an empty road through open farmland. We turned into a long bridle way, cobbled but sprinkled with ruts and holes. The car was shaken from side to side but Hugh wouldn't reduce his speed. I felt my pelvis was about to disengage.

'Hugh can we drive slower?'

'I'm driving Mike. I drive at the optimum speed.'

The headlights illuminated two stone gateposts with rusted iron hinges. There was no gate. Beyond, at the end of the track, the black bulk of the house melted into the dusk. Candlelight flickered around the edge of a door that had been left ajar. A fire caressed a wall through windows that looked the size of postcards.

We crunched through the thick wet gravel at the front of the house and halted close to a vast door. Above a knocker shaped like a brass hand was a crude Jacobean carving of a garlanded river god. We could see a nameplate over the lintel. The words were indistinct in the dwindling light.

Hugh offered the result of his brief scrutiny of the river god.

'It looks like Al.'

We pushed open the hefty oaken slab. Across the hall, we could see through into the kitchen. Thick candles, white towers of wax, melted at either end of a long trestle table. Two figures were silently hunched over bowls.

The slim shape of a woman wafted by in a tie-dyed dress that brushed the monumental stone flags.

'Hello. Is Al here? We 're looking for Al.'

She didn't seem startled by the two specimens wandering through an open door. As she approached the candlelight illuminated criss-cross lines on her cheeks, the deft etching of crow's feet around the eyes.

'We're old friends. Mike and Hugh. We've come for the wedding. Al said we could stay here beforehand.'

She opened her mouth. I noticed some front teeth were missing. Words that seemed about to form were interrupted by staccato blows from the floor above. We both looked up the bare wooden stairs to a landing. Striding above us was a giant figure wrapped in a goatskin coat, hammering the floor with a six-foot long shepherd's crook. We hardly noticed that the woman had quietly disappeared.

'Where is my acid …who has taken my ACID?' The voice possessed an innate Teutonic precision but also an extreme anger. The shepherd's crook battered at a series of firmly closed doors. Lynyrd Skynyrd's 'Free Bird' echoed somewhere in the house. Otherwise there was no sound. A face stared down at us, vulpine with straggling black locks.

'You have taken my acid.'

Any resolution I had quickly drained. I profoundly wished I had some acid to assuage this demon in animal skin. But Hugh seemed dangerously careless of terror. He looked up and called, 'We've only just arrived.'

'What do you mean, *just arrived*? This is not the Savoy hotel. I am descending these stairs to search your bodies.'

I was tempted to run. But I knew I could not run fast enough from a seven-foot giant. The enormous shepherd's crook was approaching down the stairs with all the menace of the figurehead on a Viking longboat.

'Helmut, these guys don't have your acid.'

Al had emerged from a door just above us in blue denim dungarees. Unlike Helmut's unruly locks, his hair was coiffed and curled with a requisite bounce.

'And you know we never take acid on our own.'

'But Al, how can you know these strange old men?'

'I know these old guys.'

'You mean… you are as old as them?'

And there was reason to doubt. Al's body was wiry and muscular. His face unlined in the candle light. I couldn't help wondering if he still used the same moisturiser that was so rare forty years ago.

'Helmut, they have just arrived. They wouldn't know where it is kept.'

'I would still like to search their bodies.'

'It's not necessary. Listen. You will get an extra allowance and perhaps you shouldn't be using it on your own anyway.'

Hugh gave me a questioning look at the mention of the word 'allowance.'

'Al I can look after myself now.' There was disappointment and a petulance you might show a parent.

'Nobody can look after themselves. That's what we're all about.'

I now felt relaxed enough to look at Al. He had a thin face, longer than most, the nose dominant and sharp tipped. The hair flowed long and grey and probably had been brushed in the moments before appearing on the stairs. The eyes were of an alert hound. As he spoke, he seemed to be attending to Helmut's aura, not simply listening. His soft South Yorkshire accent was still present, but overlaid with a complex of other tones and places, hints of pretty well any English- speaking country. Al spoke with the patience of an experienced angler and I could almost hear the reel singing as he talked Helmut down. Helmut mollified, slunk off to his room somewhere across the courtyard. I couldn't help imagining a stable with straw that needed changing. Al turned to us.

'Don't worry about Helmut. He's harmless… at least when I'm around. Don't know how he got his hands on the acid. Need to sort that out. God you both look knackered… or just older. Didn't Siobhan come with you? She coming later?'

'I…' I felt knocked off-balance.

'Mike?'

'Look Al, I just walked out. Your mail—it was kind of a catalyst.'

'What…' Al was open-mouthed.

'…'

'You mean you just left her and came here?'

'Kind of…' I had been here all of five minutes and already felt Al was making my profoundest actions sound like pathetic gestures.

'And what's she going to think of me?'

'It's nothing to do with you, Al.'

'You don't get it, do you Mike? I look like I'm harbouring you, giving you an escape route. You've left Siobhan, man! You're absolutely crazy.'

'Look he must have his reasons,' Hugh intervened with a lameness born of years of making excuses.

'Oh…I suppose so.' Al shook his head in disbelief.

'We'll talk about it tomorrow,' I offered. It was my only possible offer.

'Yeah okay, it's your affair, Mike. Suppose you need to crash out. Edith'll show you the rooms we've got for you.' Al put his arm around the woman in the tie- dyed dress, 'Edith's my fiancée.' As Edith mutely nodded, her hair poured forward covering most of her face.

'Well congratulations Edith. Really wish you both well.' Hugh smiled, glad the altercation about Siobhan was over. I murmured something indistinct and vacuous.

'We'll hang out tomorrow, yeah?' Al turned and disappeared into a room just under the stairs. As the door closed, I could see a blue light from a screen playing on drawn curtains. The door clicked shut and a lock turned. There was an odd beeping, then silence.

Edith gestured to us to follow her to our rooms on the ground floor. Hugh closed the door and I heard the bed groan. Edith opened the door to my room. It was sparse, more like a monk's cell than a bedroom. There was a table, a single bed, and a wooden chair on a bare floor. After Edith closed the door, I noticed a chamber pot under the bed. I assumed at the time that it was some kind of humorous ornament. The wall above the bed was dominated by a mandala, a fresco painted onto the plaster. In the middle sat a twelve handed god with figures dancing around the circumference. The door, walls and ceiling were a light green. I'd noticed Hugh's door was painted a light blue pastel.

A mirror hung from the door and I held the candle to it. What had been thick grey stubble was now the first stages of a straggly beard. The beginnings of a stranger stared back. Etched lines flowed from the edge of my eyes over my cheeks like river channels stretching from the open sea.

'I could be some sort of mystic… a wise man.' A search with the candle revealed no plug sockets.

I collapsed onto the single bed. The past few days had

been a speeded-up film. And now the frame had frozen, reality crashed into me like a winter tide. My marriage was finished. I had jumped out into the clear air. Perhaps I had expected the sensation of floating downwards, arms spread, buoyant in the moments before the chute opens, like a leaf in a gentle wind. But now the ground was screaming towards me.

Siobhan still had her own beauty. Her face was so soft. It was as if there were the finest down beneath her skin. The faces of some of her friends were raddled with deep grooves, the damage of dramatic diets. Siobhan didn't diet. But her skin was still delicate. She was sparing with makeup. There was no coarseness when you touched her face, when you kissed her cheek goodbye. She enveloped herself in a bewildering variety of long wraps above hugging jeans, a presence that still expressed voluptuousness. While I simply looked hang-doggedly fat.

I couldn't tell Al or Hugh. I couldn't tell anyone. Siobhan had stopped sleeping with me months ago. There was somebody she was seeing. I only had suspicions who. But whenever we were together the words for that question just wouldn't surface.

Still, by simply living in the same house I felt there might be some chance to repair our marriage. Alone in the spare room, I knew that touching myself would only be a joyless substitute for the experience we both had shared. Eventually the body would take its course and I'd wake to find semen soaking the sheets. But the dream was always of Siobhan. I couldn't tell Al or Hugh. I couldn't tell anyone. I'd let it all go wrong.

Siobhan, Al and Me

July 1971 to November 1972

Another hot night in the city. I walked the wine dark streets in the late evening. The air was stiff without a breath of wind. Windows forced up as far as the sashes allowed, gasped for air. An air so dense you could be wading through it. Thick Levi flares and baking polyester underpants chafed sweat welts onto my thighs. But this discomfort was normal. I hardly gave it a thought

I had circled the area for half an hour before knocking on the wide-open door. She descended the stairs barefoot. The wood hardly creaked as her feet depressed the boards. I hadn't thought this through. I was simply drawn to her door. Siobhan said without surprise, 'Mike… I thought you might come tonight.' I followed her full thighs in negligently sagging jeans into her room.

The candle flames transformed our bodies into dappled shadows and golden skin.

There was a slowness, a timelessness. Her hair was a long, thick mane, a blanket over full lips, large eyes patient, restful—on the edge of sullen.

After that night we saw each other fitfully, even though the memory of Siobhan crept through my blood stream. There was *someone else*. Al was a head taller than me, with his ranging walk and long flowing blond hair that never looked remotely greasy. When I was with them, Siobhan would dextrously remove the nonchalant arm Al placed on her shoulder and quietly look at me. Before anyone knew we were involved, it felt we were both part of some delicious secret.

Al booked all the concerts at the students' union. He wore a floppy purple fedora, floral shirts with enormous curled collars and the widest flared jeans I'd ever seen. Before the start of a gig he strolled onto the stage, leaving a trail of smoke from the joint languidly burning in his hand. He always announced the group as if he owned them. And they were big names then. Led Zeppelin, Deep Purple, and the Who all toured the campuses.

Al sometimes talked to me as if I was some bog-standard mop top, about his industrial level of conquests. In an age of groupies routinely trailing bands, Al's attitude to women didn't seem so abnormal to the average guy propping up the Union bar. He handed out passes and tickets in return for perfunctory sexual favours. Later if the women passed him, he acted as if they didn't exist. I'd read at least part of *The Female Eunuch,* and certainly enough to feel a creeping unease when Al invited me to collude in his worldview: 'So many of them are just squaws, Mike…'

Siobhan was different. She asked no favours from Al. If anything, she could seem contemptuous of him. She didn't want to see the hairy-chested music at the Union. She preferred playing old blues records on her Dansette to squeezing into the hall to hear the second-hand version offered to the young middle class in the making.

Siobhan was born into a monied Irish family from the South. They were deeply traditional Catholics. She told me she kept it from her parents that she had stopped going to mass. When she was younger Siobhan only knew England as a place women, including some of her friends, were forced to go for abortions. And now she was here as a student, it was as if the cloud of guilt the Church bestowed on everyone had been lifted. She found a refreshing quality to being anonymous, where nobody, rather than everybody, knew your family. No, she felt freer than she had ever been. She'd say that men like Al might fantasise that they had some hold on her. But that was their problem. And she seemed to feel I was a little different.

I didn't possess Al's dangerous charisma. But she told me she liked it that I didn't have the condescending certainty of a lot of guys, that my ideas never seemed clear-cut and off the shelf—yes, she liked that. And she thought I wasn't bad looking in some of the smart new stuff I'd taken to wearing. No, she told me that for a while she couldn't make her mind up about me. But she found her thoughts returned to me. And she felt I changed after my mum died, more mature, less anonymous than the other men in identikit flared denims and ex-army greatcoats.

I remember it was a metallic grey February afternoon. I was working on an essay in a modern hall of residence with rooms like identical hutches. There was a knock on the door. A porter handed me a telegram without looking at me, and walked away as soon as I took it from him. Telegrams were generally bad news. This was no exception. It was from my uncle. He told me that my mum had died suddenly. I needed to get back as soon as I could. I threw a suit into a case and drank a double whisky at the draughty station bar.

I took the train down to Coventry, to the prefab I'd

lived in with my mum on a small estate left over from the war. I'd loved my childhood there. I used to play with the other kids on the bomb sites near my home, vast craters and crumbling mysterious brick. Traces of wallpaper still clung to the inner walls. I knew mum could remember the neighbours who had been killed there, but she hardly spoke about them to me.

I'd no memory of my dad. He'd died when I was three. Alf had worked in the car factory, but I knew very little else about him, apart from that he'd fought in the war. My dad remained a perpetual ghost in the black and white photos taken on our Baby Brownie camera. He was always wearing the same suit.

When I'd left for university on the coach to the north, mum was renting a colour television and spent most of her day wandering between two channels. She never watched BBC2: 'Just for posh people, not for us, Mike.' She was proud of me, the first in our family to study for a degree, and told me not to worry about her. I phoned home less and less often from a freezing call box. Even if I wanted to, I couldn't share my new life, and she sounded increasingly remote and sad. I went home for only a few days at Christmas. It was only later I realised why her face became a rigid mask when she believed she was unseen. At the beginning of February, her body caved in more quickly than the doctors expected, from the metastasis feeding on her.

When I arrived back in Coventry, I was immersed in an unfamiliar adult world. I had to register the death. A man in a stained brown suit, shined at the elbows and cuffs, solemnly gave me a certificate after recording the death in meticulous copperplate.

Then to the undertaker's where the plastic flowers in the window needed dusting. I'd sat in the office with my Uncle Charlie and was shown a brochure of coffins. I'd chosen the cheapest. I later found out that it was the model used by the council for the so-called paupers' funerals. It was made of plywood for all I knew, but it would soon be burnt. The undertaker began to look upset and offered me a polished box with brass handles 'that somebody didn't need.'

Afterwards, I had a drink with Charlie. The pub was two streets from the prefab. We were in the empty public bar. The thick fug of Woodbine smoke ingrained into the walls brought back the memory of my first beer here when I was fifteen. Nobody was concerned about my age then. Charlie had this rather emphatic way of talking.

'You don't know too much about your dad, do you Mike? God he was a troubled man. He couldn't let go of the memories of the fighting. The war destroyed him in the end. Your prefab only has these thin walls so everyone could hear his screams in the night. They shook the whole neighbourhood. Your mum told me he often dreamt of bayoneting a German soldier as they stared into each other's faces. Well it's over now… twenty-five years.

'But us people, people like your mum and me, who went through the war—we were stoical—too stoical. We don't talk about it. I don't think she ever said much to you, but what happened here were a nightmare. They laid out bodies in rows after the first raid.'

I remembered my mum mentioning a mass grave, but I hadn't taken it in.

'I once saw a dog running around with a baby's arm in

its mouth. Even your mum—it were hard for her. She'd find bits of somebody... a leg with a shoe on... you know... her neighbours. We had no words we could find for it. It stays with you, though... but your life seems so different now. I envy you, Mike, I really do, with your long hair and your marijuana and that strange music. I just hope you never get to see what we saw.'

After a bleak fifteen minutes at the crematorium, everybody was relieved it was over. A rent-a-vicar had taken a few facts from me shortly before the ceremony and then celebrated my mother's life. It sounded a dull life by any standards, but you couldn't convey her unaffected simplicity that often cheered me up. Even this short committal was enough to make everyone feel remote from the body that was my mum being wheeled off to the furnace once the curtain closed.

Back at the prefab my aunts laid on tea and sliced white bread sandwiches; clammy ham and tomato, tinned salmon and cucumber, grated cheese and Branston pickle and a bowl of Smiths crisps. There were cocktail sausages and a salad of lettuce, cucumber and beetroot. Heinz Salad cream coagulated sickeningly with the beetroot juice on the discarded plates. Nobody stayed that long. The aunts screwed up and threw away the paper table covers and cardboard plates. Once they had washed the cups, I told them I had no use for the tea service. I asked if they wanted to share it. They became confused. Nobody gave away their tea service. In the end my Auntie Margaret offered to look after it for me, just to put an end to the embarrassment. They left, mumbling a plethora of phrases that were all folksy and useless. I kept a few sandwiches for the journey. I hadn't plans to stay the night in the prefab.

After the last aunt left, I was finally alone in what had been my home. The rooms populated by my mum were draining of meaning. The remains of my childhood were evaporating. I crumpled into her chair, head in my hands, rocking forward. Unheard sounds were coming out of me. Short, choking and hacking noises. Then a quiet moaning wail. It felt uncontrollable. It felt like it would never stop.

But I had to leave in a few hours to catch the last train back that night. I forced myself to go into each room. My face was soaked and shaking. I picked up the objects I'd want to keep and put them into her cardboard suitcase. Her brush, which still had straggling grey hairs in the bristles, her plaster donkey from Weston, and her three wise monkeys on the beige tiled mantelpiece. Then I lifted down my grandad's picture from the wall by the door.

It was taken in 1912. He was wearing a straw boater and a five-button jacket. It should have looked so carefree, but the photographer had encouraged him to maintain some solemn dignity as he leaned against a fake tree in front of a crudely painted screen, and waited for the exposure to complete. He'd ended up looking soppy and pompous. Two years later Grandad had watched the Scharnhorst gunned down and sunk near the Falklands. There were hundreds in the water. They could hardly save anyone. It was what happened to sailors then. He never talked about it. I remembered him in his flickering gas-lit house, always in the same brown cardigan, puffing on the briar pipe that probably killed him when I was ten.

I pulled out the biscuit tin from under the bed, a collection of the photos from the Brownie. Small two-inch square black-and-white snaps. Here were early photos of the dad I never knew in uniform, grinning inanely. And mum in an ill-fitting coat that did for about ten years.

Here I was at seven. I looked at the camera grimly and dutifully in the new school uniform I wore most days, whether I was in school or not.

And aged eleven in a pair of cheap jeans and my raincoat that had to do for any season. I had been excited to get a pair of jeans. But they were cheap and scratchy and I mostly ended up wearing my school trousers. In the picture I was standing in the high street. Chip-paper and cardboard were clogging the drains by my feet. People threw everything into the gutter then. Behind me, men and women in uniformly long drab overcoats pushed past me. They seemed to wear them whatever the season.

I swept up my mum's Buddy Holly and Bill Hailey singles. It all sounded so tame. I caught the last train north that night.

My mum put by some money for me. Somehow she'd saved a few thousand. Enough for me to never have an overdraft at university again. I could just about buy a flat. I returned to Coventry once, to have the prefab cleared by a second hand dealer. I can only remember the man speaking to me through a masticated egg sandwich. I never went back again. The suitcase was still in the house in London I'd abandoned. I shoved it into the loft when we moved Maddie into her own room. I don't know where it is now. Siobhan has sold the house and moved on. If she put the case on a skip, it's all I deserve.

When I came back, I had more money than most. I was able to take Siobhan out for the occasional meal in the city centre restaurants. She wasn't overly impressed but never refused. When we were out, I even wore a wide-lapelled herringbone suit with trousers flaring from the knee. I couldn't help but stand out from the sea of blue denim. Siobhan found it kind of independent and funny. Sometimes we spent the night together at the end of the evening; I never told her how much that meant.

One night we were in a newly opened bistro covered with black and scarlet flock wallpaper. I had passed it in the daytime and booked it out of curiosity. Once we arrived, I felt I'd made a fatal mistake. But Siobhan was unconcerned. The other tables were peopled with easily embarrassed diners terrorised by starchy waiters. We were served veal in a sad grey sauce with overcooked broccoli. But the food ceased to matter to me. I was lost in Siobhan's relaxed laughter bubbling through the room like a brook bursting out of the ground. After the food, we sat over the watery coffee, and as often happened, I found myself probing her feelings about Al. Even as I tried to sound casual.

'I mean I do kind of envy him. Al's kind of charismatic. You know he's come into a room before you even see him. There's that fizzing atmosphere in the air.'

I suppose I was tempting Siobhan's derision.

'Well I never seem to quite be in his force field somehow… not like some of these girls. It's like watching iron filings shooting across and sticking to his *oh so magnetic* personality!' Siobhan chuckled and skittered her fingers across the table cloth. There was melody in her laughter.

'But that's the thing, Siobhan. You're a challenge to him…'

'Oh yeah, like some wild mare he's trying to break in. Yeehaaah!'

Some old couples turned and stared at the young uninhibited Irish girl in her shawls and jeans.

'Kind of…' I felt a sort of pride sitting with this young woman, so relaxed in her skin, amidst the ramrod stiffness. Siobhan lowered her voice and leant towards me.

'Mike, you know sometimes I still do sleep with him… when I feel I'm in control.'

'I know… I mean you're nobody's…'

'Do you mind me telling you these things?'

'No…'

'Because I'm no one's squaw.'

'No.'

'I know you care about me, Mike.'

'I…'

'Not now…'

'I…'

'Don't say it—you don't need to say it.'

Seven months later Siobhan told me was pregnant. I thought we'd been careful, but these things happen. By now we had virtually moved in together. Al had drifted away. I offered to marry her immediately. I couldn't stop myself saying it and she looked at me with a seriousness and sadness I couldn't fathom.

'I want you to be the father of my children, Mike.'

Meanwhile, Al hitched off to Marrakech. The word was he had gone to score enough *kif* to pay his debts. He returned in time to attend the wedding at the local registry office. Weddings could be pretty low-key affairs then. There was no grand reception, no stag night in Prague, no hen party lasting five days. It was frankly unusual anybody like us, under the age of twenty-five, got married at all. Al insisted on paying for the drink with his new money. Nobody wanted to ask where it came from.

Siobhan's family were sour about the civil ceremony. They saw no reason for it not being a Catholic solemnisation. I was left in tatters by Siobhan's mother. She didn't think much of Hugh as the best man. He couldn't find the ring for endless seconds, and seemed incapable of simply standing still. She'd met Al several times and said to whoever would listen, what a fine-looking man he was. She told me he had 'something about him,' as she stared brutally at me out of tiny narrowed eyes framed in a face of leathery skin, stretched over what seemed an oblong box.

She asked if I had a job at all. I dutifully told her I was beginning my doctorate. We'd have my mother's money, along with the bursary. We should be okay. I just sounded like some lame plodder. It didn't seem enough to satisfy her eyes wandered across the room to our other friends, John and Ruth, both leaning against the wall talking together, making no attempt to mix, but replying politely if someone approached. John was already the successful entrepreneur, with a burgeoning mail order stationery business. His success would contrast brutally with the travails of Hugh's village shop, where window envelopes and notepads with pictures of sad donkeys on the front, were curling with age.

Meanwhile Al was laughing away with some of Siobhan's aunts and uncles. The family still talked about the time he travelled to Ireland with her. I couldn't measure up to the dashing man regaling them with tales of the Marrakech souk.

'It's a labyrinth—and you get sucked in. The place kind of encompasses a whole world. It's full of things you never knew you wanted—and it goes on for miles and you feel you won't find your way out—and the alleys start looking alike—and then you realise you've been past the same stall three times. But if you even begin to look lost, some of these guys are onto you. And they tag along and try to sound helpful. And then they offer to get you to the main square—or the leather market is a classic con, cos you really are lost if you end up there — and then they want money for *showing you round*—100 Dirham and it can get nasty—they can get quite threatening—and their friends can suddenly appear…'

'And what did you do, Al?' His languid drawl hooked them in effortlessly.

'I needed to go there on business, so I never went into the souk looking like some hippy. I'd dress smart in Marrakech—and I'd look the guy in the eyes—and I'd name this captain in the gendarmerie—you'll always get someone's name if you ask the right questions at your hotel. But you've got to be confident—I'd tell this guy I'm going to the police and I'll pay them to pick him up—and put him in a cell for the day—and then truncheon him senseless. He'd generally sidle off slowly like some cat avoiding a fight. They don't expect you to con them—they think we're clueless.'

'Well, anyway Al, you saw them off then,' one of Siobhan's aunts said slightly uneasily.

'Kind of…'

And whatever they may have thought about Al threatening a beating to a man in Marrakech, I wasn't anywhere near able to carry off the louche act the way Al did. I just looked somehow staid, but not respectable either. Siobhan was having too good a time on the dance floor to notice any of this.

Leave this World

14th May 2019

In the morning I woke to find the light from the uncurtained window picking out the bulbous eyes of the twelve handed god glowering at me from the mandala. I looked at my wristwatch, still on my arm—I'd been too exhausted to take it off last night. It was almost nine o'clock. I'd dozed from around 6.00 when I'd heard a clamour of feet on the bare wooden staircase, doors clicking shut, the pump in the yard cranked. There wasn't much talk, but I could hear Al's voice echoing from the kitchen. He seemed to be delivering a short speech. There was some laughter and then the thumping of boots on the cobbles.

I got out of bed in the long smock I found by the pillow. Through the window I saw a group silently performing slow graceful motions in the yard. Al was among them, absorbed, his arms and legs forming parabolas in the air, followed by statuesque balancing, the limbs still, a fluid moment frozen.

I changed from the smock into my grubby chinos and last night's shirt. Beyond the large stone flags in the entrance hall, the floor of the house was bare polished wood. The boards were often uneven and most steps emitted creaks or low groans. In the silence of a virtually empty building, sounds reverberated as if the house were listening to itself. The walls were a whitewashed plaster over thick stone. It was a place that in bright sunlight would be filled with shadows, sharp geometric angles of darkness. I experienced a kind of claustrophobia, as if the house was compressed, not spacious. 'Maybe it's my mood,' I thought. And at that moment the truth crept up and ambushed me. I had no other home to go to.

Six of the rooms on the ground floor were bedrooms. Each door had a different pastel shade. The door to one room was ajar, and painted onto the wall above the bed was another mandala, this time of dancing women surrounding a Krishna figure.

From the kitchen, I heard the gurgling and bubbling of hot water. On two stoves, lids of enormous saucepans rattled like exotic and intricate percussion. I had a towel and a bronze bowl I had found in my room. But as I approached the Belfast sink, I realised there were no taps.

I'd overlooked any possibility of a house without running water. There were pipes snaking down the outside wall. But when I walked round the exterior later that morning, I found tanks that captured rain water from the roof gullies. Part of the floor near the window in my room had been concreted over. A lavatory bowl had probably stood there: and the taps for a sink as well. The pipes and sinks had been removed. The house was returning to its origins.

I raised a trembling saucepan lid. There was a ladle to scoop out boiling water. I filled the bowl and left it to cool. Edith had silently entered the kitchen. She opened a cupboard and brought me out a sponge, and a functional slab of carbolic soap. I washed my face and asked where the toilet was. I had realised the chamber pot I had found under my bed last night was no humorous ornament. A tall gangly figure was carrying two brimming pots into the walled garden on the other side of the courtyard.

I turned to Edith. 'Why's that guy taking the pots into the garden?'

She replied rather cryptically, 'We don't waste our urine, Mike.'

'Okay, but there is a toilet?' I didn't want to admit I had tipped a full chamber pot through my ground floor window during the night.

Edith found me a pair of crocs that were just a little too large. She motioned me through the kitchen door, and led me across the yard. The stones were slippery with a thin sheen of mud after a recent shower. We went through a gate in the fence and into the neighbouring field. At the far corner was a wooden hut that could have been a herder's shelter. Edith left me to sit on something resembling a lifebuoy, a rubber ring supported by four thick wooden posts. Below lay a six-foot hole. The excrement emitted a vague gaseous steam when I looked down. The faecal stench was mitigated on this visit by a strong gust of wind blowing through the hut.

A bale of year-old newsprint announced its function. Neatly cut pieces hung from a string above an open bucket of screwed up paper balls. I was startled to find Helmut standing outside as I flipped up the latch.

'*Morgen* Mike. I have always my shit at this time.'

I nodded a greeting. Helmut seemed quite amiable today. I murmured '*Alles gut*', uncertainly to the giant in goatskin. I still felt timid after Helmut's ferocious welcome of the night before.

'*Ach, Sie kennen Deutsch!*'

I could only say, '*Nein, bitte,*' which didn't sound quite right. Helmut looked disappointed and I went back across the field in some confusion.

The cast-iron pump dominated the centre of the yard like an ancient idol. The spout bent its head, the handle curled like a hand resting on a hip. The yard was raked in a slope so the water flowed to the central drain at the foot of the pump. The handle creaked and I washed my hands in a freezing gush.

Several zinc baths hung from a bare space of wall by the kitchen window, like a row of giant beetles. As I returned from my field trip, I saw a tall stocky woman with grey frizzy hair and a wide chin, unhook one and take it to a ground floor room. She returned to fill two large buckets with hot water from the range, and then another one of cold from the pump.

Hugh ambled in from the hall giving out cheery 'Good mornings.' Edith didn't look up, but intently stirred a saucepan of porridge. I gave him directions for his first visit to the earth closet. Hugh strode across the yard and confidently disappeared along the path. He returned a shaken man.

'How can anyone put up with the stink in that place. What are they going to do with all that shit? Reminds me of one of those cess pits at the festivals. I remember there were these long planks that went on for several yards and you'd sit down and there'd be guys staring at you from the opposite pit… and you'd look into a ten-foot-deep trench full of shit… anyway this board at the Isle of Wight began to bend…'

I wasn't going to speculate with Hugh where he thought the communal excrement would end up, but I felt Al would probably find a use for it—and it would involve Helmut.

I suggested a short walk in the fresh air before

breakfast. Hugh tagged along. He said you didn't go for walks if you actually lived in the country. A bewildering variety of crocs and wellingtons were set out on shelves by the front door. Somebody had hosed them recently, and they dripped into a puddle on the stone floor. Hugh and I both still had the crocs Edith had given for our latrine visits. I asked Edith where my shoes were.

'We don't go out for walks. We don't discuss it much but Al wants us to avoid the locals. Al says he doesn't want them asking what goes on here.' There was that singsong quality of a true-believer in her diction. It reminded me of the tone some of my students fell into trying to lecture me sternly about politics from a playbook of second-hand ideas —'What you need to realise Mike is…' I'd always found it easier to place a cheesy grin on my face and not argue—but not today.

'Edith, they've got plenty of funny ideas already…' And that was from only ten minutes in the pub.

'Well I'm not sure. Al feels they would make up even more stories.' Edith was fiddling with her bead necklace.

'Look, you've got my shoes somewhere. Can't I have them?'

'I don't know Mike. I'm sorry but I do have other tasks now.' With that, Edith's skirt swished away.

When Edith was out of earshot Hugh whispered, 'So they can't even leave the fucking grounds.'

We found better fitting crocs and decided to just go outside the house and look around from the top of the valley. We pushed open the monolithic door. Hugh was alarmed when he couldn't see the Scimitar. Last night he'd parked it on the gravel. I told him I'd noticed the bonnet stretching out from a stall in the stable block. Hugh couldn't be sure how he gave Al the keys. As we crunched across the gravel, Hugh speculated without much concern what he would do now the MOT had run out. He seemed to rather like the idea of having to stay here a while. I had nowhere else to go, but that realisation didn't prevent a creeping unease that we were marooned.

Hugh kept stopping to shake out small stones that were caught in his crocs. The house clung to the top of the moor. The walls were of thick austere blocks, two-foot square. The surface of the stone had been partially blackened from the time when soot from the factory chimneys had choked the valley. There were no ornamental touches. The lintel was three monumental stone slabs.

We now saw the valley in the daylight. Beyond the gravel, the front lawn merged into gorse. We peered over a mile down to a river cutting through the ravine. Squat trees and bushes hung from the edge of the slope where blackened mould elided with green moss on the boulders. A steady drizzle idled towards us from the other side of the valley. We decided to turn back to the house.

Above the brass knocker in the shape of a hand was the oblong sign we had not been able to read last night. Three words were carved into the polished wood: 'Leave this World.'

We returned to the kitchen for our breakfast. The oak table was long and narrow, wide enough for only one person to sit at each end and perhaps fifteen on either side on two long backless benches. The table had probably been there as long as the house. The surface was marked by serrations from centuries of knives.

At the end of the table near the kitchen door was a Jacobean chair with the same crude carving of the River god above the head rest. I guessed rightly that it was seen as a kind of throne for Al when they sat down for meals. I plonked myself on one of the long benches opposite Hugh. I imagined I would upset Edith if I had sat in that chair even when Al wasn't in the room.

Edith handed us two sturdy plates. A freshly baked wholemeal loaf lay on a breadboard and beside it a large jar of conserve, a mix of thick figs. Edith took a butter dish from a tiled larder. I had realised by now that there could of course be no fridge. When I looked around the kitchen walls, I could see the marks of plastered-over holes where the electric points had been.

We were offered a resemblance to coffee in chunky cups. I murmured to Hugh that this was like the *Kaffee-Ersatz* the Germans drank in the last World War, made out of crushed acorns—or it could have been dandelion seeds. Anyway, the coffee alone would have forced me to surrender to the Allies.

Toni, a diminutive woman with small gold ear-rings, short purple hair and a rather formidable physique in her dungarees, came in from the yard. Hugh bade her a greeting she brusquely ignored. She informed us that while we were staying at Gritstone, we would be on a rota to bake bread with the rest of the residents. Toni would induct Hugh tonight and he would pass on the knowledge to me for the following session. Hugh thanked her for including us in the community. She clearly saw this was facile politeness, and told Hugh they must be ready for ten o'clock that evening. They would prepare the loaves and allow time for the dough to rise for baking first thing tomorrow morning.

'First thing?' queried Hugh.

'Five o'clock. I hope I'm no' lookin' at a slacker I generally know one when I see one. Most bakers are up well before then.'

After we'd eaten several slices of the moist bread with the conserve, Edith presented us with two bowls of porridge and a jar of honey. As our spoons were poised above the bowls, there was a click followed by the unmistakeable electric beeping we'd noticed the night before. As the door by the bottom of the stairs clicked shut, Al strode into the kitchen and planted himself in the Jacobean chair. There were no pleasantries. But then there hardly ever had been.

'Mike, I still can't believe this. You've left Siobhan. I mean, how could you do that?'

Hugh became absorbed in his porridge. I churned my spoon distractedly. The sticky impenetrable mass in the bowl began to resonate with me.

'We've been in separate rooms for months. I dunno, she just said it was because I snored all the time and she needed to get to work after a decent sleep.'

'Well do you? Do you snore?'

'Kind of… it might be the weight I'm carrying.'

'Yeah frankly you are. But you could've done more about it, Mike. You needn't be like this. I mean, I look after myself.'

'Well you always did.'

'You were quite good looking.'

'Yeah… were.'

'Still could be. God Mike, how could you?'

I was sinking into a dull, sullen mood. 'She's seeing someone else. Once I was sitting in the kitchen and saw she'd left her phone near the chopping board and I realised —that slim piece of metal holds all her secrets, all those little whisperings to this other. And I thought it would be the matter of a moment—I could go over and enter her secret life. But I didn't want to — didn't want to know.'

'But you *don't* know!'

'When I left a few days ago, her bed hadn't been slept in for three nights.' I was starting to feel I had been here before where I found my conversation with Al turned into an interrogation, where he forced me to justify my every action.

'If she's met someone else Mike, I just feel it's your fault fair and square. You've let yourself go, man.'

'But Al I'm in my late sixties.'

'I don't care. I reckon Siobhan isn't like some tub of lard on legs. I'm sorry that's a bit harsh—but I'll bet she's still beautiful. Probably some younger guy who's bowled over by her.'

'Yeah she is… still.' Didn't dye her hair, there were no concessions to aging, no catastrophic facelifts. She wasn't scared of age and age had backed off from her.

'Hope she comes to my wedding anyway.' That distant idea became an inevitable reality screaming closer and closer along the tracks.

When I looked up, Al had disappeared back into the downstairs room.

There were two frescoes opposite each other. One on the wall by the door into the hall; the other between the kitchen window and the back door. Both were about a yard in diameter: mandalas of red and black wheels, as if about to violently spin with the figures of gods and people frozen in the moment before they were thrown into chaos.

I couldn't remember the intricacies of the symbols, but when Hugh asked, I tried to crystallise the meaning of these mandalas as an ever-turning wheel of life. My own life lurching out of control seemed about to be depicted on the walls.

A couple came in from the garden. The man was the tall and stooping figure I had seen carrying the chamber pots out earlier. The woman was squatter and heavily built, with bulging cheeks framing small round glasses. The spectacles' thin metal arms bent round her head to her ears. Both had the same long grey pigtail. They each carried a full tray of thick mugs. They were bickering in low voices as they poured hot water from the range into the Belfast sink and glumly washed up. The mugs all had the muddy glaze like the ones we had enjoyed our *Kaffee-Ersatz* in at breakfast. I felt the colour couldn't enhance their mood. The couple hung most of the cups on hooks and put away the rest on a shelf in an oak cabinet containing even more shelves of crockery in the same shade, a combination of yellow and brown swirled into each other. They shuffled back across the yard to the walled garden. Through the open gate we soon saw them weeding with hoes, working a fast, steady rhythm.

A glistening array of copper-bottomed pans hung from metal butcher's hooks above the range. Below the saucepans, the deep red cookers had four main ovens that could probably heat the entire kitchen on a winter's day.

To the right of the range, a wooden board was fixed to the wall. Hugh called me over to look more closely at the words written in a thick black ink.

WASTE DOES NOT EXIST HERE

SLEEP IS RESPECTED UNTIL SUNRISE

WE ARE ALL GODS

DARK FORCES SURROUND US—WE MUST STAND TOGETHER

LIVES ARE TO BE SHARED NOT WITHHELD.

Hugh mused, 'I suppose it's all quite noble.'

'It's got Al's fingerprints all over it.'

'Mike, do you think people need someone like Al… rather than people like us?'

'Well a lot of people like the certainty, the kind of certainty they imagined they got from Mum and Dad. Al *always* offered that.'

And I felt that, yes, they wouldn't want me to lead or guide them. As for Hugh…

I could not class Hugh as thoroughly normal. I loved him like the brother I never had, even though we'd seen less and less of each other over the years. And even when I had not seen him for months on end, I still had internal conversations as if I were talking to Hugh, musing on even the most banal events during an average day, the random thoughts that sidled in uninvited. I also had internal conversations with Al and John. But those dialogues were more akin to exchanges with archetypes, another way of being to my own, another point of reference for my actions. With Hugh, it was as if I was talking to another part of myself.

Hugh

11th May 2019

That morning I had been woken as usual by the drill music pummelling the wall. The kid next door had his testosterone blast each morning before school. It was my only impetus to arise for the day. A day of remorseless futility, of habitual actions I slept-walked through. I often felt I'd been pre-programmed by a one-size-fits-all algorithm. My body teetered as I got up from the bed, unsupported, dizzy.

I plodded through the ablution rituals. My razor had been lost for weeks. But who would I be shaving for anyway? I passed the bedroom I had shared with Siobhan before she moved me into the spare room. The duvet was undisturbed for a third night. As I looked at the pillow without any impression of an explosion of frizzed hair nestling there, I had the sensation of stepping into a lift that closes and plummets through the floors.

In the kitchen in the midst of grinding the coffee beans, Al's invitation pinged onto my phone.

Mike,

I know you haven't heard from me for a long while. It's sad we have fallen out of touch. I want to invite you to my wedding. It's in 4 weeks' time now, the 7th June. Yes, incredibly in my 60s! I tried to contact Hugh but the mails bounce back. Do you see him?

My place is called Gritstone House on the

moors a few miles from Heptonstall. It can't be traced on a satnav. The postcode is a PO box number so you'll be best to ask when you get to the village. I've founded a community. I'm making amends for my past! You can stay here beforehand if you like. Siobhan gets her own invite. I'm not one of those couplesy guys…

Al

Al's marriage was roaring into being while mine felt like the remains of yesterday's greasy meal slithering off a plate into the waiting bin. As always at this time of the morning, I was perched on the high stool by the kitchen bar. For months I had sat there meekly experiencing the world as a bland tranquillised existence. With the news of Al's marriage, a molten white-hot pain was coursing through my veins. Nothing could feel commonplace or tolerable today.

I'd never screamed before. I couldn't recognise the sound that poured out. It came up from the earth, an ancient cry echoing through the Edwardian terrace, that would have been heard on this spot before London, before buildings, before the tarmacked roads, before books, before language. I hurled my empty coffee cup across the kitchen. The glass cabinet above the worktop shattered. Neatly arranged ornamental plates from Lisbon, Florence and Venice slid off the shelves and crashed onto the kitchen floor.

Among the porcelain and china shards, the cabinet's glass splinters glinted savagely against the terracotta floor tiles. I couldn't stay a moment longer, and face Siobhan over the destruction around me. I rushed to the spare bedroom. I knew I had been rehearsing this moment for months. I pocketed my passport and bank card. I threw a tooth brush, all of my pants without crotch holes, two check shirts that wouldn't show the crinkles, a thin sweater and a Nirvana t-shirt into a plastic bag. No time to find the mislaid razor.

I looked around at a home that for a long time had felt like some rented world, a hotel room to be vacated. All the memories of parenthood, of marriage, were strained and diluted. I was no longer required here. But if I didn't leave now, I might never leave.

I locked the front door, and after a moment's reflection, posted the key through the letterbox. I texted Siobhan and then dropped the phone into a bin two doors away.

I'd go to Al's wedding—but first I would find Hugh. Al wanted Hugh to come, but at best Hugh hadn't opened the invite. And I needed to see Hugh. Hugh would know what I was going through. He'd been there. I took the tube to Liverpool street.

I'd reached Norwich by lunchtime. It had been an age since I'd visited Hugh on his boat, but I could remember the name of the staithe and the nearby village. I took the bus that would drop me on the main road near the mooring. Soon I was travelling on the top deck through a flat landscape without a horizon. I saw miles of green wheat brushed by an invisible giant's hand. The sky enormous and endless. 'I'm small. I mean nothing. I could disappear here. I could be swallowed into this land.' The thought gave me a kind of exhilarated happiness.

I walked along an icky path onto greasy duckboards.

As I approached the mooring, I was dwarfed by swaying rushes that converged on me, furry headed stalks clattering into each other, then nodding in unison in the breeze.

I could see a line of boats now, in varying sizes and repair. But I recognised Hugh's boat immediately. It was the smallest with paint blisters and green slime waterlines. I knocked on a window. After some scurrying, a face looked out at me from the cabin door.

'Hugh.'

'Mike? It is Mike? You look like warmed up porridge.'

Hugh was guilelessly rude.

'Well you'd better come in.'

I stared around at the crammed interior of the cabin. The light struggled through greasy glass picking out rickety piles of DVDs, books, and vinyl records; but there was no turntable I could see. Watery light came from his laptop, paused during a YouTube video on cabin cruisers.

'You've been here for a while now.'

'Yeah a long time… since I left Lily. I just lose track… why should I bother knowing… can't tell you what day it is to be honest. Well I do hear the news but…'

Hugh took my unexpected arrival as just that, and restarted the reassuring film of holidays on the Broads in the early '60s with the soundtrack of an acoustic guitar picking away in the background, untroubled by the aftershocks of the Cuban Missile crisis and Richard Dimbleby on the TV prophesying war as the Berlin wall went up. Hugh carried on watching the video for fifteen minutes in what probably felt to him like a companionable silence. His limbs seemed to move independently, the thin legs like pipe cleaners criss-crossing incessantly, arms jerking as if he was continually itching. Hugh's hair had grown but it was very fine and he habitually shifted strands behind his pointy elfin ears. He eventually noticed I was vacantly staring at the small screen. I had started to experience the aftershocks of my actions. Icy sensations shooting up my spine. Even Hugh had the insight to eventually realise I could never be engaged with cabin cruisers. There was something seriously wrong with me.

So to paper over the unease he asked if I was hungry. I groggily agreed to eat whatever Hugh offered. Hugh placed a cast iron saucepan onto a rickety two-ring Calor gas range and reheated yesterday's dinner. 'I warm it up for several days.' Eventually I was disconsolately tucking into brown rice, black-eyed beans and boiled carrots, which was all that was on offer on the boat that night. Hugh made the only sacrifice available.

'You can have the last of the tamari.'

And a few drops landed on the soggy carrots.

'That's nice of you, Hugh.'

Hugh saw me staring ruefully at the fare. He could only promise, 'At the weekend we can have bolognaise.'

'With mince?' My question could only be half-hearted. I couldn't believe he'd become a secret carnivore.

'No. No meat. It's not sustainable and I can't afford it anyway. I have some tinned jackfruit... "

Hugh poured out more brown rice from the pan. The burnt residue from previous reheatings was encrusted onto the sides. He continued the patient mastication of the fibrous grains. 'Lao-Tzu says "*Eat your drink and drink your eat*",' Hugh helpfully offered.

'Did he die before the end of his first large bowl of brown rice?'

Hugh smiled and continued eating in contented silence. But eventually he put his bowl on the camping table where cup circles interlaced the surface like an out-of-control protractor.

'Mike, why have you come here? You've only got a plastic bag.'

'Just threw a few things in and walked away.'

There was a chill on the water now—and it was piercing through my cord jacket. Hugh sat comfortably back and looked with what in anyone else would pass as polite interest.

'Look before I tell you anything… Have you got an even older sweater than the one you're wearing?'

'I'm sure I have. Let's dig into this pile.'

A combination of must and the dank cool of a mausoleum emerged as the surface of a pile of blankets and shirts was disturbed.

'You can try that one,' Hugh said with touching triumph in his voice.

I'd become more fastidious than I realised, as I contemplated the thick, dirty grey woollen on offer, with the subliminal odour of sweat under the arms. But I was freezing. I was entering Hugh's world, an altogether more basic affair than my Edwardian terrace.

'You've had a few pies since we last met…'

Some of the cable knit was unravelling as I breathed out.

'I know. I'm going to lose some of this flab. A week here should do it.' I had gracelessly invited myself but Hugh didn't appear to have noticed. 'You know I've missed you Hugh. I'm beginning to realise that for a long time I haven't felt real at all. I'm so sick of being so bloody diplomatic. I need to see people I can be rude to.'

'Well, thank you for that.'

'Oh, I mean real with.'

'*Real*... whatever that means. You're starting to spout some tired old stuff, Mike. Been in therapy or something? Think I prefer you just trying to be rude.'

There was a silence. I knew that with the next few words my new life would explode into actuality.

'I've left Siobhan.'

Hugh carried on eating.

'Did you hear me?'

Hugh just ate. I looked questioningly so Hugh had to respond.

'Yes?'

'You don't seem very... anything.'

'No.'

'Hugh you are unwontedly placid,'

'If I'm honest Mike, I just don't want to know.'

'After Lily, I thought you might feel the sa...'

'I still feel numb, even after a few years. But now it's like there's this layer of snow covering everything. All of those memories. Even the good memories are now bad ones. I don't want to dig through to my past. The snow looks so clean, pure and calming.'

'Well how poetic. I'm not sure I have reached that level of contentment... but I've only been feeling this for a few days.'

'It's how I experience the world.'

I went silent a minute or two. Somewhere under that snow was the memory of his two daughters who had gradually stopped visiting him since he'd started living on the boat. In fact, probably none of Hugh's family had the first idea how he was apart from a call from him at Christmas. But I had my own grief…

'Anyway, Siobhan and the kids, they don't hate me but I make them… sad. They've watched me turn into this creature with guts that slide from side to side under my shirt. I mean I *have* let myself go just a bit. Wobbling along—I look such a smug fool. I'm starting to miss her Hugh. I still just love looking at her. And yes, she's seeing someone else… but who can blame her?' My face was beginning to crumple.

Hugh's voice contained the thin steel of a hacksaw. 'Mike, I know I'm going to sound harsh. I can't cope with all this negativity you're bringing into my home. All the pain of losing Lily is coming back—because of you. I just don't need this. Did you intend to come here to make me feel like this all over again? And I'm sorry, Mike. Of course, I know it hurts. I don't suppose it will ever stop.'

I could see I'd disturbed the waters too much. There was a silence and then I gave Hugh the news about Al's wedding. Hugh told me he had stopped bothering to look at his mail. It was part of his process of cutting himself away. But when he knew I was going, he became enthusiastic. 'You know I haven't seen him for years but he's one of our oldest friends… we've kind of got to go. I thought for a while we were estranged… if that's the right word.'

He seemed quite energised by the idea of a journey.

'You're in the nick of time. The MOT on the Scimitar runs out tomorrow.' Now he was bobbing around the lurching cabin. 'I'd better pack then.' But what he packed was a little less than what was in my plastic bag—a few pairs of pants and a t-shirt. Eventually after this burst of activity, Hugh wandered off to the site toilet by the office. I did a quiet search for Gritstone House on Hugh's laptop and found nothing.

First Meal

14th May 2019: Evening

I could hear an impenetrable hum in the kitchen. Occasionally Hugh's voice rose through the vocal soup. I was famished but on edge. The fact was that for most of the past year, I had hardly left the house. But Siobhan would still hold dinner parties and I was expected to be the husband.

I came to dread them. I'd stopped caring about my physical shape—at best appearing to be the sturdy swain who could have fought and survived Agincourt. And with my shape came the assumption that I colluded in blokiness, which admits you into the hot fug of male bonding, joshing, and bawling in each other's faces. The guys at her dinner parties often did fit the stereotype I prepared for them—the brooding testosterone, the mechanistic sensuality. Men whose conditioned responses you feel you can predict. Anyway, I was off the idea of groups, and now I dreaded this encounter with upwards of twenty strangers.

It wasn't a good beginning. When I put my head round the door, the room went silent. I was wordlessly appraised while pots and kettle tops tintinnabulated on the range. Six of the community were busy peeling and preparing vegetables. I felt unnerved and walked out again. The mumble resumed.

I overheard Hugh say, 'He can find it hard with new people.'

I blundered down the ground floor corridor. At the end

was a sitting room-cum- library. Ten figures in white vests and loose cotton trousers were in a circle on the floor. They were all in the lotus position. Whenever I tried it, I found it physically excruciating. Next to the French window, Edith sat beside Al with eyes firmly closed, palms upward balanced on her knees. A woman with long greying red hair was taking them through the final relaxation section. They gracefully uncoiled their legs and lay flat on the floor. There was a rapt silence. I felt I was intruding though nobody seemed to notice me. Equally I was frightened to move away in case a sound broke the spell. But there was an involuntary creak as I shifted my feet on a loose board.

Emerging from the group, Al's voice whispered, 'It's all right Mike.'

When they sat down to eat, the community were in the long robes they seemed to wear around the house after work, mainly in a shade of a greyish cream. That was apart from Helmut who was now resplendent in a deep red full-length dress.

Looking round the table I could see there were at least three couples. As well as Al and Edith there was the pair I had seen bickering over the washing up—and two gay men. I caught the name of the black guy, Sylvester, but not his partner. Everyone seemed at least in their mid-sixties. Apart from Helmut. Several faces were grizzled by days in the sun, a leathery Mediterranean texture. Al looked pale in comparison, and I wondered how much of his day was spent in the curtained gloom of the room that seemed to be his office.

The community ate when the sun had disappeared behind the small grove of trees at the top of the field.

Without the natural light, the candle flames playing on the walls transformed the kitchen. The wheels of the mandalas seemed to revolve, the steel pots captured the sparkle from the flames and bounced flares of reflection onto the walls. I wondered whether this was why they ate so late in the middle of the year, waiting for the dusk to allow this transformation. We served ourselves from the pots on the range, brown rice and adzuki beans, with vegetables roasted in thyme and basil. And a rich sauce everyone poured on. It had a tomato base with a mixture of freshly cut herbs and wild garlic.

Al introduced the people round the table, but there was no way I would remember their names. Hugh repeated each name and nodded to them. But I felt it was to convince himself his memory hadn't been blasted away years ago.

'I've told them you're my oldest friends.'

While I felt more relaxed though still tickled with anxiety, I might perhaps have expected some interest in our backgrounds and indeed any current political issues. Hugh mentioned Brexit in passing but was met with polite incomprehension. The community members seemed to think it was a new miracle cleaning fluid. Al explained that they had not taken any new members for four years, so no one would have heard of Brexit, let alone care. I guessed Al did know about the news, but he deftly slid the conversation away from the crises in the outside world by asking about my family.

I suppose I obliged. My daughter Maddie was married with two children and a successful husband. But Al skated over this and seemed much less interested than you might have expected in Maddie and her detached house in

Smethwick. If anything, a look of disappointment passed over his face. He changed tack to my son Billie, who rather like Al, had a few successful years in the City and then left suddenly. At that time Billie was living in a hut on a beach in Thailand. We had only been fitfully in contact. Siobhan missed him terribly, though she seldom spoke of it. I always felt a kind of exhilaration when I thought of Billie's life, partying and barbecuing on the beach. But whatever happened the night before, Billie meditated early in the morning on the shoreline.

One man, Ezra, remembered being in Thailand in the 70s. '...But I got busted man. Don't know how, but the consulate got me out from this cell I was in with ten other guys—and no one spoke English. Well suppose my pop was an admiral, and it was kind of embarrassing for him, once he got over my need for a moral lesson.'

Al had spent a year there. 'Yeah, there were plenty of fools like Ezra.' I sneaked a look at Ezra but he was laughing. 'I can understand about Billie just staying on that beach. You slow down completely, watch the sky and that edge between the blue sea and the blue sky, how they seem to be about to coalesce apart from this thin line. this tiny division between air and water... I'd just stare into that edge for hours. And they can seem to be all one...' Ezra was nodding '...but they're diametric elements that never meet. There is no horizon where they merge even if you travel right round the world. So you can feel there is harmony in the vision as you sit on the shore, but it's an illusion—the clouds are high above, and the sea is a dangerous fucking place once you land in it.'

'So, it's all just a nice comforting illusion sitting on that beach?' I turned to Al not believing I had said anything challenging. But I felt a frisson round the table. Some people stared at me with mild shock, or quietly looked at each other. Al sat there in an atmosphere of cold calm. Perhaps Al just made unquestioned pronouncements in this room, to this community.

'Yeah in a way it is Mike. It's good to live through that and see it for what it is, a beautiful dream that the world offers you. But that's why we're here. We're beyond illusion.'

There was nodding and shortly after they began to drift away, lighting candles from the two wax towers on the table. I heard the creaks on the boards as I sat there alone with Hugh. I remembered now that Hugh was mentally preparing for his initiation into bread-making with Toni. We could hear her approach from the yard where she had spent several minutes holding her hands under the stream of freezing water from the pump.

'You'll need your hands to be spotlessly clean, Hugh. Get out to that pump.'

Walled Garden

15th May 2019: Morning

I woke after the house had emptied, and went downstairs for my visit to the latrine. At the kitchen door I narrowly missed crashing into Helmut carting a pair of large wooden buckets across from the courtyard pump. Helmut gave what can only be called a cheery grin, as he clattered by in enormous clogs with thick wooden soles. These could have been as old as the house, echoing on the cobbles like generations of people before him.

'I like your clogs, Helmut.'

'I exert myself to integrate with your local culture, *mein Freund*.'

'So, what else are you doing on this glorious day?'

'I go to tend my goats. We have ten.'

'So you *are* a shepherd.'

'Ja, I was goat-herder in the Bayern.'

'I thought the milk tasted different.'

'I milk them all with my own hands. I love each one.'

'But you're wearing a goatskin. Doesn't it upset them?' I was being facetious and straightaway felt a bit worried about riling the giant in front of me.

'This is my favourite goat, Marius…'

I wasn't sure where to go with this information.

'Marius escapes from the field. A tractor hits him. The driver very upset. Marius dies in my arms. How else do I have memory of my dear friend? I wear his skin. Now he is with me to comfort me.'

'You eat your goats?'

'*Mein Gott!* If someone tries…' Again, I wished I hadn't asked. I walked away as slowly and casually as I could across the yard. On one side was the former stable block. Helmut occupied one of the rooms above, where the grooms had slept. There also seemed to be four other people living there. Later I found three of the community had vacated their rooms in the main house for Al's wedding guests. On the far side of the yard was the slatted fence and the gate. I went through to the open field with the earth closet on the horizon. After paying a visit I washed my hands in the pump's icy flow. Now I wanted to see the garden. With its simple and pleasing high walls of unadorned brick, the walled garden was always the place I went to if I ended up on a country house's estate—rather than the country house.

The bricks of Gritstone's walled garden were small, more the size of a Tudor house, redbrick amidst all this sandstone. The gateway was two bottle-green wooden doors, as tall as cart horses. They opened inwards, high and wide enough for a waggon. I pushed one side and the rusty tip of the bottom bolt grated against the cobbles in an arc incised over centuries.

Once through the gate I found a small orchard of knotty squat trunks. Pink flecked apple-blossom poured off the low branches. Beyond were lines of pole-beans, leaves curling round and covering eight-foot high stakes. The small stocky woman I'd seen washing up yesterday was balancing on a stool and pulling the beans from the frames for the evening meal. She nodded when I greeted her but otherwise ignored me. Beyond the poles, spinach grew to the size of small bushes. Gigantic cabbages had leaves with the dimensions of a triceratops crest. A man in a hazmat was spraying an area of root vegetables from an enormous canister on his back.

I introduced himself. 'Hello I'm a bit surprised. I thought you might be growing organic food.'

The man turned off the spray, pulled up his Perspex visor and said, 'Why, man? We put in anythin'… anythin' at all, to make these veggies better and bigger.'

I didn't quite feel up to giving him a lecture on letting the insects have their allowance of the earth's bounty, and the ingestion of chemicals not being terribly good for our own bodies. But mainly I hoped Hugh didn't find out. He always asked, even in a transport café, if his meal was organic. They always said *yes*…

'We spray fertiliser and put in pretty well everythin' that'll kill those pesky pests. The bigger the vegetables the better, man. I don't care how they're grown. We ain't sharing these babies with any creepy-crawlies.'

I must have looked bit non-plussed. But the man in the Hazmat continued, 'We need to eat, man. We don't want to rely on the outside world for food. So we need to grow big, man. You never talk to Al about this?'

I said we hadn't had much chance to discuss the gardening yet.

'Oh yeah. Al talked about you the morning after you arrived. We can't expect you old guys to do heavy work.'

'That's nice of him.'

'Yeah you go back, huh?'

'Yes we do.'

'Bet Al was an experience when he was young!'

'Yes, I suppose he was.'

'Yeah man, he managed that English rap band the…'

'The Savage Boys.'

'Yeah that's them. Reckon Al made 'em sound almost as good as the real thing, man. When I heard 'em I was *surrr-prised*. Where'd they come from?'

'Oh, a place called Kent.'

'Never been there. Came straight from Baltimore, man. Kind of got the summons. Anyways, plenty of work to do here fella.' He picked up the bottle and pulled down his visor.

'You were saying Hugh and I are quite old... err I'm sorry I know I've seen you at the meal but I'm useless...'

'Cyrus man.'

'Yeah, well Cyrus I was wondering how old you are yourself?'

'Round seventy-seven. Kind'a lost count.'

I walked across to the other side of the garden. The small arch in the wall had a wicket gate. I lifted the latch and found open scrubland beyond, mostly heather and the occasional small spiky bush. A metalled path led gradually up through an open field to a grove of trees near the top of the moor. Small bronze figures dangled from the branches, like the puppets that would have been illuminated for a shadow play. Some flat rectangular stones were spaced out around the tree, resting in the earth. A single letter was carved on each. The stones were not worn by centuries of rain and lichen.

The Music Room

15th May 2019: Afternoon

I'd gone looking for Hugh. I eventually found him, after I'd climbed two flights up bare wooden stairs, in a large white-painted room in the eaves. Either side were small bedrooms where the servants originally would have slept, and now seemed empty, as most of the house was during the day. The bay windows looked out to the other side of the valley. The land was dotted with farm buildings, and sheep were being driven like a horde of ants through one gate and into an upper field. Along the wall opposite the windows were shelves holding thousands of vinyl records. Otherwise the room was bare apart from two large sofas of aged brown leather. They acted as silent audience to a pair of massive speakers.

Tufts of horsehair protruded from the cushions. On the bare boards either side of the speakers stood gutted monumental multi-coloured candles annealed to the floor in their own wax.

I collapsed onto one of the sofas and noticed my impact cracked more of the leather surface. A magazine rack beside the sofa held back-numbers of the Melody Maker. I saw some copies from 1973 and then pulled one out from 1970.

Hugh was absorbed in examining scuffed record sleeves

'Carol King *Tapestry*—oh I loved her. Mike, you remember Yes's magnum opus *Tales of the Topographic Oceans*? Oh, this is my kind of music! Look Genesis!'

Before I could fall on my knees and beg him to stop, the needle had introduced the sound of crackling static. As Peter Gabriel began the first chorus, Hugh was already prancing round. For the finale he mimed pushing a lawn mower of air.

'Okay Hugh but now it sounds just a bit…'

'Fantastic—haven't heard any of this for years.'

'There's a reason…'

'Have you no soul? Now let's play Wishbone Ash *The King will come*!' The needle dropped introducing some troubling clicks.

'They used to do this bit in unison!' Hugh was picking at the spiralling melody, rocking forward one leg, stretching back as far as humanly possible, the other bent at the knee. The air guitar was reaching new heights…

'You seem to be settling in.' Al's voice cut through the guitars singing away together.

Hugh leapt over and pulled up the needle with a sickening scratch. His act of vinyl vandalism couldn't go unnoticed.

Al was attempting not to grimace. 'We won't tell Helmut about that.'

'No don't—you needn't.' The mention of Helmut returned Hugh to the present.

'Anyway, best to stop. You're using up our electricity.'

'Well I'm ready to make a contribution,' Hugh said a little too grudgingly.

'We don't get electricity from the grid, Hugh. We have solar panels. And Helmut tops it up by cycling to charge the batteries. He'll just have to do few more hours on the old pedals…'

Any apology from Hugh would have sounded too

tardy, and he drifted into an awkward sulky silence. But Al hadn't come just about the electricity.

'Guys, I was just wondering how you're getting on—it's your first day here, and I suppose it must all feel a little unusual to you.'

Hugh plonked himself next to Al. 'Well, I was feeling more relaxed until you told me off.'

'Yeah, but you needed to know that it isn't on tap.'

'It seems rather extreme. I mean no hot water—and what's wrong with having some lekky from the Grid? I mean that *is* extreme.' Hugh could be irritating with his cosy diminutives like *lekky.*

'Hmm, I suppose it looks like that. You see we don't pay any bills because we don't want to have any bills. We have our own water, our own electricity… I pay some council tax. That's about it.'

Hugh didn't get it. It was starting to dawn on me but Hugh persisted. 'Yeah but why Al? I mean everyone else… I mean what's wrong with being in the 21st century?'

Al turned to Hugh. 'Everything is wrong with being in the 21st century. Do I have to spell it out?'

Hugh opened a convictionless mouth.

'When we were young, we had hope. Do you really feel that hope now Hugh? We don't want any outside interference. You saw it over the door. We want to *leave this world.* We don't want anything more to do with it.'

To divert the conversation from Hugh's struggles, I said in a faux academic tone, 'And we were curious… about your noticeboard.'

But Hugh was more direct. 'Your little precepts…'

'Oh… yeah.'

'What? You mean it's there as some sort of noble afterthought?'

'Naaa… but you have to have lived here for a while to get into it.'

'Suppose so. I mean I'm not a god. Can't speak for Mike, of course.'

'But I think maybe you are.' Al turned his gaze to Hugh. 'All right. There's no maybe about it.'

'I could have done with Lily realising that.' Hugh dangled the knowledge he clearly wanted Al to have.

'So that's finished. Well I suppose I should have guessed. Christ, you've both messed up your marriages. Maybe I shouldn't have invited you both to *my* wedding. Pair of Typhoid Marys.' He paused. Hugh was looking at him with a face of stone.

'But sorry, Hugh when did you break up?'

'A few years ago.' Hugh spoke grudgingly. I often had the feeling he craved compassion from Al. But not the sort you beg for.

'Well I'm sorry…' Al tried to make amends.

'Don't be—it was misery in the end.' A silence crept into the room as if the oxygen has been siphoned out. Al got up and suggested a pot of tea.

'It won't be like anything you've tasted before.' Al spoke with a familiar nonchalance I now began to remember.

We clattered down the stairs to the kitchen. Al pressed a mixture of dried leaves into a large tisane and immersed it in the black enamel teapot. We sat around the kitchen table and waited for the infusion to take hold. The wood was still damp from being recently scrubbed.

After Al poured, I sipped politely. Hugh appeared

more enthusiastic. I wanted to know how Al went about buying the estate. How had he discovered it, even?

'Yeah I'd been looking to go back North. I had this whole concept in mind… Actually saw this estate was for sale soon after it came into my head to leave the sea. When I heard the house was available, I knew what the place would look like, even before I'd seen the pictures. I *knew* the colour of the stone, how it stood on the top of the moors. But even when I sold the house by the sea, this place still cost an arm and a leg—far more than I got from the sale.'

'But I thought you'd have no money worries at all after your time in the city.'

'Always spent it all. Never saved. Suppose I felt I could always get more. I travelled. I travelled pretty extensively. Went on my own. I'd generally go off after I finished a… *relationship*.' The last word soaked in sarcasm.

I remembered now. We'd get these cryptic post cards. From Thailand where he'd lived in a hut on a beach for months. From some town in the mid-West when he drove across the States and never touched the cities. And photos in an envelope of some rundown village in mainland China that could have got him arrested if the Chinese government had seen them. And a letter from a remote village in India reached by a track. His money had built toilets. He said it put a stop to the women having to go into the fields where they could be raped.

'I mean, you remember that time I went to Nicaragua. I travelled down gradually from there, but I suppose all along I wanted to get into the Amazon— to really get away from civilisation altogether and in the end I began living with this tribe. There was this guy who took me there. We travelled for most of a week on motor launches and then canoes. He was a builder's labourer in Manaus. But he'd go back to the village and bring money. I suppose I was looking for somebody like him to take me into the rainforest. And he missed living with the tribe. When we got there, I loved their way of life—and the food—fresh caught fish, the fruit straight off the trees and we all ate together in this long room—in the *maloca*. Just wore trunks all the time 'til they gave me a kind of loincloth.'

I was remembering my own life at that time. The children were young. I sat in my room in the university staring into a grass quadrangle nobody seemed able to get into, feeling bored…

'And I ended up getting married, I think—but it isn't the same there. The headman came to me one day and introduced me to my wife. It was strange at first—I didn't really know any words…' Al paused as his mind seemed to fill with recollections, the fuzzy picture of a woman he may not have wanted to remember too well, of hot slow days, the odour of the rotting forest floor, the constant rustle of the towering upper branches.

Hugh chimed in, 'Yeah sounds great…' Hugh was struggling with his village shop, even then. But immediately as he spoke, he realised we were leaving behind the idyllic part of the story.

'And then the loggers came. I got so fucking angry. The tribe didn't know what I knew, wondered why I got so upset. They were defenceless against these bastards. These thugs didn't bother us much at first. But once they'd begun their work it was clear the tribe were going to be driven off their territory. And when the headman went to them, they tried to buy him off. And when that didn't work, they threatened him. And then they took out a few of the men and women as a warning, as examples of how far they would go. Well I had the money. I went back to Manaus and laid my hands on some old machine guns and had them brought up on a motor launch, as far as it would go. Then we transferred them to their long canoes. I wasn't going to be pushed around. They were just worthless low-lifes, these guys cutting down the trees. Anyway, we learnt how to use the rifles. I'd never fired a gun in anger before I went to Nicaragua—and I didn't fight there. Anyway we did some training. And then those loggers… they had a taste of it. We ambushed their camp. The tribe knew how to creep up real close, like they were hunting wild pig, stalking right up to their sleeping bags. These guys didn't know what hit them. Nobody escaped. Some died in their sleep. A few of the tribe were killed but…

'We burnt the gang's bodies. Probably didn't need the guns. Those bullets left them unrecognisable. Once the tribe started shooting you couldn't stop them. Suppose I shouldn't tell you this, but anyway…'

'What happened to the tribe?'

'Dunno now. Had to leave. My visa was running out. The loggers' bosses knew some European was involved. Thought I might divert attention if they came after me. I shaved my head and beard…'

'And your… wife?' I was hesitant.

'I only ever knew a few words…'

'So you left her back there.'

'She was better off there. I explained to the headman—it was sort of sad—but someone from the tribe misses the other members—can't cope with being on their own. They don't understand how we can live alone. They're together all the time. They don't travel. Hunting trips are just a few hours. And they all get together at the end of each day. It's wonderful, man. Honestly, maybe I should have stayed.'

'And carried on fighting the loggers?' I tried not to sound as doubtful as I felt.

Hugh tried to be more helpful. 'Well, at least you may have diverted them, took them off the scent if they followed you…'

Al descended into an impenetrable silence for minutes on end. 'I suppose this place is replicating the communal experience.' Hugh was always uncomfortable with brooding. But I remembered when he had told me about the time he had a hankering for that tribal warmth. He'd just read *Iron John*, wanted to try a sweat lodge and ended up spending a weekend with a number of men in middle management howling in the darkness and frenetically beating something like an Irish bodhrán, but it didn't quite work for him.

'Yeah maybe…' But Al's mood was sombre now. He drifted off and the office door made its staccato squeak.

Hugh whispered to me. 'Something's got to him. I've never seen him go quiet like that. Things hardly ever seemed to go wrong for Al when we knew him… but they seem to have there…'

Rosamond

16th May 2019: Midday

There was bench by the garden wall near the herb patch. I was sitting reading Proust. I'd found a solitary volume in the green room from *In Search of Lost Time*. The long sentences were so soothing, nothing staccato and jagged, but meandering like a slow stream. It felt good to read about the human condition but with the action taking place in an unreachable world. Hugh had tailed along with me but was incapable of sitting still, let alone reading a book. He wandered around the herb beds crushing rosemary in his hands and inhaling it. As he broke off a third stem, we heard a voice behind us. 'Please don't do that. We treasure our herbs.'

She was six inches taller than either of us. We had seen her in the kitchen without speaking much. Her voice had the familiar boom and brusqueness Hugh later said reminded him of the woman who taught his girls horse riding, and yelled instructions from the far side of the field at gymkhanas. She was in the functional dungarees everyone wore for work in the garden—everyone apart from Helmut in his goatskin Lederhosen. Her grey hair was thick and tousled. Remarkably small eyes were sunken into her lids above a wide chin that stretched across a broad face. Hugh was conciliatory.

'I'm sorry, we're still fairly new here. I don't want to appear disrespectful.'

'Yes… well if you could refrain in future.'

Hugh attempted to divert the conversation but

whatever tack he took…

'We found the place a few days ago. It wasn't easy.'

'Found! Well we don't want to be found and have a place full of gawping nosey parkers.'

'No, I suppose not… err why?' Hugh asked.

'What do you mean, *why*?' She was being very curt to Hugh. I pretended to read to stay out of this conversation.

'Yessss… well.'

'We have come here to escape your world. A world neither of you look very good on, I'm sorry to say.'

'You are a very direct lady… uh?'

'Rosamond… Wyatt. Oh!' she pulled up short in surprise.

'Sorry are you all right?' Hugh was puzzled at what had suddenly disturbed her so much.

Rosamond regained her composure. 'It's just I haven't spoken my surname for a year at least. It feels so strange to think I have this married name. I'm sorry if I was too personal but Al urges us to be direct and honest, even if it hurts.'

'Well you can't hurt me that much.' I had become a mute bystander as Hugh seemed to want to share.

'Oh dear, are you damaged as well? God, is everyone?'

'Yes Rosamond, I'm afraid I am.' There was a plea in Hugh's voice. He spoke slowly and searched for her eyes.

But Rosamond brushed away that plea. 'Well I didn't come here because I was damaged. I mean I might have wanted to kill myself but that was more…'

'I know you have a deep hurt and you hide it from everyone.' Hugh was looking directly at her and found her eyes. Without his usual self-deprecatory smile, he said, 'It takes one to know one.'

Rosamond seemed to judder. She needed a few seconds to regain her poise. When she replied, it was with a lightness that still couldn't conceal that she had been hit below the waterline, 'Well if that's the case I can't win, can I?'

'No.' I probably had never seen Hugh so serious.

'But you are very wrong... sorry, what is your name?'

'Hugh... and this is Mike.'

'Yes, I remember now... but Hugh, you are very much mistaken. I came here because I wanted to leave the world. Yes I did stockpile pills. It didn't take long to buy enough paracetamol if I went to ten different chemists. But it wasn't the right choice to overdose on them anyway... horrid death. But late one night I put into a search "I want to leave this world" and Gritstone's site had the words "*leave this world.*"'

'So something had made you so desperate, Rosamond.'

'You know we hand in all of our devices, our laptops, phones—when we arrive. Al stores them away. We all have good reasons. It's a little like when my mother was dying. Neither of us wanted to know all the grubby facts, the diagnoses that led nowhere. The less we both knew the happier we were. I just feel the world is dying. I mean I could see it on a screen, read in the newspaper every day... and I don't want to watch it die.'

The Malvinas

18th May 2019: Late afternoon

It was sunlit morning, but it could not raise our spirits as Hugh and I glumly drank the coffee substitute in the kitchen. The community were out working, mostly in the walled garden, though Sylvester was sanding some of the flakier window frames on a ladder round the other side of the house. Al wandered in from the room beneath the stairs. He looked preoccupied, seeking a break from whatever was going on in there. Again, I was noticing how pale he was—how much time he spent in the curtained room. Partly to take his mind off his apparent problems, I asked if he had invited John to the wedding.

'Thought I should. Not seen him since Ruth left us.'

'Has he said if he's coming?' I wasn't sure if John was in the frame of mind to.

'Yeah well he wrote to tell me what train he's going to be on.'

So John was going to join us. But as I said, I had more immediate concerns. At that time, I was worried about Al, but didn't know why I should be. I knew nothing of what he was doing in his curtained room then. But I wondered if his pallid appearance had anything to do with money problems. Did he still owe money on the mortgage?

'Yeah I'm still paying it off.' He was sounding too casual. 'But this place demanded more than money. There was six months plastering, painting… I've got round to changing some of the windows… But I wanted to found something small—yes—*small* Hugh.' Al had noticed a

74

look of incredulity cross Hugh's face.

Hugh responded, 'You always seemed to have such grand schemes. I think we were both a bit surprised…'

'Yeah it' doesn't seem massively ambitious. I just want this community to—to reflect a world I want to return to. Obviously I could do it for myself. But I know neither of you will probably believe this—I always want to share my world or it has no meaning.'

Hugh now wore a pair of dungarees he'd been given by Edith. I've said how Hugh had a habit of waggling his limbs, as he was right now, his wide trouser legs flapping away round his thin joints while he was listening to Al. It should have been maddeningly irritating. But I could see Al was more patient than he used to be.

'Any people?' Hugh grinned, trying to inject mischief. It didn't deflect Al.

'A lot of people want to leave their life behind and they feel they only have one way out.' As Al spoke, even from the first sentence this gradual spell was cast over us. And his tone darkened as if he had put down a violin and taken up a cello. We gave into this contrary state; a dynamic lethargy, a narcotic ambience where critical faculties had no place. Rationalising too much felt a barrier to the visceral experience. I had forgotten how powerful this could be. In fact, Al seemed more magnetic than ever. His words emerged slowly, deliberately, almost dreamily.

'We can kill ourselves at any time, anywhere… we've always got the means to hand. They are never far away—pills, railway tracks, cliffs and tall buildings… water, always water… And sometimes I might feel you're right to decide to take that route. Your body could be imploding, caving in day by day and nothing can stop it. You may be screaming in never-ending pain. I'd be ready to help if it was someone I cared for—yeah, I'd help them. But some people—it's almost as if they're looking into blackened glass. They feel they're trapped in commitments they have no conviction about... or in a virtual world of bottomless loneliness. But you can escape that world. Leave that world behind. This place offers a way out. I offer a way out.'

Hugh and I had gone silent. This was no bog-standard hippy commune he had founded; but what else could we expect of him?

'The people who came here and joined this community, literally have left their lives behind. It can feel like they're entering a closed order. And I look after the flak—you understand? All the extraneous stuff. They need to feel nothing has followed them; nothing is coming after them.'

Almost as if to fight the narcotic atmosphere Al had created, I tried to be combative. 'Well that all sounds nice Al. But like Hugh was saying, *you're* running this aren't you? It's your place.'

Remarks like this used to provoke him. Now he brushed them away like dust on his sleeve. 'I had the vision Mike,' Al replied levelly.

I remembered all those years of arguments where John could forensically take Al apart, almost at will; or Siobhan would make him look foolish and naïve. And Al would storm off or get drunk and go silent on them for a few days. Now he had changed.

There was one time on Anglesey. We were pulling on a joint outside a holiday cottage we had all taken. They'd had another argument. It was just after the Falklands war. Al was laughed out the room for his modish insistence on calling the islands the Malvinas. I never baited Al in the way John and certainly Siobhan could. She was relentless…

'So Al, perhaps it's time for you to learn some Spanish. You could swap your Dalston flat and exchange it for some freezing bungalow in Port Stanley. You'd quickly get to know everyone—I mean there's only 4,000 people on the island—and you could persuade them where their best interests lie. You would be able to convince them about Argentina's almost religious belief that it has a right to those islands, where the current inhabitants look more likely to feel at home in… say, Chipping Sodbury. Yes, off you go, book your flight. I mean as a result of Argentina losing the war, they threw out the military junta who *disappeared* thousands of their own people, and they returned to democracy. You'd think they might have been grateful to the UK. A little better than anything the British army ever achieved in Northern Ireland. Not that you were ever so bothered about that—no the Malvinas, the Malvinas—wouldn't it all seem quite noble if there wasn't oil out there? So noble and idealistic. I mean Al, can't you get beyond all this corrosive nationalism in the late 20th century? Always like some little boy who has to support a team, aren't we? Can't both sides seem rather shabby and dishonest and manipulative? I mean it's pretty cold and wet there. The temperature might reach a dizzy 20 degrees if you're lucky at the height of summer… and it might snow whatever the season. Can't see the patriots of Buenos Aires moving there in droves any time soon … have a great time!'

I remember Al saying to me as the sun sank and the laughter echoed out from the cottage, 'Sometimes I hate them… even Siobhan. I'm sick of the feeling I have to measure up to them. But where's the energy in them to do anything that's going to change lives? Look at Hugh, all smugness sitting over his pint like some old fucking codger on his bar stool. The most he does is make his own home brew. What is he ever going to do—whether or not he has the millstone of Lily round his neck? I don't sit on my arse and mock. I've got a life-force, Mike. Things start to happen when I'm around.'

Al and Edith

18th May 2019: Morning

Hugh was immersed in the ragged pages of the December 1973 Melody Maker. He'd already been upstairs to the music room several times that day and brought back another copy from the magazine racks.

Meanwhile there was plenty of clearing up in the kitchen. I was helping Edith stack away the bulky plates. I said how heavy they were and all in this dreary muddy glaze. I wondered where Al got them. She just replied, 'They're all made here Mike.' I decided not to upset anyone. For all I knew Edith's might be the less than deft hands on the potter's wheel.

Hugh sat at the table successfully ignoring the activity around him. And indeed, he was reading a long review of *Tales of the Topographic Oceans*, his favourite YES album; no, his favourite album of all time. He read gobbets aloud with renewed disappointment that Chris Welch, then the kingmaker of album reviewers, just didn't get it. Hugh insisted on sharing Welch's stinging putdown, 'cohesion is lost once more to the gods of drab self-indulgence.' Hugh couldn't stop fulminating. 'Well that guy Welch was proved disastrously wrong. It has stood the test of time, a towering monument to the music I love… and it was all but washed away in the three-chord assault of the Pistols.'

Edith found herself in the slipstream of this tirade and quietly said, 'Sorry Hugh but I didn't know about them. I used to listen to the Carpenters though…'

So we were all in confusion when we heard the

electronic beeping as the door opened by the stairs heralding Al's entrance into the kitchen. I was beginning to notice that aside from the loss of colour in the face, he often looked tense when he came out of that room during the day. Hugh was rather impervious to the most tumultuous emotions and asked Al in his desultory way about the record collection on the top floor.

Al actually welcomed the diversion and became quite engaged. 'When I knew I was going ahead with the plan for this community I started buying old vinyl collections from all over the country. I'd sift through them and keep stuff from the late 60s to mid-70s, when I was young, when all these people were too. You know the Police Auctions sometimes come up with interesting stuff, Hugh. Anyway, anything I didn't want I'd dump at a charity shop. Couldn't be arsed with eBay. Not what I'm about. Same with the *Melody Maker*—just bought the yellowing scraggy ones the collectors gave a wide berth to. I've now got most of them from '70 to '74—none in mint condition but you can read them.'

Hugh started going on about the bargains he got for the boat on *Gumtree*, but was soon reduced to silence by Al's manifest lack of interest. After Edith and I had finished clearing, I sat down opposite Hugh. As usual she had been almost monosyllabic. But she seemed to appreciate that I didn't need to talk, just wanted to get on with the tasks. After she left the room and I had poured some mint tea for us, I changed the tack of a conversation that Hugh had crunched into a layby.

'You know, I was really surprised—shocked even—when you wrote to say you were getting married. You've never even got close to wanting to marry before.'

Al leant back in his chair. 'I still don't Mike. I still don't.'

My face was creased in disbelief. This was more than irritating. 'Sorry, I don't quite get it… we've come all this way for your wedding and…'

Al was unfazed. 'I feel I should… I'm doing this for Edith. She's never been married. Not really had a relationship…'

The candles' soft shadows in the evening were kind to Al's face. But close up in the daylight he looked the age he could usually conceal. Deep lines ran from the edge of his eyes, the valises under the lids seemed more pronounced. I had an urge to put an arm round his shoulder. I could feel Al's weariness as if there was some burden he wouldn't speak of.

'Guys, you've known me on and off most of my life. I've never been someone scared of being alone—I wasn't living in any kind of personal wilderness when I met Edith. I wasn't desperate for this deep kind of intimacy. No—it hasn't been like that, this has been a free choice—for both of us.'

'She seems so quiet.' I still couldn't see how…

'Look Mike, Edith is so different to the other women I've been involved with. She has her own quality and it reached me. We slowly got to know each other after she arrived. At first, she'd hardly talk.'

'Challenging…'

Al ignored my cheap sarcasm.

'Well yeah, she was when she arrived. You'd often see she'd been crying to herself. She was living with some kind of terror. I still don't know all the causes even now, and it doesn't matter, because she came out of it. We'd talk each day. I'd always find time. It felt like she hadn't really spoken properly—been comfortable with a man before. Her parents are both dead and they left her with no money worries—really for the rest of her life. But she was alone in this enormous house. Rooms she never even went in. She had a job in the local library but didn't need to work. So we were kind of a different experience for each other. I never had to try and understand someone like her. I never had to work at getting through to a woman before. I've lived with damaged women, but they'd never admit it. Cover it up with sessions at the gym, hardbody stuff. But she never pretended.

'The security she had in that enormous house was more like a prison sentence. She felt like a captive in the family home. She'd sacrificed years of her life to looking after her parents. And the way she talks about the guys she met—they all sound pretty limp. And one day she found our webpage on a pc in the library…'

'And what did she search for? Domineering monomaniac?' Hugh' s uneasiness came out in nervous joshing. But his words sounded leaden amidst a new stillness in Al. He looked at Hugh with resigned contempt.

'No, Hugh. She searched for "How to leave this world."'

'You mean she wanted to…'

'I still don't know. She wanted some kind of oblivion. She wrote down our details. Round that time, I still kept a phone on for people who wanted to join. And then—really late one night—she called and made the arrangements to come here. Left written instructions with her solicitor to sell the house. I met her at the station in

Hebden Bridge. There she was in an old duffle coat, carrying a small suitcase.'

I couldn't help speculating about all those years before. 'Al you're sure she's never been married?'

'She doesn't keep—she can't keep anything from me. It wouldn't matter anyway...'

'But what about you. I still don't get it?' I was still trying to make sense of Al marrying now, after all the women I'd seen him with. The one he brought to the holiday cottage in Anglesey where they argued incessantly. She was always on her phone and one morning she just disappeared in a cab. The rather too malleable partner who shared his house by the sea. The haughty Spanish dancer he brought to our marriage who was dramatically impressive: and all consistently, statuesquely beautiful.

Al looked abstractedly across the yard beyond the kitchen door, less speaking than thinking aloud. 'I can't unpick it—why I'm doing this. She does have money... she has helped me... her money bought things like those two range cookers over there. But the money was kind of a barrier. It got in the way. We had to see beyond me being obligated—dunno—indebted to her. And I don't know what marriage is for her, anyway. I just know I can give something to her no one else has.'

He turned to face us.

'But yeah... Edith has touched me. She lets me into her secret self... only me. I never expected that. I have never felt like this. Kind of scary really. Feels weird.'

Pumpkins

19th May 2019: Dusk

At the evening meal Al had a different persona. He seemed enthroned in the carved chair. It was when his control was accentuated, even though the community was at its most informal. The rest fitted onto the benches as they arrived. They talked about house business. That night there was a long discussion about the walled garden. Donald, an austere, towering Scotsman, sometimes wore a kilt while working, rather than the dungarees. But tonight, for the evening meal, he was in a long robe like the rest. He was concerned about the pumpkins, which were more than a Halloween conceit, but essential to the winter vegetable supply. They needed more cloches for the initial outdoor planting. Al would need to buy some. It all increased the yield.

Hugh asked how big the pumpkins got and Esther went off to her room and brought down a watercolour she'd painted of an *Atlantic giant*. 'It's the largest variety we raised. It actually didn't taste that good. We generally grow smaller ones as well as the squashes.'

In the painting she had placed the pumpkin by the wall. It was as high as eight bricks and as wide. A deep orange shade with red blended in, more like a spaceship than a vegetable.

They lit the thick white candles as the sun disappeared below the edge of the moor. The room was suffused with a ritual atmosphere. The flickering light created an illusion that the faces around the table had softened, become youthful. There was a rapt silence. It was a moment they waited for each day. Helmut's green velvet dress glistened brilliantly. But Hugh always felt uneasy in an atmosphere without noise.

'Do you have any photos?' he asked and seemed to immediately wish he hadn't.

'We don't use cameras here, Hugh,' Esther said with reproof in her voice as if he should simply have realised.

'But it would be nice to have pictures of you all. They could cheer up the place.'

'Sorry, I don't quite understand. Does our home need *cheering up?*' Esther betrayed the first signs of irritation.

'Well maybe not cheering up exactly, but there's a lot of bare wall…'

Esther turned to Al, who looked on blandly.

She continued, 'For myself, Hugh, I don't have any interest in how I look now. I can remember my appearance when I was young. As I look round the table, I can see the history, the story of our lives in our faces. But I don't feel a photo will give you that totality.'

'What about painting portraits of you all? Your pumpkin's stonkingly good.'

'I can't capture faces. Still lifes are a different matter. I'm not sure I would want to anyway.' Esther fiddled with the bangles on her wrist—the slight jingle of thin metal echoed in the room.

I made a suggestion that seemed all right at the time. 'On the top floor there's one portrait on the wall just outside the music room. I think he's Indian. Whoever did that could do a really good job on you people.'

The kitchen became more than silent.

Al said quietly, 'Well he's not here anymore.'

First Trip

20th May 2109: Evening

There was drizzle in the air so for most of the afternoon I stayed in my room reading Proust. I felt a new inner calm had settled on me and I welcomed it. From my window, I had watched the community going to and from the garden as the sodden air slowly soaked into their dungarees. The meal was early that night and I almost missed it. Heavy cloud obliterated the sun and although it was still light, the room was now in semi-darkness without the usual candles. I noticed a silence developing. Hugh's chatter echoed against the walls and got less and less response.

Around eight o'clock, when I was back in my room, there was a knock. It was Al with a strange smile, almost uncertain.

'Can I speak to you?'

'This sounds like it's something serious, Al… shall we get Hugh in?'

'Hugh's already downstairs.'

'Already…?'

'Yeah… he's decided to take part.'

I had the realisation where I was—miles from anywhere, vulnerable and alone. Even Hugh had deserted me. And I was scared what I would hear.

'What's this all about, Al?'

'We're all dropping acid together. It's going to rain tomorrow so we'll take the opportunity. You need a day of rest after a trip.'

I'd never dropped acid. I'd smoked marijuana more than half a lifetime ago. Colours seemed warmer, more brilliant. Music formed solid shapes of sound. I didn't experience any after-effects but once I started teaching, I'd heard how much adulterated stuff was washing round. I'd once been asked if I had taken recreational drugs during an assessment—it was for couples-counselling with Siobhan. And I'd asked the therapist how these drugs could be called recreational. How could the experience of smoking marijuana be equated to creosoting a fence or clipping a bonsai plant?

I'd stopped smoking altogether years ago and knew rolling a joint would land me back with nicotine. I'd tried nicotine-free tobacco, but found a caterpillar in the bag. I couldn't get past the idea of the smouldering end driving another small larva down the cardboard funnel and into my mouth. So I hadn't used anything for years. Everyone knew that the dope, if it had ever been, was not being brought back by some hippy from Morocco. No, I felt if I smoked now, I couldn't get past the ruthless backstory.

So Al was probably involved with criminals in order to score the acid? I asked him, 'Where do you get your supply?'

'There's a lab a few miles down from here in the valley. They don't make much but it's expensive.'

Somehow the transaction didn't seem enmeshed in crime. I was suddenly ready for it. It would be like an initiation. So far, I had just relinquished a past life. This felt like a journey into an unknown country. And I surprised myself that I actually did feel safe in this house.

'Will you be dropping it?' I asked Al, and for some

reason sensed the answer.

Al shook his head. 'Somebody's got to act as a guide Mike. It's not safe for us all to be in our own worlds if something goes badly wrong. Okay with mushrooms of course.'

I sort of wished I hadn't asked. But I was committed now, and there was a kind of gravity to my involvement.

As we entered the kitchen Hugh was reminiscing to Kate and Sylvester about his first and only trip. Kate was pulling up and tying back her red-grey hair, looking at Hugh with a thin ironic smile. Sylvester was more openly amused at Hugh's chatter.

'The one time I took it, I felt I was going to disappear—but I didn't mind at the time. Like everything that was me was compressed to the size of a pea in the middle of my brain. The rest of my brain was this complex mechanism, but if the pea popped… all that was left was a machine.'

'A soft machine,' said Kate.

'You know I always thought that group were too far out for me."

'I meant the Burroughs novel,' she said drily.

Hugh scuffled round in his memory, came up with no recollection of William Burroughs and descended into a confused silence.

Al handed out the tabs, the shape of little pyramids. I popped mine into my mouth with apparent nonchalance and wandered off into the hall. I felt ready for anything new, even if it was as frightening as Hugh's experience. Once I reached the staircase, simply climbing an individual step had become an amusing challenge. Each tread appeared a different size, each bent to one side or the other. It reduced me to giggles as I raised a foot with great deliberation to plant it on the next level. And then the other foot. I could feel my body in intricate detail. Feel the muscles' elasticity as they stretched and relaxed. Feel the bones' solidity like carved marble.

It felt like an hour or several hours later, when I pushed open the door to the music room. Lines of record spines, each slim confection containing the history of weeks in a studio, or the stolen hours in the afternoon and the approaching night in the club. I didn't want nostalgia like Hugh. Something challenging, not reassuring. Something a little different...

Ah... Miles Davis. Siobhan liked him. *Kind of Blue* wasn't it? Sort of exquisite. You couldn't help but be swept up by the beauty, class, swing. Felt great with a large glass of red. Hmmm, *Bitches Brew* by Miles Davis. Different kind of cover but it was just over ten years after *Kind of...* Not sure about the title though. But the music can't have changed that much. I mean U2 and REM, ten, fifteen years later, the songs are different but not that different. Let's give it a listen.

The needle landed, and I was swallowed into a brooding landscape before a storm. A massive trumpet the size of Tibetan shawm, one of those horns so large they play them on stilts, began echoing round the world. The sound was metallic, gigantic. It flew round the room, as an electronic tempest broke amid chaotic drums. And then the storm passed, the trumpet disappeared and an insidious creeping bass line led me into a forest of glass. A wooden snakelike instrument was slithering along the forest floor. Electric creatures leapt through crystalline branches. And chords from myriad keyboards became large raindrops of deep vivid colour, landing on the path I was on. And then the trumpet returned. There was a voice in the trumpet and it spoke to me about the bleakness of the world, that everything we love we will lose. And yet there was this harsh beauty everywhere in a planet that didn't need me or anyone. I wanted to be part of a planet without people.

A guitar became a brightly coloured bird calling from the tree tops. The undergrowth was heaving with sound. There were drums everywhere. The trumpet returned to speak to me again. It had more to say. Overwhelming unspeakable truths above a bubbling magma of sound. A soprano saxophone slithered down from a tree…

But I had had enough. There was something indefinably unbearable in this music. But I knew I had an infinite amount of time. I slowly and carefully raised the stylus and stood in a thick and gelatinous silence. I wasn't sure I could move. I pressed my hand against the air and felt that if I walked quietly and deliberately, I might make it to the door without disturbing the room's aura.

Once outside the room my body felt weightless. I floated down the stairs to the ground floor with a fluency and grace I was unaware I was capable of. The front door was the size of the gate to an ancient city. I wanted to be outside in the night air but the door was locked. I kept turning the circular metal handle. At first it was simply an attempt to open the door. But these fascinating creaks— each time I turned the ring a different sound emerged, like drawing the bow behind a viola fretboard, like a cat purring in a deep sleep. Every sound was suffused with wonder.

I became distracted by the patterns in the wood. They were in continual flux, flowing as if wooden oils were coagulating on the frame. The world was so intricate and beautiful. You'd need so many lifetimes to fully live the experiences dwelling in this house. I forgot about wanting to be beyond the door in an infinitely spacious moorland. The house felt like a book I could never finish. The whole world within it was endlessly fascinating. Individual moments that could freeze and last forever while I simply stood in front of this door. And yet I knew there would be change. It was inevitable. I just had to wait for the next revelation.

Edith and the Man

20th May 2019: Midnight

Into a fathoms' deep silence, a voice reverberated. I turned slowly. The kitchen door was just slightly ajar. I wondered whether I could walk towards the door if I moved ever so gradually across the stone flags. And each slab felt so cold, as if I were walking on blocks of ice in my bare feet. But like being in the sea when the wave thumps your bare skin—the cold was an enervating shock.

The kitchen was throbbing with colour—palpitating browns and greens. The walls shifted slowly like wet clay. Both mandalas were revolving madly like Catherine wheels. Nothing had solidity—colours merged, meshed, split. The kitchen table stretched on and on as if the wooden surface was elastic. And at the far end in the distance, Edith sat, smiling gently as she crayoned a large rainbow. She seemed so diminutive, so far away.

I began to speak. The walls had a cavernous echo. Each sound, each movement, changed the world forever. Every action needed care… 'Edith—are—you—all—right?'

The room was bending, curving in an arc towards where she was sitting.

Edith didn't seem burdened with my knowledge. She spoke softly, breathlessly. 'I feel so safe, safer than I have ever felt. Al is watching over me. He will be my husband.'

She drew another curve of colour and intoned, 'We're in the heart of the house—the beating heart—it's alive.'

But I was distracted by the flames in the grate. My fascination with flames goes back as far as I remember.

We never had coal fires in the prefab. A boiler almost provided central heating. That and a paraffin stove. But I loved to look at coal fires, and when we visited other houses I was mesmerised. Flames never lost their unfamiliar otherness, a marvel in the drab world of the 1950s.

And there were shapes in the blaze—faces. There was Al, a long and melancholy face. He was being punished, trapped in the flames. But just as suddenly the guilt was expiated. What guilt? Our collective guilt for what we do as humans. And Al was suffering for our wrongs. Except now all guilt was done away with at a stroke. Al could emerge...

And then Edith began talking in a slow, rapt manner. 'I haven't told anyone why I really came here. Mike. You feel different, you're not part of the community. You sort of feel safe. I want to tell you. I feel you might understand what happened to me. I just feel that no one else at Gritstone might understand...'

Some force was crushing my stomach as if it were a ball of paper. I never imagined I could feel scared about a revelation from Edith. We were immersed now—outside time. It felt like hours since the last sentence she had spoken. And I asked, 'Not even Al?'

I saw the shape of her thoughts—like a woozy ectoplasm, but I couldn't divine what they were. My question punctured the surface of one bubble of thought and was swallowed, like a cell pierced under a microscope.

'No... not Al.'

She paused as we made sense of that fact. Her transgressive feelings. And then as if a decision has been made, she began. 'My parents were both dead. I was starting to live my life on my own. A man even asked me out a few times but he tried to go too far… and I didn't really like him.'

It was if she was reporting a dream she was part of, right then as it happened. She spoke blandly, absently in her uninflected midlands accent. Everything in the kitchen felt slow, moving to a halt. The pans, the kitchen range had a kind of life but they had lost motion. They rested, they slept.

I had transcended listening. I was entering Edith's world, inhabiting it. I was moving freely around in it. The story unfolded, became a three-dimensional drama. I could see the large house with a towering pointed roof, an empty road at night and a long front path snaking up a steep hill to a large black painted door—the tall house, at least four storeys high where Edith lived on her own. This huge property with spiky gables, carved grinning dragons staring down from the roof, cavernous rooms she would never enter, with chairs and tables under dust sheets. Somewhere on a radio, a piano was playing innocent, intricate music full of regret. Schubert but better than him, more exquisite, more immortally profound…

'But he wouldn't leave me alone. He started coming to the library.'

I was transported to another scene. Now we were in the library where she was working. But not like some municipal library. I could see the shelves spreading out like the petals of a flower emanating from the large central console where Edith sat in a smart dark suit. Her hair severely pulled back into a neat pony tail. She was stern and intimidating.

Edith stood up from the desk and began turning the

lights off. It was November and the evening swallowed the shelves, the books and tables into the darkness, as the long fluorescent tubes pinged and were extinguished. But in the far corner a figure was bent over his computer screen. As I listened to Edith, I was there too, under that last tube of light. I saw the figure. I was there sitting at the next desk, watching as the face turned to Edith, a face of deep creases, full wet lips, slavering, simian. It was him. The man. That man.

Edith had told the man formally and severely to leave and I watched him meekly pack his light brown scratched leather briefcase and walk away without looking back.

'But he was stalking me Mike. I stopped at shop windows and looked round and he was there, but he didn't even pretend he wasn't after me now. I thought I would go somewhere with bright lights and crowds of people. And I wandered round the shelves in this supermarket and when I turned he was there—neither of us even pretending to buy anything. And then he disappeared and I sneaked out after a while. But he'd been waiting for me…'

I didn't want to hear any more. But I couldn't stop Edith—not now. I had lost all ability to move. Edith was not animated. There was a toneless quality as if she were watching herself. As if she were sitting before a gripping film, with the neutral gaze we see if we look round the faces in a cinema.

'I didn't know he was there until he suddenly grabbed me from behind and pushed me into a covered yard that would have been a stable. It stank of piss. And he cornered me against the wall, and his breath smelt like a gone-off camembert.

'I had a hat pin in a side pocket of my handbag. My mother always advised me to carry one. I never believed I would use it. And I was able to slip it out even though he'd pretty well trapped me. It was six inches long. And while he was fumbling at his fly buttons, I plunged it between his legs. And his eyes bulged and he buckled. And I pushed in the needle slowly until just the little pin head stuck out from his tweed trousers. I could feel nothing. Nothing. I loathed him for what he was going to do to me.

'And he crumpled over onto the cobbles, and there wasn't much blood coming out then, just a small ooze round the pinhead. I hated him for turning me into this monster. And I stared at this stuck pig lying on the cobbles. And I didn't feel sorry. I leaned down to a few inches from his face. And his skin with those deep folds, his slobbering mouth, he looked like some kind of bulldog. And his eyes were begging me to take the pain away, and his face was sopping and I stuck a dirty tissue into his mouth and I told him, "If you go to the police I'll make sure they know what you were going to do, you bastard."

'And he was just mouthing little muffled sounds and looking at me pleading.

'And I pulled out the needle and he was groaning and the blood shot up like a geyser. And I walked away without looking back. When I got home, I washed and changed. I threw the clothes I'd worn into a black bin bag. There were large wheelie bins in a block of flats nearby, and I dropped the bag in there. I saw my doctor the following day and persuaded him that I was depressed—it wasn't too hard—and sent in a sick note. Then I phoned

Al and I took the next train. Al helped me write to my solicitor and instruct him to put the house on the market and eventually it went for something huge. And when the sick note ran out and we put together a letter and I resigned. After a few months I started to believe that man hadn't gone to the police—but I was at Gritstone by then.'

Edith's voice had gradually emerged from a hazy mist of distanced recall to an urgent present. I felt a vice around my arm. She was gripping it with the strength of a woman in labour.

'Mike, I never told Al what had happened. I don't want him to know. He might not want to marry me. I don't know if that man's dead.' And we sat there in silence for a long time. The vibrancy had left the room. The dawn light was a leaden grey before the rain; without another word Edith went off to find Al.

The acid was wearing off when I collapsed onto my bed—though I doubted if it would ever wear off entirely. I had become the voyeur of every scene in Edith's story, immersed and detached. Watching like an unerring camera, I had seen the man's body swallow the spike so gradually. I watched his unbearable pain lying in the alley as if it were a film, horrific but unreal. The consequence of his action. By now it had the quality of a trance. I had experienced this release of power in Edith. She had been transformed in my mind into an avenging angel. She might—she did—revert into shyness and reticence, but this image persisted. Not for the first or last time I had hidden knowledge. The unwilling custodian of narratives I'd have done anything not to have heard.

The Day after for Hugh

21st May 2019: Morning

I woke believing my body was made of glass. Persuading myself it was safe to move, I left my room with the utmost care. I found Edith scrubbing the kitchen tiles. She turned a bland face to me. It was as if the revelations of last night had never happened.

'Mike, you'd better look in at your friend.'

Hugh was lying on a sofa shivering under a blanket in the room in the eaves. He was mumbling to himself. Then he saw me. 'Have the snakes gone? Over there. There was one crawling up the curtain.'

'Hugh, it's a curtain cord'.

'Why didn't they tell me it was a cord?'

'Who?'

'There were six of us up here listening to Wishbone Ash, but when I got scared of the snake, they all left.'

'You find out who your friends are, if nothing else.'

'Mike, I had that experience again. I was about to disappear. Everything that was me would never exist again. In fact, I'm not sure it hasn't happened. How can I prove I still exist? I may be just a robot with conditioned opinions.'

'Well a lot of people have thought that about you for some time.'

'Thank you, Mike, I'll have a cup of tea please. Acid's strange. But I'm not craving for the next tab. I don't think I'll have any more for a while—until I forget this trip anyway, which might be next week.'

Esther's Journey

22nd May 2019: Morning

Hugh was worn out with the effort of struggling with a bowl of porridge. He tried to force down a prodigious breakfast because the lunch break would only offer a cold mix of compacted rice and vegetables, made bearable by soy sauce. He said he was always starving by eight at night. While he sat back and stared at the sticky mass that still awaited him, I was helping Esther clear the bowls into cupboards. These bowls all had the same muddy glaze, which could make the porridge look rather sickening. I really didn't want to think in detail why. I washed the copper-bottom pans and then Esther burnished them. She would give each pan a final polish before hanging it from one of the butcher's hooks above the kitchen range, holding each up to the light from the kitchen windows. I was fascinated at how the pans snared the sunlight and spread glinting pinpricks onto the kitchen walls. This polishing, this dedication could become hypnotic.

Hugh and I were curious about Esther. She kept her hair severely short and looked indefinably smart even in dungarees. The denims she wore had the quality of appearing to have been ironed after washing day by day. And keeping your working clothes clean involved scrubbing them by hand in a tin bath and pegging them from ropes in the barn. In conversation at the table Esther tended to keep her replies at a fairly anodyne level, but her speech had an assertive unhurried quality. Hugh was always the one to take a risk—or not realise he was taking a risk—when he asked her, 'I'm kind of curious Esther—I suppose we both are—about what your life was like before you came to Gritstone. I don't know—I sense it was very different—I mean, am I wrong?'

Esther spoke over her shoulder at first as she carried on with the kitchen tasks. She had a light smile, and her voice transformed into the more languid drawl of someone who when she does speak, is used to being listened to.

'I came here because I wanted some chance to return to the life I had when I was young, when life was so hopeful. I mean, wasn't it wonderful in the late 60s? I know it's a bit of a cliché to say that—but I had the most searing time. We all did, didn't we?'

Hugh could only nod. He'd told me that the late 60s passed him by on his council estate in Rochdale. But he was always too embarrassed to admit it. When he started university, things opened up but he still had the feeling he'd missed the best bits of that era. It was the same for me in the Coventry prefab, but I never let on to Hugh. I always tried to seem slightly more experienced. Unlike him I did have flared jeans when I arrived at university.

Esther had her own momentum now.

'And I suppose we felt it was inevitable the world would change with us. Be transformed. We just didn't need those Tudorbethan houses in silent streets where everyone seemed holed up in secret. Most times you didn't know if anyone was living in those houses at all. And the department stores, the appalling furniture. Oh God—and the variety shows on the telly at the weekend. I'll bet you remember what it was like. Once I got the chance to leave home I went like a shot.'

She stopped and stared at the pan in her hand, her skewed reflection looking back at her. It could be the younger self immersed in a haze. I remembered watching Morecambe and Wise with my mum. Perhaps I didn't have the same drive to leave. It had seemed all right at the time.

Esther sat on the bench opposite us with a steaming cup of nettle tea. To me it seemed that a shield was being lowered, her bland responses at meal times were a confected protection. I suppose we weren't part of the community and that may have made her less guarded.

And she was absorbed in her own past now. Hugh and I might as well have been sitting in the stalls at some matinee in a provincial theatre listening to her story.

'We squatted in this abandoned cottage in North Wales for a few years—the best years really. We had an open fire and no electricity and there was a cold tap against the wall in the yard. Honestly it was great. You lived in harmony with the seasons. It was all so different then. Young people all seemed to feel the same. It wasn't about being involved in any kind of politics. We were beyond politics. We had the solidarity of the young. It didn't need naming. People like us would pass by and stop and talk. And we'd share a joint, they might stay for a meal and then just carry on. There were so many people squatting like us in the abandoned countryside.'

I wondered, 'Perhaps because the smallholders had gone bankrupt.' But she ignored me. Hugh and I couldn't hold back the roaring tide of Esther's memory. She was breathless as her past returned.

'You could trust your generation. At least the generation we knew. I couldn't include those skinheads.

Such hateful creations, you wondered if they weren't part of some government plot. It didn't seem an accident that the skinheads' first disco was at the Finchley Conservative club. You know, Thatcher's constituency. I have it on good authority.' I knew about the Con club as they called it at the time, and I was miles away in Coventry. But I also had privileged knowledge Hugh wouldn't want me to reveal—that for six months on his estate he wore DMs and a Crombie. All the young guys did. It didn't stop him getting beaten up. Perhaps he should have shaved his head as well.

Esther continued in an unstoppable flow. 'Older people were like interlopers on the earth. You weren't sure if they were really human. I remember wondering if most were robots, otherwise they would know that they were totally free.' But she stopped. There was a frown slowly forming.

'I don't know when it all started to change. It was as if we'd all been part of a fantasy. But it really wasn't a fantasy! It was a possible existence. But most of my friends betrayed the idea, gradually quietly, secretly.'

A vague tentative tone crept into her voice. We listened in silence to what she would probably call 'her journey.'

'Jack and I... I suppose you'd call him my partner... Anyway... we moved to a squat in London and I got pregnant. That was around '78. When we had our first boy, the council rehoused us and it was a nice flat. But of course, we couldn't live on the benefits we got and support a family.'

I remembered being unemployed for a while round that time. Nobody cared. You just lined up in the dole office, joined a queue under your box number and shuffled forward. It was the only time I really felt a proper part of the proletariat. It felt all right really.

'So I had to find a job. And somebody I knew got me into this computer firm. I didn't know much about I.T., didn't have much of a clue really. It was the same for most people. Anyway, I learnt a bit, went to college, and started going out on consultancy. And then there was the beginning of the internet. Not many people really knew about it then. But I suppose it was clear the web was going to change everything, even at that time when it took ten minutes to download a picture. Anyway, the firm grew.'

I'd been quite happy as a lecturer, a bit safe but not badly paid. Hugh and Lily ran a stationery shop in their village. He said it was usually stressful and they always worried about the bills. But he told me he used to feel a fool when earning money looked so easy for people like Al… and Esther.

'And then the firm went public on the stock market and I found out about these things called shares. And I got quite rich. Jack stayed with the kids. But he started snorting coke and worse in the middle of the day. I inevitably found out—him sponging off the money I earned. And then one day after who knows how many rows, he was gone and the kids were left stranded at the school gates. The bastard!'

Esther's face had gone puce. Hugh made the noises he would make in these situations, sounding both emollient and ineffectual. Esther collected herself.

'Well I had to organise childcare, but in the end, it seemed cheaper, better for everyone, to send them to boarding school. Anyway, that was what I did.'

I'd always reflexively derided boarding schools but I

didn't feel this was the moment to argue. Now we were meekly listening because we could not, not.

'And it was funny. Most of the people I worked with were round my age when I joined, so we all got rich together. But have you noticed about our generation? We did rather well from our work pensions let alone the state handout. And then for some reason the ladder was kicked away for the generations that missed the 1970 Isle of Wight festival. I mean it almost seems like we plotted it.'

Hugh looked at me as if to say, 'I'm still skint...'

'Anyway, it feels like we were always bought off at every stage: the generation with the really dangerous ideas. I don't know if it's true...' Esther drifted to a halt on a vague questioning tone.

Hugh sat silently but later said to me whoever bought off Esther lost interest in him years ago.

To cover the sudden vacuum I asked, 'So your kids have grown up. Where are they now? Are they doing okay?'

'I hate them. I hate what they have become.' She turned and hung up the last pan on its meat hook as if to impale it.

Hugh chimed in, 'Is what they're doing so different to what you became? I mean before you decided to come here.'

She stared at Hugh fixedly but her whole face was one boiling slobbering tremor.

Hugh held up his hands.

'I'm sorry. It's not my business.'

Esther was holding back an earthquake under the skin. She hissed, 'It's all right—I'd just rather not... Al urges us to be really open. But it's hard...'

I couldn't stop Hugh continuing as an innocent torturer. 'And Jack…?'

'Please!'

Hugh changed the subject… to himself. 'I split up with Lily five years ago. I've had a terrible…'

But Esther had rushed from the room before he finished the sentence.

Hugh turned to me and said, 'I don't think that went too well.'

In a few minutes we heard Al's van grinding over the gravel and reversing into the yard. He'd arrived from Halifax with ten hessian sacks of brown rice to unload. Helmut came out of the stables. They carried them into the pantry. The pantry had a solid three-inch thick airtight door, more appropriate for a bank than a kitchen. Hugh said it seemed extreme.

Al grinned at Hugh. 'There are plenty of rats. We can't afford for them to get at our supplies.'

'Can't you lay poison?'

'But I thought you could not kill, Hugh.' Hugh became rather sulky. He had told me how you would see rats, the size of a small dog, riffling through the grass and reeds on the waterfront, dirty grey coats and sickening long hairless tails. He would lock his cabin and lie there in the dark until the scrabbling stopped. Or look out of one of the little windows at a snout snuffling against the glass moving from side to side as if in a breeze, the little eyes fixing on him…

He murmured to me, 'Yes, I'd make exceptions for killing them.'

While I sat tight, Hugh offered to help carry in the

hessian bags from the van, and came close to a permanent back injury before Helmut breezily lifted the load from him.

After parking the van in the barn, Al walked back across the cobbles to the house. Hugh had been waiting to speak to him and waylaid him at the kitchen door.

'I think we've upset Esther.'

'That might take some doing.'

'We just asked about how she felt about her kids.'

'Don't see why you shouldn't. I encourage a culture of openness.'

'But she stormed out.'

'Hugh sometimes you mess up—well pretty often—but you don't seem to get it. You don't seem to realise that you're a truth-teller. And you don't seem to get it that this is your greatest strength. What I say may sound kind of offensive and I don't really have time to explain, but you're what they used to call a *holy fool*.'

Hugh seemed bereft of the vocabulary to respond. Al had never said he valued him at all—ever—even for this.

'And a guy like you has an important place in this community if you stay on…'

I just sat there. I didn't want to be Al's *holy fool* but I felt a little sidelined. I wasn't in Al's orbit now.

Hebden Bridge

23rd May 2019: Morning

It was mid-morning. I had just visited the latrine. A bird was calling over the far side of the field from the hut. Long collections of notes that could have been from a flute of glass. I followed the sound over a stile, and found I was on a path descending steeply into the valley, an old woolpack trail with rocks occasionally laid as steps down sudden descents or across streams; streams that form after storms pour from the tops and at other times are hidden currents riffling through the grass.

Eventually I was climbing the wooden steps fixed against the side of a wall, and came down onto an empty single-track road bordered by grazing fields. There were no hedges up on the moors, only the drystone walls. Ahead was a hamlet of cottages of thick sandstone blocks. I felt a dangerous exhilaration. I hadn't been on my own and away from the House since we arrived. But today, I'd decided to take my wallet. It wasn't a concerted plan. I just allowed myself to be tantalised onward from the moment I heard the bird.

Beyond the last cottage was a bus stop, a post with a timetable. A bus was due in twenty minutes for Hebden Bridge. I had never been down to the town. I'd only seen the place on the news when the high street was underwater. I sat on the wall and waited until a small hopper bus pulled up. I placed the Freedom pass I hadn't used for weeks onto the reader. The bus shuddered back into life. There were two women in their eighties sitting with their shopping trollies in front of them. At first, I thought I was imagining it when I heard one woman whisper, 'Gritstone.' I turned round to them and they went silent. A young man got on at the next stop, earpieces throbbing under his beanie. He looked sidelong at me. I wasn't used to this attention on a London bus. I thought I was quite blend-in respectable. But on the little hopper I might as well have been another species.

How could they know where I came from? I was still wondering when the bus made its final stop. I wandered round the pedestrian area. I felt I was being openly stared at by passers-by. It seemed like paranoid imagining at first. There was suspicion in the faces of the sales assistants if I looked at all likely to go into a shop. I came up to the small open market at the bottom of a steep slope. The place was heaving. Different stalls selling what the middle class—the class I used to feel I belonged to—see as a human right—sourdough bread, olives, pies and thirty varieties of cheese. I felt familiar sensations of social panic. But equally I was starving by then.

I stood in front of the pie stall. I had forgotten the etiquette of waiting to be served. You remember who else is there and gradually edit them as they go. But I couldn't keep track of who was waiting, who should be served next. I'd been at Gritstone so long, the conversation around me seemed to be at a gallop, in a foreign language similar to English. The pieman eventually gestured to me.

'Escaped have ya?'

I just felt confused, asked for a mushroom and asparagus pie, used up pretty well all my change, and scurried off to a bench near the canal. Again, the guy seemed to know about where I was from. This visit felt increasingly uncomfortable. But I needed to drink something as long as they'd take £20 notes.

I passed a crowded bar. In the semi-darkness, shadows shifted and criss-crossed, the babble chaotic and indistinct, bubbling like a cauldron. It was a long time since I'd been in one, even before I left London. The withdrawal had been gradual. I'd hardly been anywhere in the past year.

Eventually I found an empty café. The door buzzed and the barista turned round to look at me. He was even more upfront.

'Down from Crazy House?'

I was less puzzled by this stage.

'Gritstone,' the young man clarified.

'But how do you know I'm from there?'

'Might as well be wearing an orange jumpsuit. You all look same in them dungarees… and the crocs.'

I took a polystyrene cup in silence. The barista glowered at the £20 note.

It began to drizzle. I sat in the doorway of a closed-down shop, I put the cup down to shake a small stone out of my croc. Within seconds a pound coin landed in my chai latte.

I got on the same Hopper bus going out beyond Heptonstall. Climbing back up the slippery path in the now heavy rain, I was working out what to tell them and wasn't sure at all if it should be the truth.

Rosamond opens up

24th May 2019: Morning

There was a cat at Gritstone. Helmut fed him from a large sealed tub of biscuits which he kept in the kitchen safe. He was called Hercules and he was a monster, all muscular black fur and a bushy tail that betrayed his inner thoughts. When it waved violently side to side it was best not to try picking him up for a cuddle. Hugh saw Helmut fondling the purring beast, and risked cat-scratch fever by trying himself—just the once. He now cowered in the glaring animal's presence. Hercules patrolled the yard and the fields and slept in the barn, often under Hugh's car. But he didn't always need to come to Helmut for his biscuits. And that morning Hugh saw his other means of sustenance when the cat padded triumphantly across the yard, a dead rat lolling out of his clenched jaws.

Ezra cheered from the garden, 'Way to go, Herc!'

Hugh's way of forgetting this incident was to transfix himself with the November 1971 Melody Maker. He read to me and whoever was in the kitchen, the announcement of the release of Genesis's *Nursery Cryme*. But as we sat with the paper spread on the kitchen table, we could hear raised voices. Not shouting. The house culture did not admit it. A kind of semi-audible bickering approaching from the hall.

'You look ridiculous coming out your room with those great moth-holes in your sweater. It's embarrassing. I can't even look.'

'Oh really. Well you are *more* of an embarrassment in

that four man tent you're wearing. Hardly anyone is as large as you actually look in that thing.'

'But I bought it at Monsoon. Look I prefer this style of kaftan. Certainly compared to Al's standard issue…' They entered the kitchen. The woman looked around to see if Hugh had registered that comment. But he was the past-master at appearing not to.

'In 1986… You've got no business in a thing like that now.'

'But look at you. You look like Albert Steptoe. That ridiculous stubble. It might look good on a younger man with dark hair. But that and the moth holes—you're decrepit!'

'I just need to give my face a rest. I don't care. I might grow a beard.'

'At your age you might get a job as Father Christmas— but there's so many strange men like you applying.'

The voices disappeared through the kitchen door. We could see the short woman called Stephanie with her grey hair in a pigtail trailing down her back, in the voluminous orange dress. And beside her the tall gangly figure of Bruno, in his cardigan and dungarees, stooping as if continually entering through a low arch.

We realised that Rosamond was standing beside us. There was the faint whiff of the stables about her. Everyone washed but they all had a lived-in odour, individual to each.

'I reckon sometimes they'd get on my nerves,' Hugh confided once they were out of earshot.

'Well I'm not sure this is the right place for them,' Rosamond replied in her steady low-volume boom.

'Still that's how couples are.' Hugh immediately looked as if he'd made another vapid *aperçu* among so many.

'I've done my best to forget, Hugh. I am not interested in that mucky relationship business.'

'What, you mean you've…'

'Not for a very long time and I have no regrets—none at all.'

'Was it *that* bad?'

'Oh, I don't want to even…'

'Did you go on like those two?'

'No. I feel their relationship's quite healthy. They care about each other. And they're just continually disappointed. That's not the same as hatred. My marriage ended mostly in utter silence.'

'I suppose that's how mine ended up. We got tired of arguing.'

'For years we had sex only at prescribed times—by my husband.'

I didn't feel we needed this much candour, but Hugh seemed to empathise.

'It didn't matter how I felt. It was presented as my only opportunity. I had no inclination in the final… decade. It ended just being a sticky, messy business.'

'Umm…'

'Loveless! If I ever loved him, I couldn't remember in the end.'

As always Hugh wanted to share. 'Lily threw me out five years ago. But I still miss her.'

'Well I don't—not him. He can be strangled with his own guts for all I care.'

'We did love each other once. We had a quiet life in this Norfolk village. When I had to move out, some of the people were very nice, very understanding—someone said, "*It's her loss…*" I thought that was so kind.'

'Villages—I hate villages. All that gossip about you. Who you're seen with. Your husband spotted with a woman in Leeds. It gets back to you and then what do you do with that knowledge… eh? He comes home, says nothing and turns on the telly. Where do you even start with a man like that? Easier to carry on until the next day. Then there they all are, the old biddies staring at you in the local shop with eyes like plates on sticks. What else do they have to occupy themselves? This is better entertainment than *Home and Away*. I was ritually eviscerated day after day.'

'Ev…'

'Disembowelled. Well I mean not literally—obviously not—but it felt like the old crows would do it given a chance '

'Oh…'

'Yes, and in the end, I could see no way out—so I came here.'

'But how did you hear about this place? We couldn't find it online when Al wrote to us.'

'No, I think Al's taken down the website. I was able to find it then. I did a search…'

'We wouldn't have known what to search for.'

'God, I was starting to feel a bit desperate. I got up a search engine and I think I told you, I wrote "*I want to leave the world.*" I don't know what I was after. Perhaps some comfort, somebody who felt like me. Maybe I wanted the most painless way to go. I was sitting in a silent kitchen in a silent village. Outside there was this cavernous darkness. At the end of the garden endless fields that had disappeared at sunset. There's a song by John Dowland; there are these words that sum up that evening,' and she suddenly broke into a light singing voice;

'Where night's black bird her sad infamy sings,
There let me live forlorn.'

She sighed. 'I have never felt so desolate…'

I wanted to say she had a nice voice… but…

'And Gritstone came up. It wasn't on the first page of results but I ignored the search engine's pushier suggestions. Something drew me to select this site. And I read a little about the place. It was really only a few sentences. There was small clip you could play. Some beautiful electronic music that seemed to go on forever and later I remembered it was "Tubular Bells". Do you remember when it came out? I'd put it on and let the speakers play across the fields.'

I remembered it coming out, but Hugh would only have known the theme from *The Exorcist*…

'And Al's voice came over. And he was speaking in that arresting tone he has—it can be so soft as if you are bathing in it. And he spoke over the music—something like, "*Do you remember this music, this time? We can feel like we've lost all hope since then. What happened to the world we dreamed of?*" And then he said that if you have no commitments, and—you know—something like if you have a little money you can contribute to the community—to share a life meaningfully. And it ended something like, "*If you feel like you want to leave the world we are surrounded by, write to me.*" And there was this online—you couldn't call it a form—that you filled in. And a week later Al phoned me.

'He told me where Gritstone was and I took the train to Hebden Bridge. And I walked up from the station for a few miles. It was a foul day but the rain had stopped for half an hour. Anyway the nearer I got, the more nervous I became about committing myself. I hadn't told Al when I planned to come. I could change my mind. I hid my large knapsack. It had everything I wanted to bring with me. And I left it in a small drystone hut. It might have been some kind of shepherd's shelter. And I made my way up the path as if I were a walker who was lost. And I saw this man in a goatskin jacket and shorts and I must admit I felt a bit nervous. He was so tall. And his eyes. He seemed to have enormous piercing eyes—the eyes of a wolf. I mean the irises were so large and black, and they hardly fitted between the eyelids. It didn't help that he was carrying an axe. But he spoke really politely in that German accent. And I admitted I wanted to see the house. I didn't want to lie and he seemed to understand. And he took me to Al.'

Hugh had stopped crossing and re-crossing his legs. His tea had gone cold. I sat mutely but Rosamond somehow seemed to be concentrating on Hugh who was nodding as she spoke.

'Gosh, and then things were really moving quickly. I spoke to Al and he explained what they were doing here. And I really felt okay. I had that feeling again. A commonality, a shared existence. Not me alone in the world.'

'There seems to be some shared purpose.'

'We are escaping the present world. We no longer live in it. Nobody talks about it. We know very little about what's going on outside the walls. You know you leave your phones, anything that communicates—but you do it willingly. Once it was explained to me, that's what I wanted to do.

'Al told me he had felt like this for years. He'd made shedloads of money in the city, travelled the world and spent most of it. Now he wanted to share his life with people who would understand, who were of his generation, who felt this present world was not the one they hoped for when they were young.

'Some people do just turn up. One woman flew in from Connecticut. But Al could sense that itch of restlessness in her—felt it wasn't right for her. Even after the first day she was begging to check her smartphone. She was just continually anxious about her daughter, that her friends would wonder if she was safe, what was being said about her on the plethora of social media she was involved with. She was still too entangled to let go of her life outside the walls… We mean it—*Leave this World.*'

Helmut in the Bayern

25th May 2019: Mid-morning

A pewter sky covered the valley. I strolled from the kitchen into the cobbled yard. The pump seemed almost alive—the spout about to nod or make some pronouncement on what it had seen, perhaps hundreds of years of people's folly, tragedy and the experience of being forced together.

Helmut continued with the simple task for him, of drawing gallons of water into the large wooden buckets and lifting them into the kitchen. Perpetually boiling kettles and saucepans rattled their lids on the range.

A towering pile of logs, to feed the stove, was ranged against the kitchen wall to the level of the first floor. There was a stretched-out awning you'd see on a shopfront, to shelter them from the rain. Each piece was meticulously stacked, the lengths the same and the logs fitted together like a drystone wall. The edge of the pile in the yard was sheer, as if the sharpest of samurai swords had sliced down in a single movement.

I walked across the yard and into the walled garden. Outside the house I wore dungarees like everyone else. I'd almost forgotten I was wearing them in Hebden Bridge. Edith had found a pair large enough for me with the braces extended. It was just convenient to pull them on with a t-shirt. I had begun experimenting not wearing underpants, which saved washing, but there were uncomfortable rough moments. I'd found a name, Asif, sewn into the lining. But when I asked Edith who this was, she simply said, 'It was someone who lived here…'

I passed the area where the herbs grew in their separate neatly cultivated beds. Spiky rosemary, the tang of wild garlic hanging in the air, and the thicker scent of lavender merged in a strange cocktail of aromas. I stroked the lavender and held the fragrance in my fingers to my nostrils. I could remember my mother's lavender water as a polite accompaniment. I was unprepared for the sharp aroma invading my sinuses.

Nearby a bee was swallowed into the bell of a snapdragon, ecstatically diving in to gorge on the nectar. I marvelled at the bee's experience of complete abandon. And for that to continue for your whole short life in airborne euphoria. To be totally useful to your fellow bees in a delirious quest for the sensuality of the stamens. I imagined my own metamorphosis into a gigantic body of golden and black hoops, with bristles like a natural Velcro…

Helmut walked past carrying an even more than usually enormous axe. He was in his goatskin jacket and *Lederhosen* ensemble. The sight of the eight-inch blade on Helmut's shoulder aided my emergence from this reverie.

'I go to cut wood, Mike. Will you help me?'

'Ah so it's you that built that pile by the kitchen door?'

'*Ja* Mike. I come from the Bayern. My family lived in a village under the Pershing mount. Outside our houses all logs are so neatly stacked. Or you are not a respectable being.'

'You left your family to come here.'

'*Nein*, they are no longer there.' Helmut looked awkward.

'I was wondering how you've ended up here? You seem

maybe thirty years younger than anyone else.'

'I had to leave the Bayern after my parents' house was burnt to the ground and they succumbed to the fire.'

'So, they died… I'm sorry.'

'*Ja*, and then I left the Bayern. I never return.'

'Did you find out what caused…' But I decided not to enter into the intricacies of this episode. Helmut was still carrying the axe. I moved the subject on with some hesitancy. 'So how did you find out about Gritstone?'

'I was resting in the hostel for youth in *München*. I find free internet and *ich weisse nicht*… I look for words to reflect my mood, *ja*?'

I nodded. 'You'd been through this terrible ordeal… and there you are all alone in Munich.'

'*Ja* I am very shaken. And I go online and find this old song, "*Verlassen auf der ganzen Welt*". It is song my parents liked. It makes me sad when I hear it. And then I find "Leave this world" come up in *Deutsch* translation—and I find Gritstone's site and I open the link and hear Al's voice with the tinkly *Musik* playing. And I listen to his voice and what he was saying—and I thought this is *fantastisch*! And I write to him and I take an *Autobus* and then another A*utobus* and then cross the sea and *ich fahre nach Yorkshire*.

'I meet Al and I tell him why I have come and I tell him my parents did not like me in dresses but it is part of me. And he said, "*It's okay man. I have been waiting for someone like you to arrive. We need strong man.*" So, I stay and work and not pay rent because I do all heavy tasks.'

Helmut began chopping logs from a small fallen willow he had found in the field. A steady satisfying thud echoed across the valley. These logs would keep the fires stoked for just a few nights for all this effort. I found myself imagining the flames burning in the kitchen hearth. And then unbidden, the image of a far larger blaze as fire ate into the body of a large house at the base of a mountain and screaming from within as the beams collapsed. I helped wheelbarrow the logs back to the house and watched Helmut meticulously stack them against the kitchen wall.

The Police

26th May 2019: 9.00 am

I'd overslept and missed breakfast, so when I came out of my room, I was surprised to find people still fluttering around the house, which was usually empty by now. From an upstairs window I had spotted Helmut walking away at some pace carrying a black plastic bag over his shoulder. Edith was feverishly cleaning the surfaces of an already pristine kitchen.

Al was sitting in his usual chair.

'We're having a meeting right now. Just give us five minutes to get together. You'll need to hear this.'

And they were all there in five minutes apart from Helmut.

'People, some of you already know the police will be here in the next fifteen minutes. I've told Helmut to take the drugs onto the moor and bury them. So we have nothing to hide, nothing to worry about.'

I looked round the table. I guessed most of these people had not had much to do with the police—well, apart from Ezra, and he looked more nervous than most. Probably not one of them had the police set foot in their house, let alone be the subject of a raid.

Stephanie singsonged, 'Well I used to say, what have I got to hide?'

Sylvester closed down the conversation. 'Well now honey, it's class A drugs... and well...'

They disappeared to their rooms. The usual tasks were abandoned except for Edith who quietly carried on scrubbing the table top.

I found Al sitting calmly in the library, watching the drive up to the house. He had quickly transformed himself, and now wore a pair of grey trousers with a sharp ironed crease and a crisp white shirt. His hair was stretched back in a tight ponytail.

'How the hell did you know they were coming?'

'I got tipped off…'

'…'

'Charlie tells me.'

'Who the fuck is he?'

'I've not got time to explain. You'll meet him.'

'But Al, you gave all the acid to Helmut. We might never see him again.'

'He wouldn't dare. Where could he go? Anyway, I need him out of the way—he's wanted.'

I was speechless.

'Yeah. Charlie found out. His parents died in a housefire.'

'Yes… yes he told me.'

'But did he tell you there's an international warrant out for him. We're caught either way: concealing him or giving him up after harbouring him.'

'Sorry Al. Helmut is wanted for murder?'

'Well maybe manslaughter… I mean his parents didn't treat him terribly well. Didn't like the dresses…'

From the window we spotted a white police car approaching slowly up the track, driving gingerly over the potholes. There was the crunching of heavy shoes on the gravel. The knocker echoed like a blow hitting the side of the house.

Al was first to the door.

'Good morning gentlemen.' He had an unaccustomed breezy upward inflexion.

'We are sorry to disturb you sir and we don't want to cause unnecessary concern…'

So Al looked pained and concerned.

They weren't young or particularly fit looking. The tall stooping figure with horn-rim glasses seemed to have the prepared speech.

'Our chief constable has become worried about an increase in the number of burglaries in remote properties. He has tasked us to visit such places and if you are willing, we would like to offer any useful suggestions about safeguarding your house.'

'Well you are very welcome, but really we have very little worth taking.'

'Would you like to show us round?'

There seemed no other option.

Al didn't look fazed. 'Okay then. We'll start with my office.'

And to my surprise Al unlocked the office and in they went.

Five minutes later they emerged.

'Well sir those window locks would meet any security standard. And you say they're alarmed. We don't often see a digital entry for one room in a private house.'

'The community records are in there. People's personal information is stored in the cabinets. Otherwise there is very little of value in the house.'

'Would you care to show us round the rest of the property?'

They were less happy with some rotting window frames in the downstairs rooms.

I could hear Hornrims telling Al off. 'I have to give my own opinion sir, that the place isn't safe or secure.'

'But there is always someone here—and will be apart from a few hours in a week or so.'

They just looked questioningly.

'I'm getting married.'

'Oh congratulations, sir!'

'Yes we're very excited.'

Al said he would get around to replacing the windows anyway and they bundled down the track in their little white car.

Helmut was back soon after they left, and began lifting buckets of water into the kitchen. I took Al aside into the green room.

'Isn't he going back for the acid?'

'Naaa I asked him where he buried the bag.'

'So you're going to find it? Is it really that obvious?'

'Well he told me where the bag is. He's marked it. I'll just tell him I dug it up.'

'You're not digging it up?'

'There weren't any drugs. I just thought I'd better get him out the way—you know I told you Charlie says he's wanted.'

'But…'

'The drugs are still in the office. You know when we were out of earshot, those two quietly asked about a German guy they heard was living here.'

'And…'

'No Germans here are there? If I'm being honest, part of me wanted Helmut to run off. If I tell him to leave, I'm not sure what he might do.'

Halifax

27th May 2019: Midday

I was sitting on the lawn beyond the gravel at the front of the house looking out over the valley and listening to a bird calling from the bushes lower down the slope, the sound of notes being swallowed backwards. The bench was beautifully made with a curving back rest. And at the apex of the curve was another carved impression of the River God, identical to the face above the front door.

There had been heavy rain in the night. Mini-waterfalls came to life when the water ran from the tops, and poured into the river. A low mist prevented me seeing the small streams disappearing down into the ravine.

Al came out the front door out and sat down beside me.

'Are you getting a bit stir crazy here?'

'Aren't you?'

'Naaa I get out. I'm going to Halifax to buy some things.'

'You know, I've never been to Halifax.'

'Well we don't survive without my little shopping expeditions.'

We walked round to the stables to get the four-wheel drive. Helmut always valeted the inside for Al with a dustpan and brush, and washed it before it went out. The seats and shelves were immaculate.

'I think it's important the locals don't see us as a load of old hippies.'

'Even if you all are.' I couldn't stop myself.

Al didn't laugh. 'I don't think you realise there could be forces out there ready to destroy us. The locals have inklings. They tell all kinds of stories. Charlie passes on some of the worst ones. They won't say it to my face.'

'Yeah I know. I told you Hugh and I heard some tales in that pub. They're fascinated by Helmut playing the flute to his goats.'

'Yes, that's why I told you. I'm going to try and get him to keep a lower profile now.'

Al turned the ignition key. I noticed a stale odour I couldn't quite put my finger on. Al wound the window down and we hurtled along the drive at speed, bouncing over ruts leading up to the gate.

'It's better to go faster over the drive.' Al noticed I was suffering.

He turned right at the gate and eventually onto the road running along the top of the moor. We drove down the slope into the low thick mist I had seen gathering in the valley. It didn't seem to deter Al.

'I know the road, Mike. Could probably drive it blindfold.'

After a few miles and what felt like two near misses, we took the main road and soon were on the outskirts of Halifax.

Al slowed. 'D'you mind if I have a fag?'

I'd never seen any of the community smoking.

'I thought you didn't allow it.'

'No, I don't want to sanction it in the community. Mind you there's nothing written down.'

'There's a concern for healthy living…'

'Yeah well the odd one won't hurt. I don't think you realise how much I look forward to this when I go out.'

'So it's your little secret.'

'Suppose so—well it's ours now.' And he parked the van. We were in a cobbled street outside a small warehouse. Al struck a match and I heard the sizzle as the paper caught the flame. Al sank back into his seat and sighed as he took in the first draught of nicotine and smoke.

'I've heard of these vaping things, but I can't believe you can beat the first hit of the day. I haven't had one for two days.'

'But Al you haven't been out for a week.'

'I know. I've found a spot on the moor, some abandoned farm building. Mike, the pressure keeping this little community running is a lot greater than you might think. I need to know I have some escape.'

'What does Edith think?'

'She doesn't know. But nobody knows. Just you. I even change my clothes sometimes after I get back.'

'You seem to feel the need to confess.'

'Yeah, like *Crime and Punishment*. Except I haven't killed anybody… well, apart from possibly myself.'

I was trying to name the unease I was beginning to feel.

'In a way it's none of my business. But I feel even a bit queasy. I kind of wish I didn't know. You're sort of cheating on them—all these people who look up to you— kind of adore you. What other little secrets have you got?'

'None, honestly Mike.'

Al tossed the butt into the gutter. He drove the van through the warehouse gate.

'Mornin' Pete.'

'Ya right, Al?'

'Couldn't be better.' Al's voice had broadened, the vowels more pronounced. He could have been a stranger to me.

'Ya getting' wed next week then.'

'Aye it cum on quick.'

'Well I wish thee luck. Will we see t' bride?'

'Nay lad—its goin' t' be very private like.'

'Gettin' married in church tho' arncha? Thought I might pass by, like.'

Al actually did not look too relaxed.

'Well she's very shy. I want to keep it quiet.'

'Famly cummin'?'

'We don't really 'ave any... look sorry Pete... I need t' get bak.'

'Aye y'r right. We'll load t' van.'

Three sacks of adzuki beans went into the back.

'That's three hundred and fifty, lad.'

'Aye yer right.' And Al produced a credit card and punched in a code.

'American Express. That'll do nicely,' said Pete.

As Al turned away, Pete quietly said, 'And the A? D'ya want some more?'

Al nodded but said nothing.

'I'll tell 'em t' put package together for y'r next shop.'

As we drove back. Al's cheeks were drawn in, his lips a thin pencilled gash. I felt it would be transgressive to interrupt with any light chat. And anyway, I was still wondering about Al's American Express card.

At a red light Al broke the silence.

'How's Madeleine these days?'

'I spoke to her on the phone a week before I left. I told

you. Her and Brian moved—it was only recently. A four bed in Smethwick. The kids are fine. Maddie's fine.'

Al flinched as if pins were being delicately pushed into the surface of his face. The lights changed and we drove in silence for a minute. Al broke it, as if he couldn't hold back an irritation.

'I don't mean all that about where she lives. How much money they've got salted away. I mean, how is *she*?'

'I told you Maddie's fine.' My comfortable replies seemed to annoy Al even more.

'Why don't you call her Madeleine? It's such a beautiful name.'

'Always called her Maddie.'

'Yeah you always use the diminutive—little Maddie.'

'Yeah… well…'

'She's a beautiful woman now—not some little kid!'

'Al you're getting a bit heated. I mean, you've hardly seen her for years.'

'Maybe I am. Yeah maybe I am feeling angry. I wrote to her but *Brrrian* didn't like the idea of her coming to visit me at Gritstone. Fucking Brian. I invited her to my wedding—but they can't come because he's doing something more important—some unspecified thing that's too important for *my* wedding. *She* could have come. What kind of guy for her to get mixed up with—boring bastard with nothing but a spreadsheet where the brain should be.'

'Brian's all right.

Al was wincing. 'Mike you're so lame with your *Brian's all right*. Didn't you want more for Madeleine? So beautiful, so radiant and in love with the world—and she ends up a housewife in Smethwick.'

'You're getting a bit upset. It's not as if you're her uncle or anything.'

'Sometimes Mike I felt like I was the only one—the only one—to really see her for who she was—all she could be…'

Al had never been so personal about me as a father. *I was* riled now.

'And you're saying I didn't?'

'Yeah—yes, I kind of am. Maybe I spent time with her where I didn't have to be irritated by her—having to wait for her to leave the bathroom every day or pick up the clothes she left round the house… I don't know. And then that last time she brought her daughter—Martina—about ten years ago—and it was as if her little girl was Madeleine when she was five—when Siobhan would bring her for a few days. I loved it. I couldn't believe how you let her marry that bastard with shit for brains…'

'He's quite a successful commercial solicitor. I mean you can't really say that Al.'

'When do you last think she has heard just one, just a smidgeon of an original thought from him?'

'Brian cares…' but as I spoke, I realised how despicably homespun I sounded to Al.

'He just wants her to be *little Maddie*.'

Al began accelerating to the top of the moor and the higher road to the house. I wasn't so stung by Al's disdain for Brian but frankly by association, felt his disdain for me.

'But you hardly know him.'

'I spoke to him at their wedding. I was ready to like him—but what a condescending self-satisfied git he was. I mean I have made and spent millions. What right has he got to act so superior? If I morphed into him I'd top myself.'

I wanted to transcend the argument. Brian was uninspiring. But he gave Maddie security and that seemed to be what she wanted. Siobhan and I felt we could sleep at night and feel she was living somewhere else in safety.

'You seem to care about her Al…'

'Yeah I do.'

At the moment we were crawling behind a tractor with a trailer piled high with bails of silage. Al had the time to turn to me, a glance with a message he wasn't going to convey. I felt I should fathom it but I just couldn't—not then.

The black plastic cylinders bounced around with a sinister sarcastic quality just in front of the van's bonnet. Then the tractor turned left at a farm gate and up a vertiginous concrete path to the outbuildings. Al didn't accelerate away as he had on the way to Halifax.

'I'm stopping for another fag.'

He pulled over onto a grass verge near a stile. Al leant against it looking up to the moor tops and a line of shooting butts. His match flared and his face grimaced as the sharp tang hit his tongue. And I felt what an arrogant bastard he seemed.

'Al you didn't ask me if I mind being dragged further into your lies.'

'I know. I'm so used to getting my own way.'

Al's insouciance was too much for me now. 'Well I'm not one of your community—one of your fucking stooges. I've got a mind to tell them all that you quietly smoke. You expect me to keep this from Edith?'

'Especially Edith!'

'Yes well… I wonder how they'd feel with all this stress you make on honesty even if it hurts…'

'It would destroy them, Mike. They've left everything to come to live at Gritstone. Is it worth shattering that world just for a few fags? I might stop when I get married… it might calm me down.' He ended up laughing quietly to himself.

But Al seemed to quickly realise I was not amused. He turned and there was a surprising plea in his voice. 'Look come on mate, cut me some slack.'

'Mate! When have you ever called me mate? It's a bit corny coming from you.'

'I have no one else I could call mate. I have no friends in this setup. I can't have.'

'Edith?'

'Yeah, well—I *can't* tell Edith everything. You're the only one I can confide in, Mike.'

'And every time I find something new about you, I feel I'm drawn in more to your sneaky little secrets.'

'Well, you understand…'

We drove up to the house in silence and I went back to the bench without a word.

One More Guest

28th May 2019: Evening

The wedding was still over a week away and I was starting to wish they'd get it over with. Perhaps I'd leave immediately after. Not necessarily with Hugh. He seemed to have made himself at home, and the MOT had run out anyway. Maybe Siobhan might let me back…

Al and Edith had driven off earlier to make arrangements at the church. And Al had later taken the van to collect more boxes of food that went straight into the larder. There was going be an elaborate feast. But the food would be cooked either on the day or the night before. I even overheard murmurings for the first time about the lack of a fridge at Gritstone.

While I was reading by candlelight there was a knock. Al closed the door quietly and sat on the bed. He looked preoccupied, even nervous.

'Mike, I think you ought to know Siobhan *is* coming—maybe two days before the wedding.'

My stomach performed somersaults and backflips. I was on the verge of passing out.

'Why didn't you tell me earlier?'

'I knew what you'd be like.'

'Really… and what am I like?'

Al ignored this and continued without missing a beat '…and—you never know—you could be reconciled.'

'And so, amongst your many talents, you're a manager of catharsis.'

'I probably do work with some form of that every day

here. Well we can talk like this all night, but it doesn't change the fact that she *is* coming—and I want her to come.'

'She doesn't know I'm here?'

'Not unless you tell her. It's your business. I'm not suggesting you share a room…'

'Thanks.'

'She's mailed me to say she'll be staying in Hebden Bridge. She's knows some women friends who have a barge.'

'She's coming on her own?'

'Yeah.'

'That might have shown some nerve—to come with…'

'Who… Madeleine?'

'I don't know what I meant. I wasn't thinking of Maddie.' I had an idea of the identity of what you might call *the lover*.

'Well I *was* thinking of Madeleine.'

'Al, we spoke about this.'

'Yeah, it's important.'

'I'm getting royally pissed off. She hasn't seen you for years, she probably can't remember much about you…'

'She brought Martina to see me.'

'Siobhan persuaded her to come. I don't think Maddie was too interested.'

I wanted to hurt him. I was sick of him going on about Maddie. My daughter. God knows I missed her as we spoke. And I knew I could turn the blade by mentioning Brian.

'Well yes, it's a pity but she would only come with Brian.'

'I think if he turned up, I'd cancel the wedding. He

takes the oxygen out of a room. He's changed her. You've said it yourself. She has to follow his lead all the time like his pampered poodle.'

'Well there's not much you or I...' But now it was impossible to shut the conversation down.

'If she came just for a few days—she might start to see clearly.' Al had such certainty.

'You'd have talked her into leaving him?'

'I can do most things, Mike...'

For the next few days I couldn't escape the knowledge Siobhan would soon be there. Whatever I did, even while watching Hugh play air guitar to the complete 'Tales from the Topographic Oceans,' a spider was creeping in my stomach.

Charlie

29th May 2019: Midday

This morning we were immersed in a faint *ennui*. Hugh was reading one too many Melody Makers and I was finding Marcel Proust, however exquisite the prose, too inured from ordinary life to keep spending all my time in his company.

We heard a crisp series of knocks on the front door. It was closed for once. There was an unseasonable cold in the air. Hugh ambled across the hall to answer it. The visitor was a man somehow younger than Hugh, but seeking to look as old as he could. He had slicked back hair with a slight curl at the nape, a thin black moustache below a pushed-up nose, a scraggy neck just too small for his shirt collar, with a knitted tartan tie and green plaid sports jacket.

'Where's Al?' The tone was faux aristocratic, metallic and peremptory.

'He's around… Who are you by the way?'

'Most people here know me. Are you new? Just joined? I thought Al wasn't taking anyone on.'

'I'm only visiting for his wedding.'

'Ah yes—with Edith. Well I've sort of come about Edith.'

'Who will I say?'

'Sharpe, Charles Sharpe.'

But at that moment Al burst through the door from the curtained room and the blue light winking.

'Charlie glad you found the time to come.'

'Any business Al?' Sharpe's drawl couldn't conceal an immoderate eagerness.

'Just a few signatures.' Al's tone was exaggeratedly light.

Al and Sharpe firmly closed the door behind them. We soon heard the *eeyore* of a printer. Al emerged holding two sheets of A4 and sprinted lightly up the stairs. He tapped on the door of the room he shared with Edith. In less than a minute he emerged, bounding down the stairs and back into the blue lit room where we could hear Sharpe speaking on a phone.

All this activity had been compressed into minutes. Our acorn coffee still wasn't cool enough to drink. Hugh was dawdling in the hall, looking through the open door at the low cloud that seemed to be grazing the tops on the opposite side of the valley. The door to Al's room burst open and Sharpe brushed past him. The coffee splashed onto the stone flags.

'Hey fella...'

'I'm sorry. I'm sometimes in such a hurry.'

'Yes, just a few moments with Al. That's quite speedy business.'

'Well I'm afraid it is *our* business.'

'Yours and Al's.'

'Yes.'

'And Edith's.'

'...yes.'

'I know you won't tell me what's going on.'

'You are correct. It is confidential to the client.'

'Al...'

'Yes.'

'and Edith...'

'…'

'I've never seen Al act this strange and I have seen him…'

'I see nothing strange. This is business.' Sharpe was becoming twitchy, and impatient with the eager but seemingly not very bright terrier that appeared to be Hugh.

'I didn't know Al was involved in business anymore.'

'Well there's no other word I can conjure up at the moment.'

'His community is a business?' Hugh was raising his voice.

Sharpe moved towards the door.

'And your part is?' Hugh was in verbal pursuit.

'This is a personal business matter and I don't believe I should have entered into this conversation.'

'No but you have.'

Sharpe stopped and turned to face Hugh. His eyes narrowed.

'Look, you're not a member of this community? I really think I should know.'

'Why should you need to know about me?'

'I would *need* to know about you.'

'As part of the business side of Gritstone?'

'In the end everything is business.'

Even Hugh sensed this was not a Marxist apologia.

Sometimes Al just seemed to materialise. Hugh didn't know he was there until he heard Al's patient but firm tones behind his left shoulder.

'Hugh you're beginning to raise your voice. We don't have shouting in this community.'

'I didn't see it in your rules—and it didn't apply to

Helmut when he was missing his acid?'

Al *sotto voce*, 'Charles hasn't heard that.'

'Did you say acid drops? Still on sale in the village in those beautiful glass jars…' He had a repellent little snigger.

But Hugh decided emollience was in order. 'I'm sorry for raising my voice. Please forgive me Charles. I'm not sleeping well.'

'Yes Charles, this is an old friend, Hugh.' There was an uneasy handshake between them.

Hugh skulked back into the kitchen. He looked tarnished.

'What a creep—and Al likes him—seems to *need* him.'

'Well Al always had some kind of enforcer in the shadows. He used to cultivate this persona—the pony-tailed millionaire. I suppose I always felt it was pretty cheesy. You'd see him occasionally in the papers with that *'aw shucks'* grin, big white teeth shining out of his blond beard, the kind of *'I'm a bit of a rebel,'* look. But he always had a tough guy behind him to keep the workforce in line, make the threats to the newspapers or the people who fell behind with payments. He wasn't exactly Bambi… well he says he's changed now…'

'You know Mike. I hope he has but I'm not so sure—not after meeting that reptile friend of his.'

The Office

30th May 2019: Morning

I was enjoying the morning sunlight, reading in the green room. I'd got sick of Proust and picked up Pirsig's *Zen and the Art of Motorcycle Maintenance,* but was finding the worthiness hard to stomach. When I was in the house. I'd taken to wearing this long flowing robe with a hood—I still wasn't sure if it was a kaftan or even a dress—but everyone wore one when they weren't working. There was label inside with *Asif* again, written in pen.

My beard was lengthening and combined with the flowing robes I was beginning to be unrecognisable from the corduroy-jacketed ex-lecturer in History who arrived a few weeks ago. I tried not to think about Siobhan and what she would make of me. I even wondered if I could conceal myself in this new persona. Was that what I sought? That she might not even recognise me? I was all confusion.

Al sauntered in with a cup of nettle tea. He wanted to talk about arrangements for the wedding. The whole community would walk in procession to the church.

'It'll give the locals something to gawp at.' I chuckled but rather too collusively. And immediately felt ashamed that I seemed still to want to be included, accepted, after our confrontation in the van coming back from Halifax.

'Yeah we're still a mystery,' Al sounded so smug and casual.

And I turned on him, 'Well you're still a mystery to me.'

'Oh yeah?'

'Al, I'm still trying to work out what you do in that office. I don't think you know how shifty you look. You've clearly got a PC in there. You're not watching day-time telly. And then this slimy Sharpe. You mentioned he tipped you off about the police. He turns up going on to Hugh about your *business*. I saw you and Sharpe yesterday. You were both acting really strangely, like you had something to hide.'

Al held his hands up. 'Okay, Mike. Okay.'

'Don't *okay* me Al. I'm not sure about you.'

'You've never been really.'

'Just tell me.'

Al's face was briefly creased with consideration—and then a decision. 'All right you'd better come into the office. I've not really had anyone to talk to about all this—apart from Charlie. It gets kind of lonely in there.'

As soon as we began walking towards the room, I regretted the invitation I had provoked. I started to wonder if there was some subliminal trick Al had played to make me complicit in whatever he was doing in there. I had always shied away from this kind of knowledge, even knowledge I needed to know—the hidden kernel of a person's life they only reveal when they're too drunk or just plain uninhibitedly desperate. And now with some shock I sensed this in Al, this loneliness and isolation, this need to share a burden.

Al unlocked the door. Once inside he tapped a code on a keypad to deactivate an alarm. A watery light suffused the room from a PC in the other corner. The air was thick and stale. Al switched on a banker's desk lamp of green glass. The explosion of electric light was the first I'd seen for weeks.

The lamp stood on an elegant mahogany secretary with curved Queen Anne legs. Al pulled down the desk flap. There were neat pigeonholes along the back that would have been used to house papers. I could see a line of smart phones, two slotted into each compartment. Al pulled out a large bottom drawer that held several laptops and tablets. A pink post-it note was fixed on each device. And each note had a name: Helmut, Toni, Rosamond, Edith, Sylvester…

'When people come here, they want me to look after the outside world—like if their family gets in touch—any number of things.'

I had to stop for a few seconds and let it slowly percolate quite what Al was saying.

'You use their phones and pretend to be them? You impersonate them?' I didn't know whether to feel shocked or amused. So I felt both.

'Well when it comes to replying to the families, it does get quite interesting. Building Societies… not so much…'

'Al you're trying to wind me up.'

'Afraid not. Once a week I need to check all the devices to see if anything's come in. It takes time.'

Al sat in one of two dark red Chesterfield armchairs by the window and gestured me to take the other.

'Look, they *want* me to do it. They don't want the bother of being nice, being reassuring, being interested in the family news. That's why they came here—to escape all that—to not have to deal with it. Mike I'm doing what they ask. It's by consent.'

'And so you pretend to be Toni or somebody, and you write to some uncle saying "You're always in my thoughts" or "Can you send me even more of that nice fruitcake"?'

'It can get a bit more involved than that. Like when they can't bear the idea of communicating with someone.'

'And you don't reply?'

'I make a decision…'

'What, like you text back! You send an email pretending to be… Sylvester?'

'It may be better to send something reassuring rather than just a silence. I don't want the police looking for a missing person. Better to write back saying how fine everything is, health is good or better. I decide what's best for the person in *my* house.'

'That sounds pretty pompous for you.'

'Yeah, okay… maybe… but I feel the responsibility.'

Al's eyes seemed to contain a plea. I was taken aback. Al suddenly seemed isolated, so alone with his creation. I felt he wanted my approval for all this. And I couldn't give it.

'But Al you've taken on responsibility for their lives.'

'Yeah…' with a small shrug that didn't look casual enough. He could usually be so intense in his gaze, but at this moment with me, it looked like Al had removed the lid from a box of chaos and had begun to realise what he had opened.

'And you're handling their money. Sorry Al, my stomach actually starts to lurch when I think of it.'

'Well you can't always trust your body. Listening to it is only the first stage. You have to start thinking why…'

'Oh do come on!'

Al simply ignored my irritation. 'Anyway, look Mike, that's what *they* want. I even have power of attorney for a few.'

'Do their families know about *that*?'

'Some of them have no family. Charlie sorts it all out. They sign. They know what they're signing for.'

'But they don't need someone to manage their money. Nobody here lacks the mental capacity.'

'Charles sorts it all out.'

'It doesn't feel legal, Al.'

'It's perfectly legal. You can appoint your friends. It needn't be family. A lot of people here don't trust their family, and with very good reason.'

'But—I have to keep saying this—they *can* handle their *own* money.'

'I remember this about you now, Mike. You would always go flaky when there's that whiff of danger. We can't keep on looking over our shoulder if we're going to make this community work.'

'Al, are there any more…'

'Not really… I try and make that money work for us.'

'What do you mean exactly—*work?*'

Al deflected my question by shifting to a personal attack—on me. 'And I'll bet Siobhan looks after your money as well. You were always hopeless. Quite happy to have someone take over.'

I remembered now. It all came back. When we spent too long together, there was an itch of irritation that developed—and Al turned on me.

'If that's the case, it's entirely different. We are married.'

'God, who's sounding pompous now? So she *does!* She

handles all the money and now you've just left Siobhan with all the bills to sort out. Bet she's thrilled with you!'

'Listen Al. What do you mean—*make the money work?*'

But I already realised how.

'I've always been in shares and the currency markets. Even when I'd made my money, I kept stuff ticking over…'

'Bet you kept that quiet when you were chatting to Chavez.'

'Look it's what you do with it. Even Marx played the market.'

'Once he was set up by Engels in his villa in St John's Wood, and arranging the coming out party for his daughters. I *do* know that. But you're playing with other people's money.'

Al shrugged. 'Well he was playing with Engels' money.'

'Come on! These people haven't the first idea what you're doing. But it explains why you're in here all day—in your casino.'

'I don't enjoy it. I haven't for years. But we need to do this…'

'Do *we?* And how's it going Al?'

Al looked rather coy. 'I got into trouble with Bitcoin. There was some hacking in January. I'm still trying to catch up.'

'You mean you've lost their money?'

'It's the community's—not all of it but we lost a lot— but yeah, they don't know it's gone.'

'Perhaps they should know in this *culture of openness.*'

'No Mike, the whole thing might fall apart. I'll get it back. Best they don't know.'

'I'm not happy, Al. It's impersonation. That *is* illegal.'

'We are living outside the constructs here. We want to have as little to do with your laws as we can. That's not the same as being immoral.'

'My laws?'

'Yeah your laws. Even Hugh seems to understand what is happening here more than you. You're still a visitor, let's be honest.'

'And now you're getting married—the ultimate social construct.' I sensed this jeering tone of mine surfacing and felt a bit diminished even as I spoke.

And I could see that Al, this new Al, wouldn't be riled. It was as if he felt it was beneath him to rise to such cheap shots. Instead he ignored my attempt to provoke him.

'It's something I can do for Edith. And I don't mind. I'm committed to her now.'

'And you can control her money. I mean legally.'

'You're making me sound like some crook, Mike.' Al sounded no more than vaguely disappointed. 'But I already *do* have control of her money. Legally. Edith is one of the members I have power of attorney for. It only just came through. I don't need to marry her for that. It almost confirms my sincerity,' he concluded with vague sarcasm.

'I still feel…'

'Mike all the community… they all want me to do it. It's all part of living here. Do you think monks and nuns reply to texts and emails all day?'

'Look Al, it's quite simple. I could phone the police. You're impersonating these people online.'

'Interesting threat… If you did, Helmut would follow you to the edge of the land. I assure you; he would kill you if you took his world away. But really, Mike, why should you? Forget this conversation if you must. You never came in. Nobody showed you anything.'

I turned and walked towards the door but then glumly realised I needed Al to unlock it. Al was laughing quietly as he tapped the entry pad. And turned the latch.

'You know Mike, I love you really. I mean you could make me rethink how I saw things sometimes. I just didn't admit it. And Siobhan could take me apart systematically—forensically.'

But I just felt drained. Well Siobhan could. She could take me apart at will, as well.

'I think I'll go now Al.'

'Mike you look upset.'

'I'm not. I just need some air.'

But I was upset. I was snared in his sticky web. Any of what you might call—my moral authority—had drained away. I felt I couldn't ever confront Al again about what he was doing here. My silence had sanctioned it now. And then the creeping thought that Al had done it again— what he often did: a high-risk trick to reel me into this shadow world he inhabited on his own. Had he been waiting for the moment to tantalise me into that room?

'Mike, have I convinced you? I'm not trying to make money out of these people. I can show you. I would never do that.'

And I was inclined to believe Al wasn't in it for the money. I still felt an itch of unease. It was never ever about the money with Al. Never that simple.

'I don't care. Do what you like. You're right. I don't want to know.'

Sailing Tales

28th May 2019: Evening

Later that night, the community had finished their evening meal and the candles caressed the room. The cold light of day never seemed more apt by its absence. Al told a story about Hugh, and the only time Al went on a boat trip with him. Hugh was in the new sweater he'd bought at Cromer. It was extra thick with a slightly greasy texture, which he claimed was based on the woollen worn by Henry Blogg, the legendary master of the Cromer life boat. Hugh was quite the sailor and took charge of the tiller, yelling at the incompetence of other helmsmen.

But Hugh's boat became marooned on the silt in the middle of a creek. Hugh was relaxed. They'd just have to sit and wait for the tide to come back in. Five hours later Hugh was beginning to believe this might not be a tidal creek. By then they were starving. A little girl rowed across in a dinghy with a packet of biscuits, as the sun dipped. Eventually they fell asleep and the river rose in the night. They clearly floated a considerable distance, and woke to find themselves bouncing in the open sea. Hugh couldn't get the engine to work and they had to row. Hugh was insisting on his knowledge of the compass, while Al was pointing to a visible shore in the opposite direction from Hugh's course.

Hugh was chortling along with everyone else. Most of the community seemed to have taken to him, and he had settled into the role of occasional jester. Clearly some believed he was not serious or frankly that intelligent.

Meanwhile I felt my own lack of commonality with most of these people. It wasn't comfortable. A few weeks after my arrival I still found it next to impossible to start a conversation. I couldn't find a topic. The outside world appeared irrelevant to them. The everyday didn't exist—seemed to have ceased to exist—beyond the house. There was no gossip—certainly I never heard any.

And they didn't seem to read much. Earlier that day I had gone to look for more books in the green room. I suppose you would call it the library but there were only a few shelves of what looked like charity shop paperbacks. A lot of them would have been found on a student's shelf in the early 70s.Tolkien, Allen Ginsberg, Kerouac, Whitman, most of Hesse, a job-lot of Arthur C Clark, Pirsig's *Zen and the Art of Motorcycle Maintenance* that I'd had a slight dalliance with; but also *David Copperfield,* the unreadable *Ivanhoe,* and three non-sequential volumes of Proust had crept in, which I'd already sampled. Strange to think I had read most of these books before I was 21—apart from Ivanhoe and Proust. By the French windows was a closed book case with a key in the lock. Inside were the *Tibetan Book of the Dead,* Yeats' translation of the *Bhagavad Gita,* a book of Taoist stories and a leather-bound King James Bible. Also, inside the lockable cabinet were boxes of joss sticks and a set of meditation bowls, some the size of basins.

Rose had swept by as I was searching the room and I asked her if these were definitely the only books in the house. She told me that was the case. There were no more.

'I'm not even sure why they're here anymore… Nobody looks at them. I mean before I came here, I used to read novels voraciously. But now what meaning do they have when you've left behind the world they're based on?'

Her brow furrowed. 'I imagine it's a bit like when you are dying. The world and its doings lose a lot of their relevance. You're being relinquished, left behind while the wild dance continues without you.'

The Painting Group

31st May 2019: Morning

The community had a painting group. Stephanie, the short woman in the Monsoon kaftans, took a lead, but really just organised the times and set out the paints and sheets of paper. About six of them sat at the kitchen table with large powder paint trays. The absence of oil paint, the large jars full of water with the mix of colours drifting down from the surface to form a muddy mist—all of this reminded me of the painting class in my junior school.

They needed reasonable light in the kitchen and waited until the sun came round to the yard. They tacitly accepted that Al would provide the weather forecast but they would never discuss quite how he'd got his information. Stephanie once said that she thought he could forecast the weather from observing the cloud formations of the night before.

The paintings were neither figurative or abstract but simply combinations of colour. Some of the group produced endless spectrum rainbows. Edith painted simple mandalas, shapes and swirls of colour in some kind of endless revolution. I found Edith's productions rather disturbing. There was a great deal of unease in the wild combinations, scarlet on a deep black—or was I just imagining? I couldn't transcend the privileged knowledge I had of her past. She'd never mentioned it again, and I wondered if she even recollected telling her story, or simply regretted telling it at all.

And I often wondered about the mandala frescoes.

They were on a wall in virtually every room in the house and all signed by Asif, the man whose clothes I was wearing. But I couldn't get anyone to talk about him.

On this particular day, I had declined an invitation to take part in the painting group, but Hugh threw himself in with vigour. He took several large pieces of paper and sellotaped them together. He painted a square of dark blue mixed into purple around the edge and then took it outside. The largest place to pin up his canvas was the side of the woodpile. Hugh stood in the yard and watched with pleasure as the paint bled downwards in long stalactites of colour. But Stephanie materialised behind him and she was not happy.

'It's not harmonious. There's too much left to chance, Hugh.'

'So, you really don't like it, then? I mean I like some chance in art.' Hugh didn't have total confidence in his artistic integrity, but I wondered if Stephanie was expressing more than her own opinion.

'Hugh, Al likes us to be frank…'

'Well if I'm allowed to be frank, I feel a lot of this stuff is rather insipid then, to be honest. It's as if you want to wish away any idea that life can be a messy business.'

'Hugh, you seem to have a talent for upsetting people for the sheer pleasure of it.'

Helmut clattered past with his wooden buckets.

'*Sehr gut, Hugh!*'

'It is chaos, Helmut,' Stephanie corrected him. 'We seek harmony with the world, and in ourselves through our painting.'

Helmut looked imploringly at Hugh. He did not want to take sides.

Hugh marched up to the wood pile, tore his painting off, threw it onto the cobbles and jumped up and down on it until it was reduced to muddy *papier mâché*. 'It couldn't be more chaotic now, could it, Stephanie?' he shouted.

Stephanie seemed about to cry. 'I just help run our little circle. We were very happy. Until you arrived Hugh!' Her voice gradually rose to a high-pitched squeak. Hugh began to feel sorry for her. She seemed to be hurting herself far more than him. He clumsily attempted to hug her. But she vehemently pushed him away.

Al had quietly come into the kitchen and was standing with me in the doorway. Stephanie turned to him.

'Our group is finished. Wrecked by your friend Hugh. I'm so disappointed! Can't you do something about this man?'

'He tried to hug you. I'm sure Hugh doesn't realise what this means to you—do you Hugh?'

'I don't want to be hugged!' Stephanie said pettishly.

'Well what do you want?'

'I want him to go.' She had to heave out the words and immediately knew she had set up a collision.

'Hugh's not going, Stephanie. He's come up for my wedding. He's one of my oldest friends. He's not going anywhere.'

Hugh stood there mutely as a battle took place over his existence at Gritstone. Stephanie's husband Bruno had rushed over from the walled garden in a pair of green wellingtons. His towering figure was ineffectually kneading her hands and rubbing her back, wordlessly cooing to her. She seemed so habituated to his indulgence she hardly noticed, but stared ahead with a jutting tremulous lip as the chance of any compromise evaporated.

This tableau in the yard was nearing a frozen Kabuki moment where everyone awaited the next move.

Hugh broke the tense silence. 'It was only a painting—that I've just reduced to pulp. Everybody get a grip.'

But Al was surprisingly stern. 'Well I'm afraid you're right, Hugh. But Stephanie needs to reflect what the consequences her own actions are leading to.'

'What consequences?' Bruno asked hesitantly.

'Bruno, if you must know, I'm getting tired of both of you grandstanding in front of everyone. And not just today. It's your never-ending bickering. I'm sure you love each other...' He appraised the gangly haggard Bruno with his arm round Stephanie whose face now nestled under his armpit like a sulky jelly. 'But I am sick of you playing out your marriage in public—as if frankly—we—fucking—care.'

Considering he had metaphorically been slapped round the face, Bruno assumed what he seemed to feel was a nobility in his expression. His chin jutted out, his long thin face and aquiline nose were now presented in profile to this small audience. Stephanie was huddling into his protective arm as if they were caught in the middle of the moor in torrential rain.

'I've said enough. Maybe too much. You both think about it.' Al turned on his heel and disappeared back into the office. Bruno and Stephanie stood hunched together, uncertain what to do next. Eventually they trailed off to their room. Bruno brushed past Hugh with an attempt at haughty disdain on his face. The couple didn't appear for the evening meal.

The next day Stephanie announced at breakfast that

the classes would continue. There were polite murmurs. But everyone had overheard the argument in their room the night before. Al sat silently, showing neither satisfaction nor pleasure. The community left the kitchen to start the day. Al whispered to me before he unlocked his office, 'I wish they had left us. I wish they'd just packed up and gone.'

John arrives

1st June 2019: Morning

The day had come when John had mailed to say he would be arriving by train. Al had put on the invitation that the conditions in the house were spartan, but mischievously added that this might suit John.

Al and John hadn't met for years. Siobhan and I had gone to Ruth's funeral but Al stayed away. A few months later, I had visited John. We sat in uncomfortable black leather chairs in his steel and glass penthouse overlooking the river.

He told me that if there were such a thing as mourning, he had already mourned well before her death. He'd wake alone and drive to the hospice, to what he called the solidarity of the dying, hearing all the joshing humour of Ruth's neighbours in the adjoining rooms— laughter that could not conceal varieties of terror. He spoke of the faecal aroma piercing the lavender, the Formica so easy to wipe when it became soiled.

Now he said, all his experience was diluted and unfocussed. He'd shared a prism with Ruth, the filter for the life they both inhabited, and now it was shattered. Wherever they had been together, he felt they walked through the world as if it were new minted. It could be Calcutta; it could be Hull. There was always something fresh and vivid to be discovered by them. He mused whether they ever treasured these shared experiences enough. There had still been plenty of room for domestic rowing, niggles that persisted. The continual crusade to make the other transform back into the person they appeared to be at that first meeting. But now there was nothing, no membrane, no mutual protection between him and the world.

He said how he had felt excluded from the kind of excitement Ruth felt as she clasped her ticket for her mystery destination. Towards the end she said she felt less certain that she would evaporate as if she had never been. But now whatever that future was, he had no part in it.

John told me how Ruth's last days at home were punctuated with final electric experiences. She had stared at the roses of Sharon for hours, red tipped yellow stamens exploding outwards. Her world was shifting into a fizzing immediacy. She said the blooms had never seemed so urgent and so temporary. They were the yellowest yellow she had ever seen. Experiences were of themselves. They now led nowhere, related to nothing else. They could not be added to a bank of memory that was there to be shared.

After she died, he had anchored himself in the commonplace, in routines to stave off an endless future without her. But in the months that followed her death, he found himself watching for her in the customary places. He had never realised how so many other women could look like her. When she was alive, he would recognise her in a crowd a hundred yards away. It was something about the inclination of the head, the smallest movements. And for seconds, he would feel he had seen her, but in different clothes.

For those few moments he believed the present could be rolled back. He would approach, no he would rush; and then realise his mistake once again, before the unknown woman noticed anything. He told me that often he would retreat into a doorway to hide, fearing he would cry and be unable to stop.

Some people would say John had become more in touch with himself. When I suggested this to him, he simply said if that was the case, the cost was too high. He spoke with brutal honesty, sometimes detached from the self he was speaking about, sometimes averting his face and choking away tears.

That afternoon with John was very much in my mind as I sat in the kitchen waiting for Al's van to draw up. I wondered what John to expect.

I had looked him up on Hugh's plodding laptop before we travelled north. The former vice-chancellor of sundry red bricks. The man who sold off his consultancy that had then quickly imploded. Nobody could be sure if his hand had been missed at the tiller; or whether he knew it was failing. But he needed to divest himself of any responsibilities when he knew Ruth was dying.

The last online picture of John was from two years ago. He stared out in steely square-framed spectacles, the light blue suit, the compact sharp features in an open necked buttoned-down white shirt, severe grey hair, cut close. No flabby jowls. Any lines on his face etched downwards. This was the image John had chosen. It reminded me of so many of the pictures Holbein painted of the Tudor court, the men staring out with a combination of distrust and an underlying threat.

But would he be like that now? Al still had the image of that man from the online profile. He had dressed especially for John, in blue cord trousers and a striped blue shirt, an ensemble I had never seen before. I had wondered if this sartorial decision might betray a rare unease in Al. Even he was absorbed into the charisma of this unostentatious extremely wealthy man. And Al was out to impress. Before he set off to meet John's train, he'd said to me that now, with the founding of this community, he had something to rival, even surpass John's ambition. Sitting at the kitchen table he'd said to me, 'At last I can face him.'

Despite the arm round the shoulder, and the booming greeting from Al, John looked diffident and shy. He appeared a little nonplussed when he saw me, this bearded Old testament figure in a white robe.

He said quietly 'Mike, is it you?'

I nodded confusedly. John seemed more tentative in his speech, furtive even. The mental vigour that once outlasted anyone's in its relentlessness, appeared to have dissipated. Al took us both into the kitchen. He seemed to have decided that John and I should be alone together. He said he would show John round later and went off to his room. I could hear Hugh playing another Wishbone Ash album upstairs. But he'd always tried to avoid John's version of mental jiu jitsu when he could.

'You've changed a bit, Mike.'

'And you're inviting me to say you haven't, 'cos you haven't.'

John seemed to ignore my attempt at slightly offensive joshing. 'Well no... but you're wearing a robe and you've grown a beard. I've not seen you like this... and you've filled out...'

'You mean I'm fat.'

'I'd never speak like that to you. You're getting a bit...'

John seemed genuinely disturbed by my tone.

'Sorry—I am sorry—I just thought you were looking at me and thinking he's washed out, finished...'

'Mike, you're saying this, not me. Is that how you feel?'

'I'm going on a brown rice diet. Well, I'm not going on it. That's all they have here. I'm losing some of this flab. I already have, believe it or not.'

John looked unconvinced. But he was apologetic.

'I don't know how I come across any more. I don't know how I affect others since... Ruth died. In fact I usually don't feel too concerned. So I'm sorry. I can seem so abrupt and careless.'

'Well it was so terrible about Ruth. It still feels terrible.'

'I don't think I said when I saw you last how glad I was that you and Siobhan came to the funeral. We didn't speak much but...'

'I wasn't sure if you wanted to talk.' John had seemed absorbed in some state beyond mourning, like an austere existentialist who refuses to succumb to the sentimentality of loss.

'No, I suppose it seemed that way. How is Siobhan?'

'I'm... not sure.'

'Oh.' John looked momentarily surprised.

'In the end we sort of shared the house. Sometimes she wasn't there all night. I didn't want to know where she went. Anyway I ended up in the spare room. The kids don't know anything yet. No idea what she'll say to them—what she *is* saying to them.'

'But what will *you* say?' There was a tone I remembered now. Cloaked in concern. Concern that could sound practised. I felt his words concealed an innate need, which even John may not have been conscious of, to experience superiority in any situation. An inquisitorial tone John could easily fall into was emerging. I had never felt comfortable about where this would lead.

'I threw my phone away a few weeks ago so I can't speak to them. No means of telling them unless I send a letter—in Billie's case to somewhere on a Thai beach. I've left. I've talked to no one. No, don't know what I'll say to her or the kids. Not given it much thought.'

'So is it over? I mean you have really left her.'

'I don't really think... I don't know what I'm doing yet.'

'It must hurt... to lose her.'

I felt my wound being opened by John with the delicacy of diner prizing open an oyster shell. Yes, it hurt exquisitely. Suddenly the questions about Siobhan had a mosquito's buzzing insistence.

'She's still alive you know. She's not dead.'

John became silent. He pursed his lips and avoided my gaze.

'I said, she's not dead.' I couldn't understand what tempted me to be so cruel. I was shocked by my own vehemence. But then I realised what was driving me to this. I'd begun to believe that John was using my torment to escape from his own. That's what he was doing, however well-intentioned he might sound. I felt as if I was a wild animal being baited.

I began to feel itchy and unwashed in John's crisply dressed presence. We drifted into a silence without comfort. John broke it after what had been a few seconds, but felt infinitely longer. He looked at me with that familiar expression of pained disappointment and said simply, 'Well I've heard you.'

If I had wanted to build a bridge it was now too late. John had picked up his suit in its dust protector and an expensive leather bag and was being led up the stairs by Al and Edith. I had felt that release of tension that for seconds is exhilarating, and then impetuous and illusory. But now there was no next action to distract from my own version of shame and confusion. I had to wait for it to dissipate like the fog trapped in the valley.

Another trip

2nd June 2019: Evening

The community were going to have another acid trip before the final preparations for Al's wedding. I was non-committal when Al asked me. Hugh was keen to take it again now, despite his visions of snakes. Rosamond said she would look out for him, but she was taking it as well. 'It doesn't affect me terribly much, Hugh. You'll be safe with me.'

Al said he would again be the one who was able to handle any emergencies, or talk people through bumpy passages. After the evening meal he produced a red brocaded box with small reflective mirrors twinkling round the sides. Inside like minuscule chocolates the small pyramids were lined over a burgundy velvet cloth.

'I thought I'd use this box. It's more sacramental. Now people, before we begin, as usual we look out for each other. I'll be around. But whatever space you're in, if you know when someone's feeling bad, stay with them.'

'Al you're programming the trip, man. Now it's bound to happen!' But Sylvester was rolling his eyes and laughing.

'Naaa.' Al shook his head. 'And anyway we may have talked it out the room. Expect the unexpected people. Have a good trip.'

And they all leant back and dropped it into their mouths. At the last second, I had the tab in my hand, but as I put it to my lips, I concealed it and slipped it into my pocket. I suppose I felt I'd survived the last one, but didn't want to push my luck.

The community left the kitchen as if by arrangement, and I heard them going upstairs. It sounded like several went into a room together. John had not come down again since the meal. I realised he was staying remote from this activity in his own room on the top floor. I sipped my mint tea and waited. There was a cavernous silence for half an hour. I remembered that when I had dropped the tab last time, I had disappeared up to the music room. Time had become a bent Dali watch. I had the abiding memory of moving in slow motion, as if submerged in a permeable jelly, sound echoing through inch-thick layers. During that trip I had only seen Edith and had no idea where other people were. I couldn't ever remember seeing Al.

Then I heard the sound of Helmut's clogs on the cobbles.

The door to the yard burst open. Helmut's face was set. His crook was balanced in his palm like a hunter's a spear. He was also naked. I made the only possible response, 'Hello Helmut.'

'I come to root out the evil in this house.'

'Where is it?' I asked with some doubt that I wanted the answer.

'*Ich weisse nicht. Ich gehe es suchen!*'

I could only guess if this was inoffensive. Then Stephanie glided into the kitchen as if sleepwalking, carrying a watercolour set and paper. She froze at the sight of the naked giant in the flickering candle light, framed against the kitchen door. Her paint box crashed down. Shattered fragments of coloured powder exploded on the stone floor and fanned out. Every part of her face seemed not to simply tremble but wobble. Thoughts and fears were struggling vainly to reach the surface, to be differentiated, articulated and freed from their confused inner explosion. Then they were released and she screamed. Helmut's instinct was to reach out to comfort her. But as he moved towards her, arms outstretched, Stephanie collapsed into a corner behind the cooking range. Al had ghosted into the room.

He spoke slowly and patiently. 'Helmut man, d'you know you're frightening Stephanie?' Stephanie nodded vehemently from her huddled position. She was stuffing as much of her nightdress as she could humanly force into her mouth.

'*Ja* Al, I know. But I have no wish to kill her. I am rooting out the evil that is here among us… I am very sorry Stephanie.'

'The thing is man, that if you speak to her with no clothes on, she probably wonders if you really mean it.'

'I divest myself to confront evil with my true self. It is the only way.'

'Well man, do you have any particular evil in mind?'

Helmut spoke with the innocence of a Parsifal. 'It is the evil in your locked room. It is soaking into the house. It is creeping under the doors.'

Al slowly shook his head and was about to speak when an agitated Bruno loped into the kitchen.

'Where is my Steffi?'

Stephanie made muffled shrieks through the nightdress in her mouth, the sound of a collection of small animals caught in a bag. Meanwhile Helmut disappeared into the yard, gesturing with his crook at the heavens.

'I thought you were dead and nobody had told me.' Bruno's haggard face was tear-streaked. Stephanie stumbled to her feet and wordlessly put her arms around his waist.

Bruno looked down at her and his face creased into disgust. 'You're not my Steffi. A very convincing copy, but... get off me... let go. What is this trick you're all playing on me? It's very funny yes?'

Al was now leaning against the kitchen door. He whispered to me, 'I used to feel this acid was a bonding idea but I'm changing my mind. I'll stick to psilocybin in future. Some of these people are too old for all of this.' And he went over to Bruno.

'Bruno... man... do you trust me?'

Bruno nodded solemnly.

'This is your wife, Bruno. Remember... Stephanie?'

Bruno replied drowsily, 'Yes I remember her now. I am not sure I like her anymore.'

Bruno and Stephanie wandered off into the dark corridor. Stephanie's face was a soaking, trembling mass of misery. Five minutes later she returned and briskly picked her paint box off the floor, retrieved the solid fragments, put them back into the tray, filled a jar with water and began painting gentle curving shapes onto the paper. Bruno came back several minutes after, looking for her again. And there was another emotional disunion.

Al muttered, 'You know some people still believe this is a feel-good recreational drug. Man, I really don't know if I'll get through tonight.'

We then heard Helmut out in the middle of the yard, kneeling before the pump, praying at first in German, then transitioning to English. 'Spirit of the House. Drive out the Evil!' He hammered the staff against the metal. The reverberations echoed against the surrounding walls.

The sound seemed capable of travelling for miles into the dark void beyond the garden and I imagined people in Halifax hearing the tocsin above *Coronation Street*.

Al began to sound deflated. 'I kind of wish he'd stop that. But he can only stop himself.'

I left Al to sort out anything else in the kitchen, and meandered up the staircase. On the first floor there was an animated to-and-fro in one room between what sounded like five people. The red painted door was slightly ajar. I couldn't help but listen to a woman's voice. It was Kate.

'I'm soooo bored… sooooooooooooo bored.'

A male voice giggled and then seemed unable to stop. He started singing 'So-oh-oh-oh' and then giggled again.

But Kate was irritated. 'You think it's funny. It's a nightmare. I daren't leave the house. I don't want to leave the house. But I want to leave the house. I want to go into…' and she paused to think and pronounced vaguely, 'a town.'

And there was a long thick silence.

I thought I heard Sylvester's voice in increasingly slower tones, 'Well that does like sound kinda scary. I haven't been in a crowd for—dunno—a few years.' The sentence slowly ground to a halt.

Kate became more animated. 'All those people walking round like robots with their strange ideas… You can see their brains wobbling like blancmanges and someone presses a button in London and the same thoughts pops up… like… pop tarts.'

Two of the men started giggling. 'Ping, ping, ping!'

She continued, warming to the theme, 'We could see what the BBC was doing… programming us. I ended up getting my news from this comic on You tube. He was sooo funny. He made all those politicians look sooo ridiculous…' the voice became more and more languid.

'The walls are starting to curve again.' Sylvester was suddenly uncomfortable.

'Mmmmm… don't you like it?' Kate was mocking.

'And the mandala's moving—in circles—all those figures—dancing round the god, perpetually.'

'Asif knew what he was do…' Kate trailed off.

A silence descended like a camera shutter.

As I got to the top storey, I could hear small noises, exhalations. I pushed open the door to the music room to find Hugh and Rosamond on the battered sofa in the beginnings of an embrace. They didn't seem to realise I was standing there.

I left them alone and knocked on John's door. When he opened it, clearly I'd woken him but he still let me in. I was apologetic about my words yesterday. John was forgiving. 'We've all been under strain… well apart from Al apparently.'

I asked if John was invited to take acid.

'Yes, Al did knock to tell me they were going to take it. He obviously felt it was pointless inviting me. But I started to wonder after he left whether I would particularly care if I took it or not.'

'Well you like to be in control.'

'So does Al.'

'I've been here for two trips now and Al hasn't taken it.'

'Oh, I see.' John paused. 'I wonder what he's trying to achieve.'

'Is he trying to achieve something?'

'When it's Al, yes.'

'Not sure if he thinks it's working then. He was just saying how some of them are far too old for this experience.'

'Yes, maybe the wheels are starting to come off.'

'What makes you say that?'

'Oh, you just get a sense of these things. I don't talk much but I watch. They all seem to have their jobs, but some of them aren't getting done any more. You're trying to patch up too many cracks Mike.'

Toni

4th June 2019

Toni was terse in her conversation. She seemed to carry certainty with self-assured ease. Her whole bearing pointed to a disciplined concentration. She alternated two pairs of dungarees encasing thick thighs and muscled arms. When I'd asked her a few weeks ago what she did in the community, she told me she dealt in earth and fire. Hugh had learnt how to bake bread from her and looked well and truly educated afterwards. He was almost shaking before the morning baking.

But I was curious to see a potter in practise and asked if I could watch. She kneaded the clay and concocted the mould on her wheel under a jet of water. She had constructed something like a watering can that acted like a concentrated shower. Her eyes skinned to the point of squinting, in total concentration as she formed the bowl. She lifted the finished article and gently carried it off for firing. I made us a cup of tea and asked Toni how she paid for all of this. Toni liked to sound canny and in this case she probably was.

'Eeee, Al paid for everythin'. I brought my wheel and we were able to build a kiln in the stables. We plan to sell the—you know—the ceramics. That's the word. Just have to organise a buyer.'

The bowl emerged and Toni placed the finished article reverently onto a shelf to cool. I felt it looked rather robust and stolid, the qualities—err—of Toni herself.

The glaze was that coppery muddy brown, replicating

the thick shape and colour of cups and plates throughout the house.

'You seem to like this glaze.' I was stating the obvious.

'The community use it. Why change a winning formula?'

Toni could sound hard-headed even if she was disappearing into quicksand.

Later that day Al flung open a pantry door. Rows of muddy brown cups and plates stretched back into the cupboard's gloaming.

'Mike would you like to buy any of Toni's work?'

'Well they're not quite my style…'

'Well they're nobody's style. I can't get rid of them. She said she would pay her way with her pottery when she arrived. But she only produces these clunky pieces. You wouldn't let her near porcelain.'

'She says it's her winning formula.'

'It's her only formula! I don't know what to do. She's so impregnably self-assured. She will keep saying she doesn't take any nonsense from anyone. She can't see I'm taking it from her.'

At breakfast that morning most of the community didn't notice the subtle change in Al. He made it his business to speak to the members about their day. Helmut on the logs they needed for the next month, Rosamond on the herb garden, Claude on some work on window sills. If Toni noticed his indifference to her she didn't let on.

Hours later there was a hubbub in the locked office. Toni was screaming, 'I want the money for my pots. If I leave here, I want the money you owe me. Al you bastard.'

'Toni please just take them!'

A taxi came gingerly up the drive an hour later. Toni

crunched across the gravel with two crates, one after the other, and spurning the driver's help, heaved them into the boot. The driver tried to conceal anxiety for his back axel. Her face was rigid as she pulled away. She did not turn once. I saw her mobile go to her ear as she disappeared down the slope.

I ran into Hugh and we went for a brief stroll in the garden just before the evening meal.

'That's the first time anyone's been thrown out,' Rosamond said. You know Toni wasn't exactly popular but it's shaken people up. Left a bit of a sour taste just before this wedding…'

The Last Guest

4th June 2019: Evening

We heard the sound of an engine and the gravel crackling. Then light footsteps on the flagstones in the hall, and a figure stood at the door of the kitchen. A woman, stately among the dowdy end-of-day human flotsam and jetsam she found sitting at the long oak table. She was draped in a brilliant red scarf over a long paisley shirt more the length of a skirt, and lycra trousers.

Al ran over and hugged her. 'Siobhan!' He turned to us. 'I've known her most of my life.'

'Al... a long time.' She allowed a collusive reproof. But that was as far as she would go with this kind of corny joshing. Her eyes seemed to have a sparkle in the gloom of the kitchen and the encroaching dusk. She'd applied careful makeup, an unusual use of shadow, a not too heavy mascara. Her way of feeling inviolable.

She had the quality of an actress, meeting no one's gaze as if she were in front of a darkened auditorium. I had wondered how I would react to her entrance. And here I was cowering at the end of the table, concealed in another identity, hiding in my long robe, my beard in a frizzy chaos. But she would still have known me. We both had found ourselves on this stage with no script. I had been terrified of this moment, but now it felt flat. Siobhan was ignoring my presence with contempt. I was no longer part of her world. And nobody would know she was my wife unless she acknowledged it. Our relationship was under-wraps—as secret as when it first began.

Siobhan continued with a breezy upward inflection, 'So Al, where's the bride to be?'

Edith could hardly raise her head on the long bench, bent in concentration chopping tarragon. I felt a compassion for her as Siobhan's presence filled the room. And Siobhan persisted. 'Hello Edith. I hope we can have a talk sometime.'

Edith mutely nodded and nodded. She was heartbreakingly like the models of dogs that used to be on the back shelf of any car, necks shaking interminably as the car bowled along. Al sat beside her and enfolded her in his arms. She gripped his hand and looked up at Siobhan.

'You and Al were together …'

'A long time ago… most of a lifetime ago.'

'What went wrong?'

There was pause. Anyone pretending to be absorbed in anything else stopped and looked at Edith. There were seconds of agonised silence. It took a great deal for Siobhan to be taken aback but she registered a vague surprise.

'I think it's for Al to say…'

'I'd like to hear it from you, Siobhan.'

She looked at Edith, her lined face, her missing teeth. With a sudden gravity in the full knowledge of what she was really saying to our little sparrow…

'I was too strong for him, love.'

Edith's eyes were throbbing with tension. She choked out, 'I can be strong too, you know… Siobhan.'

'Yes you are… you will be.' Al tightened his embrace.

Siobhan could have said something like 'I'm sure you are,' but she was never instinctively emollient. She drank her tea and didn't make any further attempt to converse with anyone.

And she did what people do when a conversation dies, what most people do when they are bored or in an unfamiliar place. She checked her phone. The community watched with something approaching horror as she continued with what appeared a crass innocence.

'Siobhan, I'd love to show you the house.'

There was a firmness in Al's voice making it difficult for her to refuse. They left the room.

A minute later we heard her voice raised.

'No phones… are you all mad here?'

But the rest was lost in a murmured undertone from Al.

Decorating the Stairs

5th June 2019: Afternoon

The afternoon before the wedding I was helping Edith prepare a floral decoration for the main stairs, an intertwining of ivy with the cut stems of flowers to climb between the banister rails. We created the impression of a trellis-like growth winding upwards. An illusion of harmony. Had it been living ivy it would have strangled the flowers.

While the arrangement crept up step by step, I asked about her wedding dress. 'Siobhan has been helping me. I didn't know what she would be like but she's lovely. I think we were both sorry about yesterday. I don't know what was happening to me speaking like that. But anyway, we only needed to make a few small adjustments to the dress. My figure hasn't changed too much since I was young… And then Siobhan sat on the window seat and watched me twirling in it like someone at a ball, and we both were laughing. Mike, I don't remember when I last laughed with another woman.'

'Never here?'

Her voice went to a whisper. 'Sorry it's horrid to say it, but no… and I didn't have many girlfriends after I left school either…'

'Al said he saw the dress in a charity shop,' I was cutting long strands of ivy. Edith threaded the vines up through the spindles into this tangled illusion of a single plant.

'It was just luck… I wasn't planning to have a wedding

dress at all but Al found it.'

She continued gently threading a lily through. There was a gravity that was touching in her concentration. I had often wondered what Al had seen in her that set her apart. Now I saw an innocent, not a childlike or naïve innocent, but someone for whom the world still seemed fresh and full of unknown possibility. Different from the knowing hardbodies Al had incessantly seemed to be involved with. Her nose crinkled, her lips pursed, her eyes were gimlets. And for the first time I saw the Edith who was not cowed by other people's presence. I used to feel Al wanted to give her a life she'd been denied, and somehow make amends for his own past. But now, on the eve of her wedding, I saw why he'd fallen for her.

She said, 'Siobhan told me you got married in a registry office with no fuss. She wore a trouser suit...'

'She told you... we're married?'

'Well Al told me already but he said I mustn't tell people here. It's your business.'

Hugh also felt Siobhan hadn't recognised him. It had been years, and he wore a robe as well. But in all honesty, she'd always found him tiresome and never wanted him to stay at the house—'He might never leave'—and I suppose she had a point. So she may have blanked him as well as me.

But the mention of Siobhan had set off... well, the closest comparison was the image of a malign barman with his cocktail shaker of emotions. I had abandoned Siobhan—I yearned for her—I had been betrayed by her—I had smashed up the kitchen and walked out. The grinning barman was making no sense of this; he was simply concocting it all into one confusion. My jaw clenched frantically, but Edith was continuing in her absorbed work and noticed nothing. And then jolted me out of this reverie.

'She asked about my teeth. I told her.'

'Oh…' I didn't know what had happened to her missing teeth but I thought it might be too rude…

'She asked if the dentist ever suggested a crown or a bridge or something. So I told her. My teeth were bad and hurt a lot but I'd always avoided my dentist. He'd made me feel creepy and I didn't go back. I told her how Al took them out for me. He gave me this thick draft to take away the pain and I closed my eyes. He had some metal thing, like silver pliers. When he started, I thought my head would crack open. But he was quick and then we just let the blood wash away…'

'Christ…'

'That's what she said. But Al says Simone de Beauvoir had her front tooth missing and she was still beautiful.'

I searched back in my memory and felt Simone did replace the tooth. But you can't quite tell in when in the pictures.

'Well Siobhan was a bit shocked—but she knew who Simone de Beauvoir was.'

'Yes she's a fan.' She'd read *La Deuxieme Sexe* in French.

'Anyway, she wasn't impressed about how Al was looking after us. She doesn't believe in the old cures. But Al has studied the apothecaries. He doesn't want to get us mixed up with all these pills. My parents took medication just to counter the side-effects from all the other stuff they put in their bodies. And they were so unhappy. Honestly the mandrake and henbane work better for pain…'

'I was beginning to wonder what would happen to me if I felt a bit under the weather.'

Edith tried not to look irritated and with an exaggerated care completed the arrangement on the stairs.' Al has studied the use of herbs. We grow what we need in the garden… Though Siobhan said she would stick to paracetamol…'

'If I'm honest suppose I might too…' but I didn't have any paracetamol tablets left.

Edith's face reddened. 'I don't want to become a walking pill box like my parents. I don't want to end up like them. I remember taking my mum to the hospital when she had the cancer. And you would just sit there and wait and everyone looks like they don't want to be there or anywhere. It looked like they came because they felt they had to; they just did as they were told. They seemed to resent it all and they're supposed to be the ones who want to get well. And there they are on the screwed down plastic benches, sitting on this precipice on the edge of death, miserable and bored out of their minds.'

'Did Siobhan talk to you about her cancer?'

'Yes, she said she got away with it. I was so glad to hear that.'

'But you wouldn't have the same treatment?'

'No Mike. When it's time I am not going to argue.'

'But death is hardly ever nice and clean. It's messy, usually painful and awful to see, and when someone's dying on the ward…'

'Alfredo died here. He knew it was hopeless. Al gave him poultices and prepared these brews. And he died peacefully almost in his sleep. People could die comfortably four hundred years ago. They weren't all in pain. Al doesn't want to get us mixed up with all these pills.'

She came down to look at the display.

'I loved talking to Siobhan. I sort of forgot she'd been involved with Al.'

'Well as she said, that was more than half a lifetime ago.'

'Anyway I forgot everything. It was just so lovely talking to her. She's going to give me away. That feels so great. It was so different talking to another woman about me. And I told her Al was a wonderful lover.'

'What did she say to *that*?'

'She said she supposed he was probably efficient.'

Edith looked at me and clearly could only take it seriously because Siobhan had said it, 'Can you love someone efficiently?'

After Edith had gone, her experience of Siobhan left me with a vile shaking feverish sensation. It stayed for hours.

The Night before the Wedding

6th June 2019

A few hours later we had our usual simple meal, even if it was the night before the wedding. The wedding food had been prepared earlier and stored in the larder. Siobhan had stayed on all day. She and John were given carved chairs Al produced for the occasion. I'd not seen these chairs before. I sat at the end of a bench near the range. Siobhan had clearly decided to ignore me when she came in and Al enthroned her opposite John by the kitchen door. But I steeled myself to look at my wife. She listened with concentration, directing black olive-stone eyes at the people round the table, the rubicund lips holding a hint of a smile, an expression that could switch from sympathy to sarcasm in a moment. Her snub nose wrinkled with amusement or quiet distaste. After we'd eaten for a few minutes, she looked mock-confidingly over at John.

'What do you think of the grub here? A bit of the hair-shirt?'

John was more diplomatic. 'I just eat whatever's in front of me now. Not really that concerned about the niceties. It's a kind of fuel really.'

'Ruth was a great cook. A mistress-chef.'

'Yes, well that was different… we shared a life. Food was part of that. Now it doesn't mean…'

'I really loved her. And she was so beautiful. She always had this exquisitely cut bobbed hair, like Louise Brooks.' John returned her gaze with a drawn face over almost transparent skin.

Siobhan turned to Al. 'She didn't like the way we took the piss out of you.'

Al gave her the thinnest of grimaces, uncertain how to react to this in front of his flock, seeming to sense Siobhan could depth-charge his authority with a few more well-chosen remarks.

'You're right she was kind to me. She wasn't combative. A kind of lesson to us all.' He stared back at Siobhan with a cold smile.

'She knew how to handle you when you got upset.' Siobhan persisted.

'She understood, Yes. But we were all so much younger…'

After a pause Al quietly said to John. 'I should have come to her funeral. I'm sorry, I just don't cope with conventional ceremonies.'

John replied in bleached tones as if correcting a statistical error. 'It wasn't a conventional funeral. It was woodland burial… I would want something like that myself.'

John turned back to Siobhan. 'I remember you read that beautiful poem by Helen Dunmore—*My Stem was cut*—and Jacqui sang "*September Song*"… and…' When I looked up at Siobhan, her face had gone grey, glacial, but with the hint of the discord thrumming under the skin. I had read '*Fear no more the heat o' the sun*' after Jacqui's song.

John continued after a few moments, speaking quietly and obliquely, consciously calming the waters. 'I was glad you came. It was a difficult day for me. Everyone seemed to expect me to break down for the first time. It must have been disappointing for them—the idea that I was going to reveal my hidden self—as if there was one. The whole thing was inhibiting. I suppose it actually took me away from the grief—the visceral grief that's there all the time.' And John looked at Siobhan as if she was the only one in the room.

Siobhan was beginning to experience the hawser power of John's depthless melancholy. She stood and spoke briskly, 'I need to get a cab. I'll see you all tomorrow. Edith, we'll fix your dress.'

Then she walked out the room, the front door closed and most of the community heard the first person speaking into a mobile for years.

John rose and left without another word.

There was period of silence, of tongue-tiednesss. I felt Al seemed as shocked as anyone by Siobhan's revelation that he had been a figure of fun among his old friends. Nobody but Hugh and I knew how much derision he had suffered at the mercy of our group.

We continued eating mostly in silence. Hugh's attempts at wedding bells humour sank without trace. Al reminded us about some of the plans for tomorrow but it felt like a planning meeting rather than a celebratory event. Siobhan had opened a little garden gate into Al's past and carelessly sown dragon's teeth in the field beyond.

Wedding Day

7th June 2019

On the day of the wedding we assembled in the courtyard for the planned procession down to the church. The weather was breezy and cool but there was no danger of rain. We were going to walk down a steep road and into the hamlet where the church nestled into the side of the hill. The community formed a column with Al and Helmut at the head, and Edith with Siobhan a discreet distance at the back, observing some convention of the couple not seeing each other. Helmut wore his best dress but with crocs rather than heels. The women had helped him with some stunning makeup. Al was in a white kaftan with a red scarf round his neck.

Al had bought thirty kaftans from a wholesaler's in Rochdale. He'd told me how he cut his teeth in the souk of Marrakech and still felt the extra excitement you get haggling. He wasn't sure if the wholesaler shared the exhilaration, but in Morocco he told me that it was the second most popular sport, and he became good at it. He couldn't remember what the *most* popular sport was. He reckoned he saved £100 to go towards more food.

Helmut had been given the job of dipping the kaftans into the dyeing vats, improvised from two large barrels. He and Judith mixed a shade of blue into a red base with salt for a much more luxuriant shade of crimson. And the same with black on a blue base to obtain indigo. They rinsed the fabric for days in cold water, and the results were dramatic. The kaftans hung across the courtyard for two days. Helmut had hoisted the rope to almost the first floor where the wind caught them and they bounced like spirits playing in the upper air. Now on the day of Al and Edith's wedding, we were all dressed in these flowing robes. I wore a dark blue robe with maybe two inches of beard. Siobhan and I still had not exchanged a word or a glance since she arrived. I felt the robe and the beard gave some kind of protection. John would only wear the suit he had brought with him and met us at the church after a longer walk round by the road. Siobhan had brought the clothes she intended to wear and refused as well to melt into Al's community… like I had done. Al had chosen a church in a small hamlet a mile and a half from Gritstone. The vicar was ready to do a Friday wedding for the money. For some reason weddings are usually on a Saturday but funerals are whenever it suits you.

The procession wound down a footpath which was dry as a result of no rain for several days. Our feet kicked up the dust as we trod on the husks of ruts. As the community reached the single-track metalled road, we ceased being a straggling band and became a procession two abreast. We broke into 'Here comes the Sun.' Helmut kept a too rudimentary tumty-tum beat on a small drum slung round his neck. Ursula played a flute, but quickly lost the rhythm as everyone sang the first chorus. Her high-pitched thin tone continued to struggle with the melody and gradually lost any resemblance to it.

A woman pegging her washing out gasped as we passed her garden wall. Al indicated they ought to end the song that by now was veering out of control. Ursula's reedy melody died halfway through a chorus. We were nearing the church now. Beside Al, Helmut had changed his crocs for high heels and now looked completely resplendent in the long electric blue dress. A few minutes behind the main procession came Edith with Siobhan. Siobhan wore a black tuxedo with a red velvet bow tie. She and Edith both changed into heels and waited for the rest of the community to enter the building.

The pews just about accommodated thirty people. The walls were cold. The sun had not reached through the stone. At the altar the vicar was waiting for them.

When I sat in a pew near the front, I saw the vicar was staring at Al, and his best man who towered above him in his blue dress, with deeply indented mascara, purple highlighting above the eyes and discreetly applied lipstick. Today Helmut spoke in an even more pronounced Teutonic accent and was formal in his address.

Al's intricately embroidered white kaftan clearly did not originate from the usual purveyors of the ill-fitting penguin suits the vicar usually faced. Al stared ahead unsmilingly. He looked the Norseman of his Yorkshire ancestry. I felt this Norman church, built by the conquerors after the harrying of the North, could be safely said to be witnessing an exquisite vengeance that not even the Vikings could have contemplated.

The couple must have seemed so compliant when Reverend Marshland had met them. Al told me how he had quoted liturgy to the vicar from memory. Now the vicar seemed about to translate his unease into a reason to stride off and abandon the ceremony.

But the vicar's face changed to a reassured expression as if some order was restored to the marriage ceremony. Here was the bride in a white flowing… wedding dress. In continuity with years of shy figures approaching the altar with their... but then Siobhan could not be her mother... they appeared to be from the same generation. Well, you could almost see the vicar's thought process. Siobhan was fine looking but what was she doing in a man's suit? An ageing hipster brother might have whispered in his ear that he was being 'put on'—I could see the snarl about to rise in him. But was it a snarl originating from years of officiating marriages?

After all, how many couples had he ever seen again after the meeting when they earnestly voiced their intentions to begin regularly attending his church? How did the appearance of this congregation compare to all those respectable liars? The hatred for the Traceys, Keiras, Jasons and Kevins who trooped through his induction talk, the men soppy stern, the women rather too accommodating. I had to admit that Maddie had appeared just the same kind of hypocrite after her church wedding—her hubbie cheesily posed in his obligatory hired tailed suit. The Reverend might have been suspicious when this couple cancelled the rehearsal at the last minute. Al had said they'd assiduously studied the ceremony on YouTube.

I could imagine the reverend ready to take a whip to this congregation much as Our Lord in that problematic episode when the Messiah lost his temper and drove the buyers and sellers out of God's house. If he struggled with that passage at seminary, perhaps he now understood. He could go even further back to a biblical past and drive us all into the desert to die of thirst and hunger.

And his thoughts seemed to lead him into turning the innocuous marriage ceremony into something akin to an exorcism. He began with a new unheard-of venom. Yes, this time he felt the permission for that snarl he may have often wanted to inject into proceedings. This time he didn't blandly speak the sanitised version. Now he went back to the 1662 Book of Common Prayer which he intoned with a new savour.

'Marriage is not by any to be enterprised, nor taken in hand, unadvisedly, lightly, or wantonly, to satisfy men's carnal lusts and appetites, *like brute beasts…*' On these last three words he glowered at Al and Helmut. Al stared blandly back at him. '…that hath no understanding…'

The words hung in the air and echoed against the ancient stones like a curse. The ceremony seemed likely to grind to a halt.

Al coughed. The vicar continued but never seemed to have placed more hope that *any man may shew just cause*, pausing for what seemed an eternity waiting for the raised voice. The service then finished quickly without graciousness or celebration. Helmut was much more efficient and graver with the rings than Hugh had been. There was a weary, 'You may kiss the bride…' As the congregation burst into prolonged applause, the vicar scurried away and then remembered he had forgotten to collect the fee. I must admit I rather enjoyed it.

We returned for a party at the house. There were no family. If Al had any they would never know. Echoing hundreds of years of brides crossing the threshold of this ancient mansion, Al swept Edith up and carried her through the door into the main hall. The flowers Edith and I had prepared, snaked up the stairs. There were candles at midday in the kitchen. The table was covered with food this house had never witnessed. Tabbouleh and couscous, pungent curries redolent of cardamom in rich red cream sauce, flat breads fresh from the oven sprinkled with sesame seeds, spiced cakes. There was no alcohol. Cordials were poured from the solid brown jugs Toni could not take with her.

Hugh and I brought the two copper-bottomed saucepans from the boot of the Scimitar. Edith found more butchers hooks and hung them over the range. I think they were the only wedding presents. Siobhan had arrived in a cab that morning with several bouquets of flowers to decorate the kitchen. John clearly considered the idea of wedding presents an inappropriately sentimental and rather ridiculous custom.

He sat in a large oak chair by the kitchen range. People seemed to be nervous of him. He didn't encourage or discourage conversation. His replies seemed only as bland as most of the questions. I circled him but then sat down. 'You're quiet mate.' I always tended to cope with difficult social situations with this brand of corny folksiness. I don't now.

John replied, 'Yes.'

'Do you think we did the right thing coming here?'

John stared ahead and spoke quietly without much enthusiasm, 'I hadn't thought—I mean it's Al's wedding. One just comes…'

'Yes, but I feel I'm on the outside all the time.'

'Well don't look at me Mike. I've never remotely felt inside any group.'

'Anywhere… even when you worked?'

'Always in charge. Never worked for anyone. Always been able to be in control. You can't afford to get close. And I suppose I didn't want to uncover the secrets in my employees' lives. There might be secrets, but no mystery, if you understand. There was nothing that tantalised me.'

'Well I could be cruel and say we project ourselves onto the blank slates that seem to be other people's lives.'

'Hmmm… yes… that could be seen as cruel. Unless you're talking about yourself and I'm the blank slate.'

'No, I suppose I believe everyone has a story.'

'So, you are talking about me, then?' John's steel frames augmented the concentration in his face.

'It seems I am.'

'And that's how you see me. Living in a kind of observer-created universe?' John turned to me with neither aggression nor much curiosity, but a kind of combative weariness.

'I hadn't thought of that. Thine own words hath said it.'

'Mike, you don't seem to realise even in yourself that you want to be cruel to me. Why? What have I ever done to you?'

I laughed humourlessly. 'Yeah well, I always felt you just brushed me and my ideas off your shoulder casually like dandruff. Some kind of offhand remark to make me feel smacked down. When I saw you come through the door, I realised again how much I had avoided feeling terrified of seeing you.'

'Terrified? I don't suppose I've ever considered that other people have thoughts, have ideas about me. Never even speculated how other people experienced me. I don't suppose I thought I could be of that much interest to them.'

'Well if you just sat in your office and looked at spreadsheets…'

'What a stereotype. Yes, okay Mike, *that* is a second-rate cheap remark and I don't care if that makes you experience personal shame.'

'Maybe I deserve that. But that's the thing. I always felt I deserved the psychological drubbing I got from you.'

'Was this *my* fault? I don't do you any good by saying what a first-rate mind you have.'

'So you were giving some kind of service?'

'By being real. In that way… yes.'

'And now?'

'I just don't care. I am surprised I have the energy for this little… chat.'

'You just don't care.'

'Yes, I think I am done.'

'Sorry John, what do you mean?

'Exactly that.'

I sat in silence.

'Look this is a special day for Al and Edith. Why don't you go and talk to them… or anybody else?'

'But…'

'Mike, I have realised, I have only just realised that all you wanted to do was try to measure up to my standards for some reason. You never really cared about me much.'

'So much to be concerned about …a guy who is married to beautiful woman. Far richer than me at any time…'

John replied with increased weariness, 'But I always expected to be rich. There is no more effort involved in getting rich than training to be your plumber. That is not what I am talking about. You could have been a friend. Now I have none.'

'Not even Hugh…' But John was laughing in a hollow way.

'Well I'll leave you to it.'

'Yes, leave me.'

Around us laughter swirled and cutlery chimed on plates. And echoing down from the eaves was some lumbering bassline and the screams of dancers. I looked in to see Hugh with the rest leaping and punching the air to Jefferson Airplane's 'Volunteers'.

Al produced dried magic mushrooms he had been saving for this party. A psilocybin haze descended on the community. As the wedding party broke into groups, Helmut was still in his long dress dancing by himself around the pump. Having eaten more than his allowance of mushrooms, Hugh played 'The King will come' repeatedly in the eaves room. I'd declined the offer from Al, who looked at me as if he expected no less. I felt that in Al's eyes I'd become a timid, ageing man by refusing. But when I had seen Siobhan also refuse, I wanted to be in the same state. She might at last speak to me. And now she was briskly getting ready to leave. She came downstairs with a red leather bag. John had already disappeared up to his room after bland remarks of congratulation to Edith. She was virtually monosyllabic in his presence.

Meanwhile I was skulking in the kitchen. I'd excluded myself from the range of perception the rest of the community were experiencing. Jean and Alex were sat either side of the table, staring unblinkingly into each other's faces. They exclaimed as their physiognomies became transformed into infinite varieties of expression. But they shifted, with a jarring suddenness, into feeling convinced they both possessed a series of masks, with nothing behind but the musculature. Both started to wish they had not begun this adventure. They moved upstairs to be immersed in Hugh's air guitar.

Siobhan looked round the door. I was overwhelmed how her face possessed a new loveliness, a mature hard-won beauty… she at this moment. My wife… still my wife.

'Mike, I have words for you.' Her tone was curt, strained of warmth.

I felt myself being ripped away from Gritstone House, back, back to the world I shared and then left, in that terraced house I had walked out of only weeks ago. I found myself sidling out to her, as if accepting a summons. This was not the way I would have planned it. My jowls hung loose. My hands dangled lifelessly.

'God you look a state. I've been pretending not to recognise you in that shroud and it's not been difficult…'

My body sagged. I meekly stood like a bullock about to be stunned in a slaughterhouse.

'How the fuck can you stay here and watch Al run this disaster?'

I spoke and realised my voice sounded sulky like a child who's been found out. 'He's letting me stay for a while. I didn't have anywhere else.'

'Al hasn't changed much. Once he goes off the rails he can't be stopped. And he's gone off them again and he's taking all these suckers with him.'

'We're… they're not suckers.'

'Do you know what's going on here? Do you really know?'

I looked at her. She could see I did.

'Edith told me. Al has control over all her money.'

'They're married…'

'And she knows he dips into everyone else's accounts.'

'We all know this… they want him to look after their affairs and forget everything about the outside world.'

'Glad you're okay with this because Al never stopped playing the market. Even when he'd "*retired*." You'd find him on his PC at one in the morning checking the Singapore opening exchange rates. I was at his house once and he told me he'd remortgaged the place a few months before and the short sale paid off. But he's older now. I can't believe he won't come unstuck. He's a gambler to his fingertips. You're not telling me he's not chancing all the money coming in. In fact, I *know* he is. When we had that argument about my phone, he took me into his room, and the moment I saw the screens I could see the prices… all those little grids on one screen and another with graphs, red and green lines like sliced mountains.'

'He thinks he can turn it round.' I sounded like the supporter of a dilapidated team on the edge of relegation. But maybe not so fervent.

'You lame muppet, Mike. You do know! Just listen to yourself. One of his cronies now aren't you? Back in that hero-worshipping routine. Like Hugh. Hugh always adored Al.'

I could feel my belly shifting like a wobbly blancmange under my gown.

'God that's disgusting seeing your guts heaving about. Aren't you ashamed at all?' I could only mumble incoherently. 'Mike, you left our house and just disappeared. You think I was wasn't frightened, that I wanted some reassurance? Yeah, thanks for the text. I happened to phone you when I was leaving the house and heard your ringtone from Colin's bin. But when Al's invite arrived, I felt you would be here if you were anywhere. And when I mailed him…'

'He said…'

'He didn't have to say anything. He only invited me. He clearly knew you weren't with me. And he asked about Madeleine. I told him I was coming alone so…' Siobhan stopped beating about the bush. 'Mike we're finished. I think you know that.'

The words I'd rehearsed vaporised. The flagstones in the hall were heaving as if an earthquake was shaking the moor. 'I'm being lopped…'

'Mike you sound so pitiful. You've lopped yourself.'

'…'

'You know Kelvin…'

'I know Kelvin… he's thirty years younger…'

'Everyone's younger than us. I don't need to say it…'

'Fucking say it.'

'I'm not marrying him. I don't give a fuck how long it lasts. But I'm going to buy you out of the house. The money's waiting to go into your account. I've told the kids. When you know where you are settled you can mail them.'

I felt neatly crushed up, a cardboard box stomped on and flattened for the bin.

'I can't…'

Siobhan hesitantly began to see the damage in front of her. 'Mike this can't be a total shock… I'm sorry I didn't realise…'

'No, I don't feel much at all…'

'Well I'm sorry Mike. You were lucky I was round for so long to look after you. But when you disappeared, I realised I'd finally stopped caring. I couldn't take any more.'

'I think you'd better go. I think you're right.'

I must have frozen for minutes on end, a statue in the hall people seemed to avoid as if it was transparent what had just happened. I dragged myself into the kitchen and heard Siobhan talking just outside in the yard. She had found Al chatting to Ezra and Alec.

'I'm off Al. Not sure when you'll see *me* again.'

Al was taken aback but ploughed on, pretending he hadn't noticed the hostility behind her words, replying with some bland expression of thanks in front of these men. 'Yeah, so glad you could give Edith away. It meant a lot to us.'

'I liked Edith. You be careful with her.'

Al could only stare at Siobhan's departing back as she swept by me.

A few hours later when the party was breaking up, I was reading in my room. Well, trying to. A knock and the door opened. Edith stood there, still in her wedding dress.

'How did I look?'

'I thought you looked wonderful. The dress possesses its own kind of magic.'

'I knocked because Siobhan gave me this… to give to you.' And Edith handed me the mobile I threw into the bin weeks ago. 'Here's the charger in this bag. She wanted to make sure that I gave you the phone.'

I have the phone with me now. I haven't used it yet.

Moor Walk

8th June 2019: Morning

The house slept after the wedding party. I hadn't been able to close my eyes since Siobhan left. I shifted in bed with the same incessant sensations. You could hardly call them thoughts, but unremitting physical shocks. I waited until dawn and dressed. Now I tapped lightly on John's door. I needed to make peace with him…again.

'Oh, it's you Mike…' John looked weary and drained. I already was beginning to regret knocking but I ploughed ahead and suggested a walk on the moors.

'I don't think I've been on any moor,' John said ruminatively.

We fitted on wellington boots from the racks in the hall. I watched John select his boots with the solemnity he devoted to anything, scrutinising the soles and the size of the instep. We pulled them on at the kitchen door. Not much was said. We walked across the yard, through the kissing gate to the field with the earth closet and then up to the grove. The crude metal figures in the branches chimed together in the wind. John paused by the stones under the trees, scrutinising the single capitals carved on each.

He nodded. 'This would do,'

I formed a question, but John was already walking ahead of me. The top of the moor stretched before us, and the last of the flowering deep yellow gorse.

'Yellow was her favourite colour…'

John's grief was visceral. I couldn't recognise the man I

associated with devastating logic and calculation. I felt a shock of tenderness for this figure now striding up in front of me, along the track to the shooting booths ranged along the edge of the summit. Something indomitable in his motion. We began walking across the top of the moor. Soon we had lost the track amidst a mass of springy moss and puddles of deep black water.

John said, 'I suppose we were mostly happy—sometimes deliriously happy…' but stopped as he saw me looking blankly at the flat unvarying landscape that stretched out from the tops.

'You know Mike, I am glad to be here but I won't come back.'

'Never?'

'No never.' John seemed not to be looking at the moor but its emptiness.

I was in the company of a lost soul. I could do nothing for him. I tried to name my own thoughts as they floated before me as slowly as the clouds overhead. 'You know there's an idea you can be healed emotionally, if you really name what you're feeling. This place is doing that, this landscape's so empty and featureless. It's doing that.'

John stood beside me surveying the flat horizon beyond the pools, tufts of grass on mossy hummocks, piles of rocks that landed after an explosion of matter before man walked here. And into this vacuum, I couldn't stop myself saying, 'Siobhan ended our marriage yesterday—just before she left.'

John turned his gaze to me. He wasn't radiating compassion. He could only share his pain with someone else. And silently and slowly, it was as if he injected pure pain into my veins.

I felt that John believed he could forensically apprehend the diametric difference in grief between us; as if he could incise and remove some palpitating chaos and make a scientific evaluation, surveying my grief like a diseased organ under a microscope. No loss seemed to rival his own. And this morning, in the stinging wind when I looked at John, his face was set as if he'd come to a decision.

I had wandered off in a trance. It ceased to matter where I was. The landscape was an unvarying expanse of dark green and brown. I felt John was somewhere behind. But I didn't bother to look back. I carried on trudging through a clinging mire that clutched at and sucked the wellingtons in with every step. Soon I was perched on soggy moss surrounded by small deep pools. I was hopping from tussock to tussock. I needed to leave the moor.

When I turned, I realised I had now entirely lost sight of him. Above me there was the mocking cawing of crows swirling in the upper air. I struggled back over a landscape that seemed uniform and endless. There was still no discernible path. Only sheep tracks that abruptly died away. All I could do was head for a horizon. When I crested the ridge, John was a good mile from the track we had taken up to the tops. I saw his green cagoule zigzagging at speed down towards Gritstone. When I reached the house John's room was silent.

CPR

8th June 2019: Midnight

I was woken by glass splintering in one of the rooms above. I lit a candle and mounted the stairs with a practised delicacy on bare feet treading on the parts of the boards that wouldn't set off creaks in the wood. A silence engulfed the house and stretched in the darkness onto the moors. There were no sounds on the floor above my room, no candle light under the doors, no rattle as someone swept up the glass. But now I could hear an indistinct grumbling moan, like a cat too ill to howl. It was coming from the next floor, where John had been sleeping. I knocked but the same long low keening continued. I pushed open the door. John lay in his clothes collapsed on the top of the bed.

On the far side of the room shards of glass fanned out towards the window. John's body was clawing for air, the tendons in his neck like rods about to snap. I knew, I immediately knew, what had happened and it had gone badly wrong. John whispered between gasps, 'Took… beta… blockers… not enough…' A fit of coughing rattled his body.

I instinctively decided not to wake the house and augment the panic. I found myself flying down the stairs on bare feet in virtual silence, and firmly but lightly knocking on Al's door. Al pulled on a pair of dungarees. As we reached the second-floor we could hear the gasping. John's lips were dry and cracked. He was in a losing fight to breathe. His eyes contained an expression I had never seen from him: an imploring look.

Al motioned me back into the corridor. 'I've seen something like this before, man,' he whispered. 'Don't think he's got much of a chance. I'll find out what to do about Beta-blockers, yeah? Keep him awake Mike. Keep him talking.'

I sat beside John feeling as useless as I have ever felt. John was looking at nothing now, mumbling indistinctly to himself.

'Al's going to get help... John, are you able to talk?'

John was making strangled attempts to form words. 'I... don't... want... to...die... Mistake.'

'We're going to help you mate.' My voice reeked of lame conviction. I struggled to say anything beyond vapidly asking if John was *all right*. But John had gone quiet. The struggle to live was becoming too much. Time stood still until Al returned. He whispered to me, 'Is he still conscious?'

I shook my head. 'Barely.'

'Okay. Have you ever done CPR?'

I remembered some first aid course twenty years ago. I didn't like the idea of mouth to mouth resuscitation... but I nodded mutely.

'Right well better start. It's his only chance. Just do what you can. I'm going down to keep phoning for an ambulance.' Al silently wafted down two flights and in seconds I heard the beeping as the alarm in the office was disabled.

I had nodded to Al but once he left, I couldn't remember the details of CPR. I wasn't sure what I had learnt. John's limbs were flopped out and flaccid, a discarded doll in the playroom.

Five minutes ago, I had been tucked in bed reading Pirsig's nostrums about a couple's inability to get round to mending a faucet despite it driving them crazy—a First World domestic crisis. Now it seemed long ago, unreal, fatuous even. Now I was the powerless observer of the worst crisis of my life. Except I had to act. I was the only one able to save John. I knelt next to him, tried to control my voice and attempted a hesitant reassurance.

'John I'm going to do CPR… is that okay?' My words emerged smothered with hopelessness. There was the vaguest inclination of John's head. His lungs were packing up. I couldn't remember where to place my hands so opted to press down onto the middle of the rib cage with my fists. The house felt immobile, as if they were in their beds, afraid to even move. I was not sure how many times to do this before…

'I'm going to do mouth to mouth,' I hesitantly murmured. John's mouth was gaping. His breath stank like rotting slurry. I forced my mouth onto John's but as soon as our lips locked, my stomach lurched. I jerked away and reeled towards the door. Before I could reach it, a stew of yellow curry, rice and vegetables exploded onto the floorboards. I flopped against the cold plaster wall. When I looked over, John's breathing had stopped.

Al seemed to be away a long time, but I was too limp to care. When he quietly pushed open the door, his face creased with disgust. Ignoring me, he squatted beside John to scrutinise the waxing face. He took the arm and felt for a pulse without conviction. John's arm flopped back heavily.

'Christ almighty, Mike, you know he's dead!' Even Al

seemed stunned. He looked at me, crumpled in the corner, gawping at the corpse. My robe was splattered with yellow vomit. 'Didn't you try CPR?'

'When I tried mouth to mouth it made me sick.' I was drained of energy, transfixed by the first dead body I'd ever seen. A friend I couldn't save.

'I couldn't get a signal to call for the ambulance. Sometimes you can't up here. Kind of why I chose the house in the first place. It's all a bit late to try for that now...' The stench of bile filled the room. Avoiding the stray splinters, Al pulled the curtains and opened the window wide.

'Rather than just sitting there looking so fucking useless, you could clear up this sick. God Mike, you're so pathetic. I don't know... get a rag and a bucket from the kitchen.'

The water on the range was lukewarm. I couldn't pour straight and spilt most of it on the kitchen floor. Upstairs I wiped up the regurgitated food with the rag. The vomit slopped around in the bucket like sewage on the incoming tide.

Al sat on the bed coldly contemplating John's corpse. 'The bastard. Coming to my house and doing this—just after my fucking wedding... Let me take that fucking bucket. You'll drop it all over the stairs.' And Al lifted it down to the kitchen. I heard the back door open and then the click of the gate as Al went to empty the vomit into a ditch.

In the slowly dawning light, I noticed a sheet of paper on the bedside table. It was a neatly written note, which a calm and collected John had written before he began this last chaotic journey. He may have felt the overdose would have the simplicity of flicking a switch on a life-support machine.

> I'm sorry to do this to you but I couldn't take another moment. I would like to be buried up in that grove. Nobody knows I am here. There is nobody to tell.
> I apologise.
> John.'

I could hear John's innate restrained politeness behind the words, but couldn't take my eyes off the skin that had enveloped a vibrant face on the moor yesterday, now reduced to the cutaneous layer stretched over the skull.

I began to shake. What had been a cold tremor shooting up my back was a wind whipping in and out, hurtling round my limbs as if I was some hollow vessel. I staggered out mechanically along to the music room, two doors down, and collapsed onto the battered sofa. In a few minutes, maybe half an hour later, I heard light footsteps slowly mounting the stairs. Al sat down beside me and spoke in a low voice, 'Look Mike, it will soon be breakfast. The community will come together and we'll decide what to do.'

I murmured, 'I didn't save him. I couldn't do it. I felt so sick.'

'I think he was a goner. We did our best. We'll decide as a community what to do next.'

I nodded automatically. It felt good that this group of people would make the decisions I wasn't remotely able to. Who else could sort it out? But when Al left, other disturbing thoughts—questions I'd prefer not to answer—circled and crowded in on me like a pack of hounds that have run down the stag. I surely knew what John intended when he said,'This will do'—and I'd done nothing.

I thought again about what Al meant when he said the community would decide. Surely they would call the police?

Al's Plan

Al waited for the community to finish breakfast. His face was unaccustomedly pale and stretched. I slowly came down the stairs—I'd avoided breakfast, and poured a cup of cold water when I sat down. Al ignored me. Edith was mechanically crocheting.

'People, I've got a bit of shock for you. You might have heard a commotion last night. It was in John's room. He was on the verge of death when we found him, and now he's gone. He swallowed a large dose of beta blockers. There was nothing much we could do. He died in front of us. And he left a note to apologise.'

There was a silence as most of the people round the table tried to come to terms with the fact a total stranger's body was stiffening upstairs.

'Poor man,' murmured Edith.

But Al scythed in angrily, 'All he could do was apologise! The bastard came here and killed himself. He had to do it here, not in his fucking penthouse! Just after my wedding. I'm sorry, I'm really angry.'

The people round the table stared in disbelief at Al's outburst. Apart from Helmut who thundered, 'Bastard!'

Rosamond asked, 'Al, are you all right? I've never seen you like this.'

'I'm angry Rosamond. We've always kept out the neurosis that comes with the outside world. But he was a close friend, and I invited him. If I had even the suspicion he was capable of doing this... But I had no idea how much he'd changed until I saw him. I suppose I wondered if coming here, seeing his old friends might help him. But yeah… from the moment I saw him, I suppose, I knew he was lost.'

They still sat there and waited.

Hugh asked me, 'Did he say anything to you, Mike? On that walk?'

I knew now that John might as well have told me outright. But I shook my head. And stared at the knots in the wood in the table.

Hugh had words for the departed.

'You know I could sense a change in John from the moment I saw him. He hardly spoke to me the whole time and I said "*Come on John, let's talk it through*" and he made me feel like some obscure form of pond life. Nobody should be treated like that. I thought, "You rude and arrogant cunt. You haven't changed. Even losing Ruth hasn't changed you." You'd think he was the only one to lose someone. It's a sight worse when they're still alive…'

Al had to stop him. 'Hugh please… Look people we need to decide what to do. We have to deal with this now.'

I broke the hesitant silence. 'But that's quite clear, surely. We call the police. There'll need to be an inquest. You're all looking so nervous as I say it, but… it's the law.'

Al looked at me as if he expected no more.

'Mike this man has come to my house, to this community, and contaminated us with discord and fear. And now you want the police as well. We have abandoned that world, the world that has destroyed John. We want no part of it. And that includes your forces of law.'

I looked around the table. I saw glance-avoiding heads, eyes fascinated by tiny wax spots on the wood. What kind of laws were enforced at this table by the lords of this manor? Whippings, beatings, burnings on faggot-stacked pyres as the crowd jeered. The culture of a tribe here as long as memory. But nobody else appeared likely to equate this small transgression with those barbaric times. Even Hugh had been beyond any moral compass I could identify with for some time, and seemed mesmerised by his tea cup.

But Helmut spoke. '*Du hast Recht…* you are right Al. He has laid poison here and we do not wish to imbibe more. What shall we do?'

Al gave a slight nod. 'We do not want interference. Mike hasn't told you that John's note asked that he be buried up there in the grove. John clearly understood what happens there. We will bury him ourselves. It's what he wanted. We will do it with dignity and we will do it today. We will not do any work. It's a kind of way to honour a friend.'

I struggled to form words. I was still catching up with Al saying *He understood what happens there.* And my sudden realisation of what had happened in the grove. I could feel the weight of the room, it felt that the air had been sucked out of it. 'But nobody knows he's dead—his family.'

'He has no children. I don't know about his parents. To be frank I'm not sure there's anyone to care about John. His note said nobody even knew he was here. I looked at his phone…'

'You looked at his phone, Al?'

'Mike he is right. This is our house.' Helmut was unquestioning.

Al continued, 'No one had sent him a message for

weeks. And then it's just bills, standing orders and notifications. He'd abandoned the world in his own fashion.'

'But how did you activate the phone without a password? You generally need the phone to recognise the finger…'

I didn't feel Al was looking at me, he was looking into me.

'He left a password in his notebook , Mike.'

I was about to say 'What fucking pocket book?' but I felt a heaving animosity in the room. Helmut's crook was tapping the floor. Others were giving me sideways looks. They wanted me to stop. They wanted all this to end, to go away, the nightmare of this dead stranger.

'Mike, all you need to know is that I did activate that phone. You always thought you were—what was it? "*A bit of a rebel*"? But you never were, were you? Not like me. What did you intone like some kind of mantra? "*By any means necessary!*" Well man, I meant it then and I mean it now. You never did.'

I got up to leave. I could feel a force in the room pushing me through the kitchen door.

I sat gazing across at the moorland where I last walked with John. Yesterday morning. There among the heather and scrubland I felt I'd lost my way. There was no route back to a former life now. I was part of Al's community. I had nowhere else to go.

And I had a secret knowledge I could never share with anyone. John's calm set face conveyed everything before he spoke. And then he had said, '*This will do.*' I had known all the time on the moor and back in the house.

John had radiated grief. His body was phosphorescent with it. While I was in the house yesterday, I tried not to picture what might be happening on the other side of that door. The cold balancing before the final actions, the calculation of how many beta blockers he would need. I noticed John had left an unused packet. A fatal fastidiousness. But I hadn't knocked. I'd pretended I had other tasks and rejected the idea. And now I could tell no one. What would I say under oath at an inquest about John's state of mind? I'd lie, wouldn't I? Unwillingly, this is the world I found myself immersed in. But John had thrust this on me and I felt a cold rage. I owed John nothing.

I hardly realised as Al silently sat down beside me. 'I'm sorry man, I didn't mean all that. I was rude to you.'

'Well what bit didn't you mean, you bastard, taking me apart in front of your cronies?' Al laughed and put his arm round my shoulders. I didn't want to ask now what he meant *by any means necessary*.

I had nowhere else I could go. 'Well you'd best get on with it…'

Helmut and the Bread

9th June 2019, 9.30 am

I found Hugh and Helmut in the kitchen. I sat down quietly but I felt I'd been welcomed back into the flock. An unearthly normality had descended on the house while we were waiting for the burial. Hugh seemed to want to talk about anything rather than the dead body upstairs. Helmut was an unquestioning companion.

'You know Helmut, we did start off on the wrong foot.'

'Now we are on the right foot… but I never find that acid.'

Behind Helmut I saw Al emerge from his room and quietly ascend the staircase. He was barefoot. There was a small sliver of silverish metal stretching down from a black handle peeping out the side pocket of his dungarees. And a sealed jar in his hand. It was filled with a clear liquid.

Helmut was talking about Bavaria. 'I miss the bread most of all, Hugh. You don't have any idea of the variety in a small village bakers. People queue at opening time out of the shop… there is honey and bran, a *Landbrot, Funfkornbrot, Schwarzbrot…*'

There was a faint grating noise, an in-out rhythm.

'I know they sell tragedies of these breads in the supermarkets on this island, but they cannot attain the serenity, the richness …'

The noise became more insistent, faster…

'It is the only thing I miss, Hugh. *Mein Freund*, you seem… how do you English say… out of it?'

The noise stopped.

Al emerged and came down the stairs quickly. He was carrying something covered by a napkin. There was a faint odour but for Hugh it was distinct. Hugh whispered to me after Helmut wandered off that it was the pickle reek in the brightly lit rooms with steel surfaces, where he worked for one week and then left because he couldn't overcome the nausea of dead bodies in filing cabinets. Hugh didn't want this knowledge—it could be anything in that jar.

Al went up again with a gigantic roll of what appeared to be a bandage or gauze. In a few minutes he called Edith up to help him.

Funeral Rites

Later I was back sitting in the garden on the river god's bench. I was still coming to terms with my collusion. Nobody would call the police to begin the inquest into John's death. I was sinking slowly into a quicksand of moral qualms. In the face of Al's refusal to involve anyone from the authorities, my doubts felt as fragile as a paper lantern in a downpour. Concealing a death seemed akin to homicide. And the unspoken certainty that Al pressed John's lifeless but perhaps still warm forefinger against his mobile to activate it…

But as I struggled with my personal *Tristeia*, Hugh had been sent out to find me.

'We're all wanted in the kitchen.'

Al stood at the head of the table in a flowing black robe with woven patterns at the neck. The community seemed about to be inducted into a secret rite. They were also dressed in black. Hugh had quickly donned a robe as well. I had not been included in the plans but then, I didn't need to be. And then the slow realisation that to have these robes they must have been used before…

Al began speaking.

'We are going to bury my friend John. Who will help me to bear him?'

Minutes later Al, Hugh, Helmut, Rosamond and Sylvester slowly lurched down the stairs. Helmut descended walking backwards taking the weight of that shape that was John. Soon his body was lying on the long table, stiffly wrapped in white bandages like the Egyptian mummies I had seen in the British …

'I'd want this for my own funeral. I once saw a picture of Alan Clark's burial—he was this roguish minister in Thatcher's government. Anyway in his wife's book there was a photo and his body was in a winding-sheet wrapped like this. I think they used a table cloth. His family were around him and they took a photo and he was in front of them on the ground tightly wrapped—and then they buried him in the garden of his castle. It was a great way to end.'

'Yes Al, I remember. They had to get permission from the…' I was the only one who could possibly remember.

'Well we won't be needing that. Are you coming?'

'What's the red spot in the middle of his right side? Al, is that blood?'

'I cut myself during the wrapping. Scissors had to be sharp. I'll roll another layer on.' And with some skill Al enveloped that part with another layer of gauze.

The community formed a neat oval around the rigid swaddled shape. Edith had gone to the bookcase in the green room and brought incense sticks she set around the kitchen. An undertow of what I remembered as the distant odour from the bins at the back of the local butcher's shop in Coventry pervaded the room.

In a voluminous black sari Esther begun a wordless keening song in a shaky voice that elided between three notes she appeared unable to escape from. After minutes she clearly had no idea how she would conclude. Her voice quavered with vestiges of uncertainty. Al touched her shoulder and she ended immediately—a needle raised from the turntable mid-song.

'Thank you, Esther, that was beautiful. And now we will go up to the grove to bury John. He will need only a simple marker just as will we when we are buried there. He joins Alfredo, and Monique and Asif on our beautiful hillside.'

With shocking strength Helmut cradled John's corpse and lifted it off the table. Rosamond and Al and then Hugh and Sylvester shouldered John. Helmut took the weight of the body from the rear on his own. The cortege slowly moved across the courtyard past the dripping pump. A light insistent drizzle soaked into their black robes. We moved more quickly up the metalled path to the small grove on the ridge, the trees gesticulating shapes in the stiff breeze. It was only a matter of seconds before I was staring at a gaping dark mouth. The earth was piled and there were turfs of grass neatly laid by the mound.

Al turned to me. 'Do you have a farewell for John?'

I made a gesture. I was bereft of any emotion I could remember or identify for John. I was immersed in an action that felt like a crime. I was now part of that crime.

Hugh was attempting a suitable response to the last rites. His head was bowed with an impression of solemnity. He seemed to be searching for the emotional vocabulary for what was taking place.

Al asked with some hesitation 'Hugh?'

'Yes… yes I do have a few words. John was always superior to me in almost any way. He was more intelligent, better looking after a fashion, richer… he had a lovely wife who stayed with him. And yet inside him you sensed something hollow, unfulfilled, a raging discontent that could not be satisfied, a screaming need for what he could never be, because of what he was. And so it has led to him being buried on this beautiful hillside and it is beautiful, if rather wet at the moment. He is buried by people who were acquainted with him but could not say they really knew him, and some total strangers…' Hugh trailed off.

Al's black kaftan was clinging to his body as the drizzle increased.

'Thank you, Hugh. John spoke to me at our wedding. He told me how this community had touched him. He wanted to support it. I don't know if this was part of a planned farewell. Perhaps it was recompense for what was about to happen. But he transferred £50,000 into the house's account. So we thank him and he will always be part of this community, even though he was drawn to taking a path of despair.'

'That was very good of him,' Hugh said with an attempt at solemnity. And Helmut lifted an enormous shovel and began to fill the grave with a little too much alacrity. Hugh and I watched the bandaged form disappear under a shower of clods. The community returned to the house as the rain became heavier.

Helmut's Discontent

13th June 2019

Helmut and I were getting on better. I would help him with the wood collection. If I made gentle fun of him, he never seemed to mind or sometimes even realise. A few days after we buried John, we passed each other as he was carrying two pails of water into the kitchen. He looked at me imploringly. I asked if he wanted help but I could see he was deeply distressed. He said he needed to talk to someone. We crossed the yard to the stables and up to where he slept. This was a compact, room in the hay loft partitioned by hardboard. A pallet bed took up half the space. There was a box of clean underwear and more importantly boot socks which Helmut, like any Bavarian, wore with his sandals. And a rail of brilliant ankle length dresses—spangled, deep coloured silks, dark green velvet.

'Mike I must talk to someone. There is no other body. I feel bad. Al takes me… you say *for granted*. He needs me for my strength. I carry those buckets every day. I sometimes slip on muddy stones or the ice. I walk miles for wood and seek fallen branches so I cut no living tree.'

And indeed, had Helmut lived in the Soviet bloc, they would have put up a statue to him, one of the Stakhanovites.

He told me that when he lived with his parents in the Bayern, he would secretly wear dresses in his room. He would sneak away and jump on a train to Munich and buy them there. Sometimes he'd find somewhere to change and walk around the city streets for a few hours. He felt nobody appeared to notice. Or cared. His parents never asked where he went but always seemed pretty taciturn, according to him. Though from what he said, they sounded too reliant on Helmut to challenge him. And then there had been the fire.

When he arrived at Gritstone, he'd explained to Al he wanted to wear clothes that expressed his mood. Sometimes as a goatherd. Sometimes in the dresses he saved from the fire. Al had just said, 'That's all cool man. Be yourself.'

And it had been great. The women helped him with the whole range of makeup, all sorts of advice. In fact, when he wore heavy eyeliner and vermilion lipstick, he was dramatically different to them. The women here had scrubbed faces. Nobody had told them not to wear cosmetics. As Esther said she was just tired of all that fuss. But it was still fun to help Helmut. He felt Esther treated him sometimes like a doll. But no matter. And then Al had asked him to dress as the emotion took him for the wedding. He did his best and Esther produced mascara she never used herself. And it was wonderful. He had never looked so beautiful. It was only once they were in the church that he realised they were returning to the world he thought he had escaped forever. The minister or vicar, he could not remember which, was even worse than the Catholic priest in his village. The Reverend's behaviour to him was truly shocking. Al told him to forget it. But he couldn't. All of that cruelty came back, the trembling before confession and the feeling he was the only boy in the village who masturbated, the stiff thick suits on a Sunday. Why did he tell the priest about trying on his mother's dresses? And the priest knowing his secret and looking at him with a veiled threat. Helmut began to weep. The flimsy walls, the bare boards shook with the force. 'I hate the Church. Al cannot understand… he has no time for me to say…'

'Al doesn't have much time for anyone when they fall off the train, Helmut.'

'*Ja,* I understand, Mike. I would just leave but I have my goats. It seemed to get worse after the *Polizei* visited…'

Hugh and Electricity

14th June 2019: Afternoon

I'd accompanied Hugh to the music room. He had the intention of listening to *Nursey Cryme* for the first time for twenty years. Hugh was feeling quite excited. But as we collapsed onto the sofas, he had other things to say.

'You know, there's been this big change, kind of a transformation in you these last weeks. You arrived all stubbly in grubby chinos with grass stains at the knees…' And I remembered flab hanging over my trouser belt. 'You know, I quite liked that sloppy relaxed look. You seemed so unselfconscious. But this bushy beard.—and you wear this—it's a burnous isn't it? Like Arab men wear in North Africa. Well actually I only remember seeing them when Lily and me went on a package to Tunisia.'

'Yeah well I think I like the look and my hair's longer…' It was resting on my shoulders now and hadn't been cut for some time before I left London.' And these oils they use here that they mix themselves… the unguents… it's one of the good things about being here…'

Hugh persisted. 'And they listen to you, even if you don't say much. I feel like I'm some kind of fool after the bread baking… I don't think I recovered from that.'

Yes, that second bread baking when he'd initiated me. The result was an unplanned flat bread. Cyrus described it as more like a ship's biscuit. Hugh had consulted me at the time about quite what a ship's biscuit was. I'd whispered to him, 'It's in all the pirate films. They're the last things you eat before starvation sets in. The weevils always live in them.' White grubs wiggling through the little holes. Toni had taken over the next night to tutor me. Hugh had disappeared from the bread rota. But now the rota had ground to a halt anyway after Toni's exit. Rosamond and I tended to make it every other day.

'But I've got skills. I'm a competent electrician in a house with no plugs… well, apart from Al's office and nobody's allowed in there…'

'There are *some* plugs in this room', I said unguardedly and then regretted it immediately.

'Yeah I could do some good things given the chance.'

Rosamond put her head round the door.

'I heard your voice up here, Hugh.'

'Ros, I'm just saying I could do so much here with my electrical skills.'

'But Hugh we don't want electricity. Al needs it for his work with the outside world. He takes that weight off us.'

'But I could do more in the music room. We could have a giant screen…'

'Hugh, I don't feel anyone's explained properly about the music room. It's not like listening to the radio, which I think is the way you sometimes treat it…'

'I treat it with great reverence.'

'We ask Al's permission. It's for special occasions.'

'Nobody explained that to me…'

'Well you're a guest.'

'Yes but…'

'Hugh, you are rather a scrounger.' But she said it with some affection. 'Well you do seem hardwired just to take. I mean I rather like it. I think it's rather funny.'

'I'm not a scrounger. If I'm invited somewhere, I

consider myself invited.'

'Well some people make an art out of not disinviting themselves…'

'Okay, I can see when I'm not wanted! I'll speak to Al.'

'No, no, not on my account… no… I've come to treasure…' and she paused and Hugh started examining his hands minutely and Rosamond straightened up and left the room.

Hugh waited for her steps to recede. 'Mike, I don't know what happened that night… the last trip. But she never mentions, even hints at anything. I've got this memory, an image of us on the couch in the music room… I'm not sure if it was all some hallucinatory dream. And I think we had sex… or something like it…'

Buzzy

15th June 2019

We could hear raised voices in the kitchen garden. The rusty bottom bolt grated against the groove in the pebbles as Sylvester pushed open the gates and marched across to the kitchen. Al had left his office when he heard the commotion and stood in the kitchen doorway.

Sylvester hissed, 'I don't know what's happened here, man. Ezra's daughter's snuck in through that back gate. She's letting him have it in there.'

We could hear a woman's voice yelling 'Baaast'd!' I thought it could be a New York accent but I'd only ever been there in hundreds of films. Al was quietly ruminating, contemplating the gate with its flaking green paint.

As if in mid-thought he asked, 'How'd she find us?'

I'd come up beside him. 'All she'd need to do is check in the village. You're really quite well known.'

'Yeah… but not for having Ezra.' Al strode across the yard. 'Let's sort this out.'

The daughter was berating her glum dad amid the monolithic cabbages.

As he approached, Al called out, 'Good afternoon.'

A woman in her early forties turned to him. She had Ezra's thin face and a birdlike curve to her nose. Her red cagoule looked like a recent purchase in some outward-bound store, perhaps after arriving in Hebden Bridge.

She glowered at Al's breezy greeting. 'And who the fuck're you?'

'We might say the same.' Al didn't forsake the jovial voice of a seasoned host.

'Sorry Al,' Ezra mumbled.

'Nothing to be sorry about, Ez.' I wondered whether Ezra's American daughter still thought Al was being painfully polite in an English way, rather than about to be threatening in a very English way.

'Would you like to come into the kitchen?'

'Whose fucking kitchen?'

Al smiled pleasantly at Buzzy, enunciating each word, 'Our—Fucking—Kitchen.'

'I'm sorry Al…'

'That's okay Ezra. Introduce me to your daughter.'

'This is Buzzy. Buzzy, this is Al.'

'Hello… Buzzy. What's that short for?'

'It ain't short for anythin' fella.'

'It's just when you have bad news, I'd prefer to use a proper… well, anyway, when you decided on her name, Ezra… I suppose you and her *mom* were so optimistic that nothing bad could ever happen to somebody called…'

'Look fella…'

'Come with us.' This was no longer an invitation.

And names like hers… names like hers… the name Ezra and whoever the mother was bequeathed to her, chosen in the euphoria of mischievousness. These names can suddenly seem so inconsequential when life catches up with you. Names that can never comprehend the tragedy of being human.

'So, Buzzy… what suddenly makes you want to have an emotional reunion with… shall we call him *pop*?' Al poured a cup of tea for her from a willow-pattern teapot that was seldom seen.

'He left his family and took all of his money—our money,' Buzzy replied in a flat sulky monotone.

'Evidently.' Al looked at her in her £300 anorak. 'You must have had to save up for years to fly here.'

'I work, man… I mean… I shouldn't be in this position. I can't pay for my kids to go to college.'

'So, you come to find dear old pop.' Al turned to survey the incoherently mumbling Ezra. 'Well I'm afraid Buzzy… all the money…'

Buzzy opened her mouth…

'It's all tied up in this venture.' Al calmly stared at her.

'You think I'm gonna accept your little story. I want his money pal… I ain't leavin' until… I'll get lawyers.'

Al quietly ploughed on over Buzzy. 'It's all gone, Buz. He's living off me now. A lot of people over here have things we call pensions. So the other people who live here pay their way. The money arrives month after month after month, you see. But *pop* here… he kind of paid upfront with money he'd stuck under the metaphorical mattress… I don't think Ez attracts *social security*. I'm not even entirely sure he paid all the tax he could…'

'I got nothin' Buzzy…' Ezra was hollow and guilty.

'How long you been here Ez?' Al asked. Buzzy didn't quite get the tone that could command a ship to sink.

'Seven years this September Al.'

'Hmmm. Well… as Ez has used up his deposit now… Perhaps you should take him back to the good ole U. S. of A with you… Sound okay, Ez? Put him back to work. He can still do gardening as you can see.'

Ezra was back to mumbling incoherently. Al waited for the words to sink in and then continued, 'Look, maybe we can sort something out for you. It's not like *we* have *no* money. It's just Ezra doesn't have any. You got a place to stay?'

'I was gonna stay in that Hebden place…'

'Yeah but you could stay here. Look, come in the office Buzzy. Let's see what we can do.' Ezra was not included in the invite.

When Buzzy emerged from the office she let slip, 'That's a lot of cash to keep here.' She was now carrying a small suitcase along with her knapsack.

'We had a donation recently. Not much point in putting it anywhere really with interest rates the way they are. Suppose we could bet… Look, bring the car round, we'll put it in the garage.'

Buzzy drove up in a small hatchback. Helmut directed her to where she could park it in the garage, between Al's van and the Scimitar. Ezra spent a dismal few hours with his daughter.

Two days later the police who visited a few weeks ago were back. They asked to see Al. They spoke quietly outside the front door. Al nodded gravely. He took them into the green library, and Edith went to find Ezra. After the police left, Al came to talk to me on the bench looking over the valley.

'Buzzy's car came from some dodgy online firm. The brakes gave up just outside Todmorden. Lucky she didn't kill anyone else. The locals knew she'd come here. I've decided Ezra ought to follow her body to the States. But he won't come back. I'll pay for the flight. He's outlived his time here and I had to do something about him.'

Ezra was crumpled at the kitchen table repeatedly

moaning the name that began as two parents' gesture against the darkness in the world, 'Buzzy... Buzzy...' Edith sat silently with her hand on his shoulder. Hours later I noticed Charlie arrive and go straight into Al's office. He was carrying a small suitcase. The one Buzzy had in her hand when she walked out to her hire car while Ezra waved feebly from the doorway.

Several days later Ezra left in a houndstooth sports jacket, shirt and green knit tie. Nobody spoke about him or Buzzy at the evening meal that night. In fact there was little conversation and the community quickly melted away to their rooms.

Stephanie Disappears

22nd June 2019: Morning

Bruno had been out on the moor calling for her. He had knocked on all the doors but nobody had seen her today. His desolate voice echoed back to the house. Al sat in the kitchen angrily staring at the dancing lids on the saucepans.

'Has she walked out before?' I asked tentatively.

'No, not from here.' Al's voice was tight.

'Did she pack anything?'

'We don't know. None of them have kept more than a few changes of clothes.'

'They gave up their clothes?'

'I suggested giving a lot away to charity shops. They don't need much here. We kept Ezra's jacket and trousers in a wardrobe—until he needed it.'

'So she's walking round in that orange kaftan and a pair of wellingtons. The police won't take long to pick her up.'

I saw Al imagining the police escorting her back to Gritstone.

'Yeah I don't want them here again. The outside world—the law. Bad enough with Ezra. Lucky Charlie knew those policemen but I can't risk that again.'

Al paused before speaking. 'I'll drive out. She can't have got that far. Want to come Mike?' Al had resumed at least a veneer of relaxation, the resourcefulness, the conviction there were always solutions. 'We'll find her.'

Al revved the engine. The van grumbled as we waded

through the thick layer of wet gravel at the front of the house. He drove faster as we got on the road to Halifax, but then swung left to head up to the shooting booths

Al climbed on top of a wall and took in miles of moorland. But there was no orange shape. 'Well perhaps she's down in the village by now...'

An insistent drizzle was soaking into my white robe. I realised what I would look like when I returned to the village where Hugh and I had stopped only weeks ago. Like a second coming, a retired lecturer turned into Old Testament prophet.

Al skidded at a curve in the road. He shouted above the engine, 'Fucking Stephanie. I've had enough now.'

In the village we combed the main street. And then, there she was: sat in a cafe, a silver pot in front of her and a slice of parkin on an ornamental plate. Her chin was crumpled into her neck, her eyes more bulbous than usual. Al sat opposite her. My robe attracted all the attention from the weekday oldies. The waitress wasn't rushing to serve us.

'Do you have enough money for your trip, Stephanie?' Al leaned forward with practised compassion.

'I don't have the money to pay for this tea,' she whispered.

Al nodded. He never shifted his gaze from her.

'Al sometimes I can't bear him. Just the idea of spending the rest of my life in that house with him. We can't leave. Don't you think it drives some of us spare? We can never leave.'

'Look Edith will be upset if you're not around.' Al was back to his soft reassuring tones. 'She would miss you, Steph.'

Stephanie had the look of a rabbit in a gin trap. The life of springing across fields and grazing was ending. She was at the mercy of the approaching trapper. However Al expressed it, she was returning to the community.

Stephanie made a last appeal.

'Al you could give me some money. I could disappear and never see Bruno again. You could do that. You could give me enough money to pay this bill and get a train...'

Al was slowly shaking his head. At first Stephanie seemed to inwardly collapse. But then the skin on her neck corrugated. Her eyes disappeared into narrow slits as she hissed a final threat.

'I could tell the police about Asif. That would finish you.'

Al sat in silence and looked at her intently. The teashop seemed to recede. The three of us were sitting at a table that might as well have been floating in the air.

I asked, 'Al... Asif?' The name on the label of the gown I was wearing.

Al ignored me and maintained his gaze on Stephanie. He began in that narcotically soothing tone. 'It was so sad wasn't it, Stephanie?' He looked at her with sorrow pouring out of his eyes. Stephanie appeared pacified. She nodded with a child's gravity. Her eyes trembling, filling.

'Are you going to tell me about Asif?'

Al didn't turn his head. 'Later Mike.'

But I had broken his spell. Stephanie rallied and ignored Al's offer of collusion. She repeated pettishly, 'I could tell!'

The hypnotic compassion drained from Al's features. 'It depends; it's a complicated situation. It involved you and Bruno...'

'We did nothing!' she hissed.

'Precisely.' Al's voice was now measured and icy. 'If you get anyone to interfere with us what do you expect? The police and the courts won't be impressed by people who *did nothing*, Stephanie. Bruno helped me bury him for God's sake.'

Stephanie walked into the house where her gangly husband was waiting, his sagging face streaked with grimy tear tracks. They regarded each other with a melange of anger and irritation.

I took Al aside. 'What's this about Asif?'

'He just died, Mike. We buried him like John. No inquests, no doctors, no fuss. But if people hear about it, we're in more trouble than necessary. We did nothing wrong. Nobody here refused to be part of our ceremony... we buried Asif with respect.'

Asif

23rd June 2019: Evening

Edith and I often cleared the evening meal together now. Al had returned to the office as soon as he'd eaten. I was scrubbing the table with a stiff brush, while she washed.

'Stephanie started talking about Asif when we found her in the café. She threatened Al with the police—that she'd tell them what happened to Asif.'

I thought Edith would be shocked but she solemnly nodded. 'He's buried up in that grove. He was dying. And he was in terrible agony. Mike, he was screaming. Al couldn't do any more to ease the pain. And then on the last day Al went to see him and the screaming stopped. And then he came out and got us together and told us Asif had been released. You could hardly say he passed away. We didn't ask questions. I don't know what he did and never asked. But I felt Al put him out of his misery. You know the way those people who must travel to Dignitas to die because nobody will help them.'

Despair

30th June 2019

Edith and I were alone clearing up after the evening meal—again. The community went off to their rooms after some desultory conversation. It had followed that pattern for the past week. In the air was a waning of involvement, a feeling of exhaustion. The preparations for the marriage had focussed everyone. Now Al participated less and less at meals. He and Edith hadn't sat next to each other for weeks now. When Al looked over at her, she averted her face mutely. If anyone noticed, nobody said anything to me; but there was a *froideur* developing that permeated the table.

Tonight, the meal had been a combination of brown rice, spinach and lentils. The very colour, a greenish tinge mixed into a muddy brown seemed to engender dejection. People seldom bothered to pick the herbs that would enliven the food.

I'd finished scouring and polishing the pans until they sparkled in the candle light.

But when I looked around after hanging them up on the butcher's hooks, Edith had collapsed on a bench, lolling against the wall, her cheek smeared against the cold white plaster. I sat down with her. The silence lasted for minutes. When I spoke it was a whisper, 'Edith?'

One cocked eye turned to me like a bird awoken, jarred into alertness.

'Edith, something's crushing you.'

'I suppose so,' she murmured. The words the merest

impressions on the air, grazed the silence in the room.

'Hardly a word from you for days.'

'Something has happened to me, Mike. It's as if I've been hit and left in the road.' Edith spoke slowly, wearily.

I waited for her to say more while the light drained away, the candles guttered.

'I argued with Al. We've only been married a few weeks now… but I can't go back to him. No. It's more than that. I think I have to leave the house. I can't stay here after…' She stopped. Her whole world could be swinging on a loose hinge in a heavy wind. '…after what I know about Al.'

She spoke vacantly, drained of emotion.

'I'd been saying to him… *I'm your wife but you never let me into your office*. So once when he had just opened the door, I ran in. I barged past him. I didn't think there was much in there at first. One of those cabinet desks—think they call them secretaries—where the flap opens into a writing table. And a computer, an old grey plastic one, on a desk. And then I saw something, a jar by the window— but not clearly—the lights weren't on—and I said, "*What is that*?" And he went all awkward and quiet. I hadn't seen him like this. He was so solid. He was my rock. And I went closer and it was a jar with something in it.'

Edith pulled her face away from the wall leaving an oval of wet plaster, and turned to me.

'And then he told me. And his voice was changed, and it wasn't that safe reassuring voice, it was almost like a stranger, like his throat was all tight and he spoke quickly. And he told me it was John's finger in what— formaldehyde—he was trying to make it all sound so natural but he couldn't. And he said it didn't work when he'd pressed it to try starting John's phone… he didn't know what to do with it now. He tried to make it sound like some useless gadget…'

Edith was suddenly woken into a ferocity I hadn't seen. 'And I felt—I'm part of this criminal thing—I'm implicated—I'm his wife and he's done this revolting thing—and he said it was just too tempting to get so much money for us—that he could have accessed the phone and got into John's account—and I'm horrified…'

Edith crushed her hands together as if a prayer couldn't be answered. 'I mean I've left everything to come here and I married him. And he was saying it was for all of us, not for him. He was doing this horrible thing and we didn't need to know. And I left him there, and I walked out and I can't speak to him. I've gone back to my own room. I wrote him a note saying I need time on my own. And last night he knocked and I just pretended to be asleep. I felt terrified of him, Mike. I don't know what to do now. I'm tied into all of this.'

I was almost ashamed for what I was thinking. As I listened, I was mentally totting up how deep we had all descended. An illegal burial, no coroner's court over a death, another death covered up. And now she tells me this.

'Edith, I think it's too late for any of us to distance ourselves.'

'Mike, what are you fucking going on about?'

'We should have called the police when John killed himself. Now we have all concealed…'

'I'm not bothered about all that. I am married to a man who…'

'He's always had this kind of thing in him.'

'He's done this sort of thing before?'

'Kind of… Al could be ruthless. And he takes you along with him if he can.' Something I had decided to forget—when Al and I found a man literally lying in the gutter in an old torn sports jacket in this area near the university, rows of derelict back to backs waiting for demolition. And it was not too uncommon to see this, but this man was almost comatose. I had run off to find a phone box; but I turned and saw Al with his hands inside the jacket pockets, working with a too practised speed. And I had phoned the ambulance and told them where to find the man, but Al and I had melted away—I'd almost forgotten because I wanted to bury the memory—Al scored some dope and shared it with me, so I bought into the theft…

And then I asked 'Edith do you know what Power of Attorney means?'

And Edith had never heard of it.

Cleaning the Kitchen

1st July 2019: Evening

Over the past few days, I was still plugging even more gaps, where the tasks were no longer done. Today again, I washed the crockery and pans in the Belfast sink while Rosamond was busy scrubbing the table. We could both see the withdrawal of most community members, almost like a strike. I suppose we just carried on even amidst a growing atmosphere of drift and disillusion, because inaction felt pointless. I waited until the rest of the community had drifted away and then broached a concern with her. 'Al seems to have looked after so much—well I mean—every aspect of the community.'

'Yes, we wanted to have as little as possible to do with the outside world.' Rosamond still could be guarded speaking to me. She seemed less so with Hugh. She could be dogmatic in her answers but they were not schooled. She had always been someone who must feel convinced about her actions. There was no room for ambiguity.

I hung the cups on the hooks by the sink. As casually as possible I asked, 'Did Al ever ask you to sign some papers?'

'Oh yes. But it was more that slimy Sharpe chap. I'm not sure how Al got to know him. Al trusts him and I suppose nothing has gone wrong. But he did get me to sign something. I just trusted Al. I didn't even read it. God Mike I'm not sure now…'

'But do you have family who might have had some interest in the money you donate to Gritstone?'

'Not to speak of. No kids. Don't know where my sister is. We tried to find her and couldn't. My mother died and then my dad... passed away if moaning with pain is passing away. And then there's a husband I never want to see again. Look, Mike, what's all this about?'

'Oh, just something I overheard Sharpe say—that he was dealing with a Power of Attorney.'

'Well Al was in control so I didn't mind. I think it made it easier to transfer my monthly pensions into the house finance. I gave him my bank passwords. I think we all had that done, some way or other—apart from Helmut, I think. But we never wanted to have anything to do with any of that money business. Anyway, talking of Sharpe... there's always some nasty enforcer behind the people who do things. Remember John Lennon and that terrible accountant Alan Klein?'

But then Rosamond looked doubtful and went quiet. She asked me to explain more about what a Power of Attorney is. And she nodded and said, 'Oh... so I lack capacity.'

Rosamond and Hugh go for a Walk

2nd July 2019: Evening

I made my visit to the shed before dusk turned to darkness. I had seen Rosamond and Hugh leave the house a short time before. It was a surprise as community members hardly ever went beyond the estate boundary and seldom further than the yard and walled garden. I had heard Hugh say to her that he didn't go out enough. But it was Rosamond who'd suggested a stroll. They had laughed together trying to wedge on the wellington boots in the hall. I cheekily asked Rosamond if Al approved.

'You know I'm not sure Al approves of people like us going off for walks.'

Hugh was equally roguish. 'What do you mean, people like us?'

'Oh, you know… unattached.'

'Al was unattached himself 'til he attached himself to Edith.'

'Well you know…'

'I'm not a member.'

'No, you're like the serpent who entered the garden— no I'm only joking.'

'This place used to be an Eden?'

'Yes Hugh, there was a time…'

But their voices were disappearing beyond the yard.

As I returned from the shed I noticed two huddled shapes in an embrace further up the path to the moor.

Hugh knocked on my door two hours later.

'Rosamond's really unhappy.'

'She seemed happy enough a few hours ago.'

'Yeah but… she'd like to leave but she's scared. Nobody has looked to me for anything for years… if ever. I don't think Lily ever did. She was tougher than me. But Rosamond just wept on my shoulder. All her tears, all the yearning soaking into my thick sweater. I wanted to store the tears, preserve them in the wool…'

'Hugh, I think you're in love…'

Later I found Rosamond sweeping the front hall. 'Somebody has to. But I feel it's just Edith you and me who seem to do anything now. I mean you can't expect Hugh, but the others seem to be losing interest.' I went down with her to empty the dust into the compost bin. When we were by the garden wall, I said things seemed to have changed in the past few weeks. She nodded.

'You know there was buzz of excitement when I came here—when I began living here. But it had stopped being like that a while before you and Hugh arrived, to be honest. It can seem so dreary. We just do tasks. There was the tai chi and the yoga—and now that all seems to have stopped. But the evenings and the nights can seem everlasting. You know none of us are really friends. Everyone's very guarded. I think it's because we don't want to discuss the lives we lead here and openly puncture the balloon.'

Rosamond looked surprised at herself, even a little scared.

'Did I actually say all that?' There was a frightened animal behind her eyes; edgy, watchful, but somehow trusting me.

'It's all right, this isn't going to get back to Al. Anyway, he hardly talks to me now. But you were such a real true believer when we've talked about Gritstone before.'

'I know. Well you want to believe in it. I mean I sacrificed everything to be here. I put everything into this place. I put all my savings in, for Christ's sake! I trusted Al. He has complete control over all my money now. I might as well be a prisoner.' Her eyes narrowed into slits, her chin was shaking. 'Al is in control. I pretended it's okay. It's not okay, not at all. I want to leave. I want to leave.'

But then she whispered.

'I know if I wanted to leave, Al would talk me out of it. And he might be right, Mike. I don't know if I can face the outside world anymore—and I don't miss any of it. But this isn't working out. We're like those people who were in asylums for forty years—how can we cope out there?'

The Mirror

3rd July 2019

The house was convulsed by a short crash and then the fizzing sound of glass spreading over the stone flags in the hall. Al exploded out of his room. 'That's a fucking Louis Seize mirror!'

'Did anyone touch this mirror?' His voice echoed against the silent closed doors. The mirror had been hanging in the hall when Al bought the house. The frame was four-foot square with a gilded filigreed edging of faded and peeled gold leaf. Apparently when they did take it off the wall one day, they found it concealed a large discoloured mark. The mirror went back up again. In its own way the mirror reflected a growing inertia in the house. If Al wasn't interested in resolving a situation nothing much happened.

Helmut's voice was approaching, from the yard calling, '*Was ist los?*' And the click and beep of the lock as Al collected himself and habitually secured the office door. There was the grating sound of a tide receding from a shingle beach as Helmut swept up the glass from the stone flags.

Al went back into his room. I thought I could hear him shouting at someone but there couldn't be anyone else in there.

Two hours later Edith passed me on the stairs.

She whispered, 'Mike, I have to tell you something. It needs to be private.'

I suggested meeting her in the room where John died. Nobody slept on that floor and no one went to the music room apart from Hugh. We would hear the stairs creak if anyone was approaching. I was there a few minutes before Edith closed the door behind her. I tried not to look at the stain by the bed.

She spoke in a whisper, 'I always hated that fucking mirror.'

'You…'

'I put some twine round the hook, hid under the stairwell and pulled and it came off the wall. Al just rushed out roaring away. I loved that shivering sound when it crashed on the stone flags. Anyway, I sneaked into his room. I banked on him running out and not locking it for a minute. He was sort of transfixed. It seems like it was the most expensive thing in the house.'

'Why did you? I mean he'll never forgive you?'

'As if I care.' Even I was shocked at how disparaging and contemptuous Edith could be about Al. She continued, 'Anyway, I'd already worked out where I'd hide. There's the floor-length curtain by the window.'

'By the Chesterfields…'

'Yes—it's like a men's club in there isn't it? And I stayed rigid behind that curtain and shoved a headscarf into my mouth to make sure I didn't cough. And the door clicks open and then there's these electronic squeaks as Al resets the alarm. His computer keyboard scuttles away. And then—I knew it. I heard a phone purring. He's never talked about using a phone. I thought he'd got rid of it when he stopped taking new members. And he called Charlie. And I remember most of what he said—it was like listening to a stranger—not the man I married—and he was shouting down the phone, '*That fucking mirror's come off the wall… yeah how much insurance do we have? …Oh, fuck it, that hardly covers the value… where did you get this policy? …Sorry Charlie, but I'm royally pissed off with you.*' Edith was imitating Al with her own sardonic version of his little inflections. It was a bit of a shock. She was so mischievous about this man she'd adored.

'After he'd finished the call, he was still muttering to himself "*Fucking Charlie…*" I was inches from him on the other side of that curtain. There was some large animal prowling around the room. I suppose it was like you read about bears bursting into camp sites and you've only got the tent canvas between you and this enormous beast. And he was shuffling papers, opening filing cabinets, slamming them shut again. And this incessant scurrying on the keyboard like a rat on bare floorboards.

'And I heard the phone grumble again and it was Charlie. And Al was still angry. You know, it was something like, '*It's nowhere near enough… you didn't get it valued—why didn't you fucking think of this Charlie? And they're paying? That's not much good to me.*'

'And more rattling on the keyboard, riffling through papers. And he'd stop typing and murmur; "*Oh my God, Oh my God…*" And he was muttering and farting…

'And Mike, it was strange. I realised I felt as close as I ever could to him—not like in love—I was inhabiting this world of the real Al. Not this man who pretends he's next to being almighty. He was never so open with me. And in that room, he seemed lonely. I mean, we've only been married a few weeks and there I was feeling intimately close to this stranger, inches away on the other side of the curtain. You know—within touching distance of this secret self. Not sure my parents ever had that sense of what it was to be in the other's skin, in the way I did now. I became so lost in the experience I almost forgot I was hiding at all.

'And he made another quick call. "*Did you organise that power of Attorney? Nah not the first one, but I don't think there's much in that account anyway…*" And then he said "*You know sometimes I want to tell these ungrateful fuckers what I go through to keep this going…*" and then he went out for the evening meal.'

I was laughing at the imitation and Edith doing this devastating take on this man she'd worshipped. But there was much more…

'And the door beeped and clicked shut. I was there to find out what was in this room—what were his secrets? I'd no idea how I might access the computer and so I decided not to even try. I went straight to the desk and pulled down the flap. And there they were, all our phones with a neat label on each—a postit note. I'd handed mine to Al and knew the others did as well—and there was a really smart new phone without a label and I'm guessing it was John's. I pushed the flap up again. I yanked open the drawers. In the top one were larger devices, the laptops, tablets and I noticed Helmut's name.

'And then in the bottom drawer there were about ten bundles of envelopes in neat piles, perhaps fifty in each, tied so neatly in different coloured ribbons. There was this… kind of obsessive preciseness, like Helmut's log pile. I took one bundle that had my name on the top envelope. I thought he might not notice one batch was missing. I pressed to open the door. I couldn't put the code on. Just hoped he'd think he'd been negligent. I wondered if he'd realise someone had broken in. Would I be top of the list of suspects?'

'*I* probably would be,' I said without thinking.

'And Mike, I realised I wanted to spread doubt, I wanted to cause trouble. I wondered if these letters would blow everything sky high. But I quietly went into the kitchen and sat down. Didn't say anything. it's really difficult at the moment. He keeps trying to catch my eye. After eating as little and as quickly as possible, I went to my room and worked through the pile in candlelight.'

'Al had asked me to give my forwarding address as a PO box number like everyone else. He said he would tell me if there was anything important. Most of the correspondence was about the TV licence not being paid and bank statements. But halfway down the pile was a solicitor's letter on headed paper. I ran the candle close to the script to read it, and the flame trembled I was shaking so much. Anyway, here it is.'

Edith has that letter now. The only one she's kept.

Berwin, Marks, Charnley
Bulcaster, BU 9RT

Dear Miss Jenkins,

We have recently been contacted by a lady who states that she is your sister. She has traced you after discovering the family home had been sold, and contacted us as the solicitors. She gives her name as Mrs Ursula Banks formerly Jenkins. She has requested through her own solicitors that no personal details are provided at this stage, but has asked to meet you.

We are aware of your instructions that you wish to have absolute privacy, and await your decision on how we proceed.

This lady's appearance may also have implications for the legacy from your parents,

Yours Sincerely,

J Charnley

Senior Partner

Edith and her Sister

3rd July 2019

I remember I was in my school uniform running across the lawn from the back gate and there was this tracery of spiders' webs holding droplets like jewels from the recent shower... and that was my last truly happy moment... the last in my life, Mike. And I went through the French windows and into the lounge where my parents were sat like statues on the sofa. My dad was in his suit, looking solemn and ridiculous. and he began saying...

'Edith there's something you need to know. Your sister has become increasingly difficult to live with. She attacked your mother yesterday. We didn't tell you but your mother was terrified. Mother thought...your sister was going to kill her in our own kitchen. We decided she needed to leave and from now on she will live somewhere else.'

I asked, 'Is she still having the baby?'

They were angry. 'Wherever did you hear that?'

'I heard her talk about it.'

'We will miss her. But it is better for you to believe she never existed.'

'But I know she exists, Dad!'

'Better for you to forget her as if she had never been.'

I ran upstairs. And my sister's room was now vacant as if waiting for a guest for bed and breakfast. I pulled out the bedside cabinet and found the book Ursula wrote in. I would see her conceal it last thing at night. I still have it.

Edith still has it now though she has never read it. There was a second letter.

Dear Miss Jenkins,

We have received your instructions that you do not seek further contact with Mrs Banks. As a response to the question in your last letter, Mrs Banks informed us through her solicitor, that she has no interest in your parents' estate. She will now cease in any attempt to contact you further. We have respected your wish for privacy and remain,

J Charnley LLB
Senior Partner

Edith silently rocked from side to side. All the time they were planning their marriage, eating and sleeping together, he had been concealing this from her. I held her as she shook and wept silently. When the candle went out, we didn't dare leave the room.

More letters

The next day Edith and I arranged to meet at the small stone hut. We separately went into the fields above the house and past the grove to the former shepherd's shelter. There were numerous cigarette butts stubbed on the floor. I told Edith Al had come here for some peace and quiet.

'Looking back, I suppose I could smell it on his clothes, but I've never lived with a smoker. You know in the end it's almost amusing seeing his feet of clay.'

We began to read the other letters in the bundle with the pink ribbon. Edith skinned her eyes in touching concentration and lifted each letter from its envelope carefully, like a spy who does not want to leave a trace. She planned to return everything apart from the letters about her sister. But still she opened the envelopes with the conviction there couldn't be anything else that was worse. Her TV license was finally revoked. There were no more transactions on her credit card. Her solicitors had cancelled her council tax once the house was sold. There was a solicitor's bill. Al must have paid it in her name. She then moved onto similar letters for Rosamond, which were part of the bundle. And here were more bank statements, the closure of accounts: Edith felt Rosamond would probably approve of all of these. However there were transactions that had occurred clearly after Rosamond had moved to Gritstone; a standing order to Gritstone Holdings.

This was the first inkling of how the money entered

Al's account.

Then she opened a handwritten letter and realised she should not have. She couldn't stop herself seeing it.

Rosamond

I don't have long. The doctors say maybe a week. The body is packing up. now I didn't know it would be like this. I am lucky that so far it has been so gentle. I am ever so gradually detaching myself. Nothing engages me, I can no longer connect with anything in this world. I don't care anymore about what happens to someone whose life is not draining away from them. How can they be attached to the pettiness that consumes them? But I want to see you again. It is the last and only thing I want. Please come. I'm not asking for anything else,

Adrian

The letter to Rosamond was dated six months ago. Edith was on the verge of tears when she put the letter back in its envelope. 'I love Ros. I really care for her. I mean he'll be long dead months ago, but I can't face it when she finds out…'

Later I asked Edith, 'You've got all of these letters, burning holes in your pockets—but what are you going to do with them all?'

She shrugged and quietly laughed. 'I feel I've got some power over him, Mike. At the moment I am just enjoying it. But I will decide what to do.'

'Well don't you think people ought to know?'

'They probably really do already, you know. I mean they all pretend. They never seemed to discuss it but they must have wondered how the place is run.'

'You don't seem to think much of them.'

Her nose creased. 'Yes I think you're right. It feels great to say it to someone else.'

Edith paused. 'But they won't be able to avoid what has been happening if I do start talking. They can't carry on with this pretence'

The community seemed not to notice that Edith had stopped speaking. She made simple acknowledgements and got on with her tasks. Otherwise she was silent around the house. She wrote another note to Al saying she needed to be alone for a while and never stayed in the same room as him on her own. The next night she asked me to come to her room in case Al tried to speak to her. Soon we could hear him shuffling outside her door. We tensed for a knock. Edith gripped my arm, pulled me towards her and silently began a long slow kiss. It went on until his sandals flapped away on the creaking wooden floor. She giggled quietly while I lay there rather stunned, 'Thank God he never actually knocked. After all I'm a respectable married woman. I can't think what came over me.'

Edith wanted me to leave before dawn.' There's no knowing what he might do to either of us if he found out.'

The Green Room

Al continued with his work but seemed increasingly detached from the everyday. He had told me the office was becoming too stuffy to work in on hot days. Edith remembered more than stuffiness. The room bore the thick reek of stale sweat, farts, and electric heat. The carpet had absorbed the dark fug into the weave. There were thin layers of black oily grease. The only ventilation came when he opened the door.

So sometimes you would find Al working in the green room. The daily yoga sessions had wordlessly stopped. Nobody discussed it. They just never resumed after the wedding and John's burial. So the room was vacant and little-used.

I had walked in to look for another book after finishing the Pirsig. Once through the door, it was too late to make any exit. Al was at the table, surrounded by papers, writing into a ledger. I plonked onto the thinly upholstered chaise longue. My *burnous* needed a wash and I was conscious of how my belly sagged under the thin cotton fabric, shifting almost independently from side to side when I sat down. Al looked over with some distaste but then went back to his figures.

I asked 'Busy?' The deathless question didn't amuse Al.

'Do I look like I'm darning socks. I'm doing the accounts—look I actually do real books. When I used to earn money, I had to use accountancy software programmes. Now I do all the figures by hand. It used to be a pleasure to balance all these nice neat columns. It had its own—you know—symmetry and beauty. But if you must know, I'm staring at these figures hoping something will magically change. But the numbers aren't changing.'

He looked at me pointedly.

I went quiet. Any mention of money was embarrassing. I didn't have any to contribute. My invitation had been to his wedding, and that had come and gone. Now I was there for no good reason. I helped as much and more than most people round the house but… I had nowhere else to go, now Siobhan had finally finished with me.

'I have to keep this place running. I've protected these fucking ungrateful people from all the dirty little facts. I have to pay a mortgage every month. And I'm drawing more and more on my own reserves…'

Al went for an oblique use of a sledgehammer.

'And fucking Hugh. He's happy to sponge off us for as long as we'll tolerate him.'

I felt I had to make some sort of excuse for Hugh. 'He was saying the other day he'd like to help with the electricity. He's a kind of amateur sparks. But he's never been asked. He's trying to help out.'

'Trying…' Al made what I'd call a hollow laugh.

'Al, I don't know where I can get any money. Not right now. I'd have to go to Leeds or Halifax. I've forgotten my bank codes. Siobhan said she would put money into my account soon.'

'Oh just fucking shut up.'

'I can't help…'

'Look Mike I'm sorry but you're riling me big-time. I have to tell you all this before you even begin to apologise.'

'I thought it would embarrass Hugh to bring it up…'

'How pathetic you sound. You've been here for weeks and never offered anything. And if it's been difficult for you to do that, you've never mentioned it before now. Hugh's just a sponger. You know it, I know it. But I thought you might have been a bit more ashamed.'

I sat there absently pulling at the cord round my waist like some lost child.

'Mike you've always been useless, always.' Al was now beyond restraint. There was a furnace behind the eyes.

'So this pretence that I'm your friend who you trust with your secrets. It's all false. After all the things you confided in me.'

'You know… it was kind of a pretence. I'm not sentimental. I don't want to talk about *the old days*. I want to see change, a different world. And I'd hoped you'd change even in the past few weeks.'

'Well I have. I mean look at me!'

'Yeah. But up here Mike,' tapping his head. 'And then there's Siobhan and Madeleine…'

'Can't you lay off about Siobhan and me…'

'And Madeleine…'

'What do you…?'

'I think you know very well. You can't not have realised when you asked Siobhan to marry you. I mean come on Mike… she was pregnant and you always took precautions. I know that. She told me.'

I had casually wandered into this room a few minutes ago. I was unsuspecting, without purpose. I might never have been here at all. Now I was in some bleak empty space echoing with Al's voice—Al's words—reverberating from some distant place. But the words still reached me.

'She's my daughter. She's my blood. You must have known even if you said nothing. Siobhan would bring her to see me. I'd live for those weeks—just a few a year. But all along I've never said a word to Madeleine. Can you imagine what that's like? I wish I had now—rather than let her think that you—this pathetic specimen—that *you're* her dad. Look at yourself Mike. Aren't you ashamed?'

I was trying to form words, but my body was slowed, unresponsive. I lolled on the couch, as if I had been physically pounded for minutes on end, staggering, dopey.

'No I refuse to—you're lying to me Al. It's all some kind of trick. Why are you doing this? And Maddie. How can anyone tell her…?' My speech was rambling, slurred. Whole swathes of love for my daughter. As I woke every morning, my first thoughts were of her, part of me, coursing in my bloodstream. Now no longer and never my daughter. Someone else's. All these primeval emotions that can be rationalised as our DNA. Al was shifting my history into a parallel universe where a total revision of my life story was taking place.

My mind couldn't catch up. The new knowledge was haring away from me, but always just in sight. I was still in this fantasy, still the other side of a border where I was Maddie's father. I slowly got up and left. I would willingly have killed Al. I'd have liked to kill Al. I wished someone would kill Al.

Al visits my room

6th July 2019: 4pm

Hours later I was running over the years that would all need reframing, when there was a knock.

'Mike can I come in?' Al was hesitant, almost polite.

I stood at the door as if letting a guest into my room.

'I'm sorry mate. I know it was a shock. I've been stopping myself from saying this about Madeleine, and then it's burst out when I'm angry. This has been brewing up for weeks. Since I saw you, and then Siobhan again, I started to yearn for Madeleine. I thought I had got over never seeing her. But I clearly haven't. You see when she was old enough to choose, she said she didn't want to visit me anymore. It was that Monica who upset her. I never forgave that woman for her behaviour to Madeleine. But I didn't tell Monica about…

'Look Mike, I know you're really shaken and you may not believe it. It was underhand of me but I just waited for an opportunity to get definite proof. There were some strands of her hair on a brush in the bathroom. And I sealed them in plastic and sent the sample away. It came back with my DNA. And I did it again on another visit. I didn't even tell Siobhan. We never talked about her anyway. I have the test results here.'

I stared at the letter. It was some private clinic and it stated that as a result of tests that were all listed, Al's DNA was near nearly 50% present in the samples.

'Look Mike, surely you must have wondered why Siobhan kept on taking Madeleine up to Uncle Al? Well it was a cheap holiday by the coast, and you didn't have much money. But Siobhan felt an obligation to me. We hardly talked about it over the years to be honest. The only thing she said right at the beginning was *'Mike will be a better father than you, Al.'* You know how direct she can be.'

'Yeah—up until I knew all this.'

'And I agreed. She was absolutely right.'

'Anyway when she was in her teens I'd write to Madeleine but she didn't reply. And soon nothing from her for years. I mean she came up once with her daughter, and you said she'd been told to. I got my invite to her wedding and I wish I hadn't gone to that. To have to see what she was letting herself in for. That creep you smugly watched her marry. That father of the bride speech you made. So cliched and predictable and sentimental. All those fucking embarrassing reminiscences about when she was three, the traditional tired old slideshow of baby pictures. It should have been me making that speech, man. A proper farewell to a beautiful daughter. Not your little *Maddie*. This radiant woman who wished her life away while you stood by with your cheesy grin. All these years I've kept quiet!'

'I'm supposed to feel sorry for *you*? After what you've just said? Banging on about my failures as a father. Well I'm not her fucking father am I?'

'I don't expect you to *feel* anything. I just want to tell you what it's been like for me. You may not take it in now, but when you have calmed down, you might realise…'

'Al, I don't feel I'll ever… calm down as you put it. At the moment I hate you, I hate Siobhan, I hate a life that has been a complete delusion.' I spoke with a lifelessness that concealed a latent willingness to hurt if given the chance.

'My life bereft of my only child, or your life with a beautiful daughter who believes she's yours. I know what I'd prefer…'

I had sat in a dazed silence waiting for Al to leave. I suppose I had known for hours that it was true before seeing his official letter. And then quite suddenly he handed me the opportunity, that felt delicious in that moment, to quietly torture him.

'I don't know if you've noticed… but Edith and I are having problems at the moment.'

He sat down on the bed beside me. I tried to look surprised. I think I convinced him. I suppose that's when I realised I'd become quite practised in deceit. Not sure if I still am. I suppose he saw me as a pretty straight kind of a guy. But there was the pleasure of omniscience to be had at Al's expense, a nasty distasteful pleasure like pinning a live butterfly onto a board. I might feel guilty about it, but only later on.

'Oh?'

'Yeah she's gone back to her old room.'

'But you've only been married three weeks!'

'Yeah well…'

'What's gone so terribly wrong?'

'Not sure…'

'Let's get this straight. You don't know why your wife's left you?'

I was turning a knife. After all he'd told me that day, I was starting to feel good.

'Yeah… naaa… I think it was John's finger.'

I looked uncomprehending, shocked. Actually, I didn't

have to pretend. I was shocked Al could be this disinhibited. 'John's finger?'

'Yeah… I mean he didn't need it anymore…'

'But how did *you* need his finger… what have you done with John's finger?' I don't know how I was able to keep up this subterfuge. I was taken aback by Al's readiness to do so much—well you could hardly call it—*sharing.*

'I mean the state would have taken it…'

'I'm sorry?'

'His money… unless I'd been able to get at it.'

'Sorry Al… his finger?'

'I needed it to activate the phone.'

'But after he was dead…'

'Yeah I hacksawed it off. It's in the office still. Can't decide what to do with it.'

I didn't say anything. There was nothing to say. Al continued, 'I mean he had no family So who else would have his money except HMRC?'

'You seem pretty sure he had no family.'

'I mean, I told you I looked at his phone on the day we buried John—no family calls, texts, mails. If they're out there they didn't care much about him. Anyway, it didn't work. I took the thing out to the hut and pressed it against the phone but it didn't open again. Still there was a load of money in John's bag—I don't think he cared any more. He carried around—well it was mostly £50 notes—just over eight hundred of them—small change for him.'

By this time I was trying to look shocked in case I didn't.

'Yeah lucky—enough to use some of it to buy Buzzy off—and then Charlie got it back safely.'

'Al what is happening to you?'

'Dunno… It all hangs together for me…'

I just shook my head.

'Yeah well I'm still getting some money in. Their pensions are still being paid into the house account. I mean it's not enough. Might be able to get over this blip, get new people. I dunno. Need to think about it.'

He paused, pulling at his beard. 'But Mike I miss her. I don't know what's happened to me. Never felt like this. She—I don't think she knows—she has this loveliness, her own loveliness. I kind of didn't want her to realise. She's been hidden away for years. I loved the way she took the piss out of me when we were on our own. She'd imitate my voice—it was wicked. I didn't let on how much fun we were having. I can't believe I've lost her. I haven't felt like this before…' He was shaking his head. I was scared he might actually burst into tears, in my room.

'Al you know you haven't just lost her.'

'Yeah, well… I don't care about the others.'

'You're losing your mind… I mean it is kind of barbaric, cutting off John's finger?'

'You know I look at it in its glass jar and realise I am finally outside of laws, outside this society…'

'I've just watched you sliding, Al. Sneaking round concealing your smoking habit seemed serious a few weeks ago. It's nothing now.'

Al's eyes were glazing. Nothing I said was being let in. He waited maybe until there was no possibility I would say anything more. Then he stood. 'Anyway man, I'm starting to feel I'm getting past caring about anything. Maybe I'm finished here.' The door closed and the light slap of his sandals disappeared up the stairs.

Ultimatum

7th July 2019: Evening

The corridors were harbouring balls of dust by the doorways, the corners of the skirting. If a draft caught them, they swirled across the floor like swift eyeless rodents. I never knew whose job it was to sweep the floors, but they had abandoned the struggle. Even Rosamond only did it when she felt like it. I went to visit the latrine. It was now almost filled and becoming revolting. You had to bat off the flies. I'd pretty well given up cleaning the kitchen.it had become a Sisyphean task

Hugh stopped me as I came out my room.

'Can I have a word?' he almost whispered. 'Al wants us all in the kitchen.'

'Okay...'

'He's not speaking to anyone. Ignores me completely. He looks different... like he's had some horrible revelation. I mean he's looking like it's something he can't cope with. It's feeling pretty vile in there.'

There was a haze of crumbs on the kitchen table. A pile of unwashed dishes cluttered the Belfast sink. A large stoneware jug still dominated the middle of the table like a household god. But the lip had recently chipped.

Al sat astride a bench at the head of the table, brooding. His face appeared carved and immobile. He was staring fixedly at the plaster wall. Then he turned to the community.

'Someone is betraying us. Someone in this room.' His voice was curdled. There was a profound weariness behind each word. The community sat in silence.

Al's voice was sepulchral now, the words emerging as if from deep in the ground. He looked slowly round the table.

'Mendacity cannot be tolerated. If you know who has done this, I swear even if you are concealing them, you too will feel the consequences of their action.'

I felt I was the only one who appeared to know what mendacity meant. The very mystery of the word spread even more alarm. Avoiding each other's gaze, the community melted away. Hugh and I were left sitting opposite each other on the long benches.

'I don't feel comfortable here at all, Hugh.'

'It's Al isn't it? He's really become the genuine megalomaniac... he really is now.' Hugh began intoning, 'The horror, the horror...' He'd first heard the phrase in *Apocalypse Now* at the Rochdale Odeon.

'Well it is a bit like that...'

'Except this is on the Yorkshire Moors, not up the Mekong river.'

'Hugh, the words came from *Heart of Darkness*. It's set in Africa. I'm sorry to contradict you but...'

'No, no... Yes. I see It's not about Vietnam at all, that book.'

'It's a bit early for that...'

'But it is about some charismatic explorer who becomes a cupcake.'

'I am sure Conrad would agree with that succinct summary.'

'And it applies to Al.'

'Not so loud, Hugh.'

The bare stone flags and empty benches accentuated

our voices.

'Oh, I see… yes…But he is,' Hugh whispered.

'No, I suppose he always was.'

'He's worse now. You know, I felt quite scared just then. He can be quite frightening.'

Breakfast

8th July 2019: 7am

The previous evening had been close and humid. I woke to the odour of stale vegetables. It was coming from the sealed larder. There would be a fur like interlaced spiders webs forming, the pulpy beginnings of putrefaction rotting like bodies after weeks in the ground. When I came into the kitchen for the community breakfast, I heard a whirring from the sink. A mist of flies buzzed above piles of crusted plates. There was now a tower of crazily stacked bowls in the Belfast sink. Further towers of crockery stretched onto the draining board. The table was dotted with gobbets of candle wax. A film of bread crumbs from last night had not been swept.

Al was already in his chair. He didn't speak but stared grimly ahead. The room felt hungover and heavy. The community served themselves from the pots on the range without speaking. The only sounds were the scrape and tap of spoons on the echoing bowls. Nobody offered to fill a bowl for Al. There was an edgy politeness amidst an expectant silence. Helmut was immobile at the end of the bench in dungarees. I hadn't seen him in a dress for at least a week.

They were waiting for a vacuum to be filled. Nobody knew how, but there was the fizzing inevitability of an unpinned grenade in the room.

Edith quietly came in and sat near the range at the other end of the table from Al. Edith couldn't look at Al. Or anyone. She had told me weeks ago she always found it hard to speak in front of the community. And she had hardly spoken for weeks. She whispered now. It was as if everyone in the room could hear scissors cutting through silk.

'I took the letters Al.'

'Edi…'

She looked round the table and gradually raised her voice.

'I never felt comfortable with the idea—you know—of Al reading all our letters. But we agreed to this when we arrived. We didn't want the outside world interfering with our lives. He decided it was best for us not to see anything. We knew without wanting to ask too many questions He was seeing everything, all our correspondence, emails…I suppose that's what we agreed when we came to Gritstone. but maybe we didn't realise—maybe didn't want to think of the extent.' Edith's voice became stronger. She continued with a chilly precision. 'That included a letter from my sister who I had not seen since I was twelve. She wanted to meet me. And Al wrote back—in my name—and refused.'

Al attempted to speak patiently, 'She was only after your money, Edith. You asked for protection. Like you just said. You asked me to take decisions on your behalf—for you—to protect you from that world.'

'But she wrote back. And said she wasn't interested in money. And then she broke off contact. My sister Al!'

'Edith, you agreed that you wanted no contact with that world.'

'My sister, you bastard, and you kept the letters. They look so neat even the way the envelopes are cut open. So precise, so… sadistic.'

'I thought I might show you but there never was a right time.' Al's reply sounded so feeble in the silent room.

Edith spoke as if she was slowly pressing in a blade. 'There never would have been a time would there, Al? I think you can even fool yourself that you mean well. Maybe you can rationalise the whole thing to make yourself feel like that. But I'm starting to wonder if you like your dirty secrets. The power it gives you—gave you—over us.'

Round the table there were glances that grew into frank expressions, nodding heads. Rosamond sat stonily. It seemed the last illusions were evaporating. Sylvester shook his head giggling uncontrollably.

'Al, how much else have you concealed?' In the febrile atmosphere, Kate still sounded bewilderingly polite.

'This place was for you… for you people… Not for me.'

Edith spoke as if repressing a scream. 'But you can't stop yourself. You have to control everything… every part of our lives!'

'Edith, my love, I wanted to free you.' Al stood and held out his arms. but didn't come down the table.

Rosamond put her arms around Edith who was beginning to shake. I remembered a bird I once saw crash into a plate glass window and lie on the sill with tremors like a small breeze running through the feathers.

Rosamond tried to speak calmly. But there was still a haze of doubt in her voice. 'Al, surely there is nothing else?'

'No. I just did the accounts, closed down things…'

'But did you reply to people… to families?'

'There was the occasional anodyne text. I sometimes just sent an emoji.'

Edith looked up at the trembling monumental chin of Rosamond. 'No Rosamond, that wasn't all. There was a letter for you. It was six months old. Your husband wrote to you. He was dying and he wanted to see you for one last time.'

Rosamond removed her arm from Edith. She strode round the table and hissed into Al's face, 'You take things pretty literally.'

Al regarded her levelly, and slowly replied, word by remorseless word, 'You said you hated him. The marriage was a disaster from start to finish. How can you look at me like that? I did what you asked me to do. You aren't ready for this life if you can't accept that something like this would happen. You were expecting me to protect you from the world... *not the selected bits.*'

Esther's cool voice had an ironic edge, 'Well Al. I can't believe that was the sum of revelations we can expect. Why not tell us about all the other *little* ones?'

'*Mein Freund*, I think you had better tell us,' Helmut said.

Al seemed to fumble for words, for the right combination to turn this moment into a dream. 'This is not the time,' he murmured.

Rosamond hissed, 'When is the right time, Al? I think we need to look at this little office.'

'Yeah, show us your office, Al.'

'This is not the time...'

Al was hiding behind this mantra. This was a role he had never studied for. His charisma was draining out of him. His face sagged, his body sagged. He shuffled out the kitchen.

But once in his office things seemed to crystallise for

him pretty quickly. He probably felt he'd had enough of all these ungrateful creeps. He had reached for the phone…

Half an hour later we heard a car pulling to a halt on the gravel. Sharpe walked into the kitchen, to find the community waiting for him. His face was more drawn than usual, but with a strange forced smile. Al locked the door of his office and came in to join the solicitor. The two of them hardly looked at each other as Al spoke.

'I'm closing this community. There's nothing to hold me here anymore. I feel nothing for any of you now. I've lavished so much care on you, with little thanks at any time. Well you leeches, you can all fuck off and the sooner the better. Pack your belongings. You need to leave immediately. You have no rights. You are not tenants. You are effectively squatters and I want you to leave my house. Charles can show you in writing if you need to see it. Here are your individual letters of notice. I will be calling taxis and will pay for them to the railway station. You need to get your things together.'

Sharpe unzipped a slim brown leather brief case. There were envelopes with their surnames typed on each one.

'So, Al. This doesn't feel exactly spontaneous. It looks like those letters were there waiting!' Rosamond was laughing but it was brittle laughter like the thinnest of ice over a deep dark lake.

Sharpe spoke before Al could reply, 'I just printed off the form of words. It is quite standard.'

Rosamond stared up Sharpe's trembling pointed-up nose, 'As if I'd be so interested in your—fucking—form—of—words…' and hissed, 'Charlee.'

Then she turned to Al. 'I want my money, Al. I've put money into this place…' she was shouting into his face, 'We all have!'

Sylvester spoke in his usual drawl. 'Al we're not leaving just like that. I don't think that your slimy friend's letters are worth the paper they're printed on. I'm not even going to open mine. We want our share of this place. That's going to need some work. The community's finished. We all accept that, man. But we need our share. And that's going to take time to sort out.'

Al seemed to have regained some of his poise while he sat in the office waiting for Sharpe. He may even have been concocting words for Sylvester, someone he had clearly been waiting to skewer.

'No, no Sylvie. This was *my* vision and you bought into it. We're not suddenly business partners… just because it suits *you* now. You've shown precious little interest in how this place is run. Quite happy to just forget everything including two kids who don't know where their dad is—and are waiting for the money he promised. Well now's your chance to make amends. Their daddy's coming home. I mean they're kind of fortunate I did send them some money as it seemed their pathetic father was ready to forget them… Anyway, anything to keep your family from coming after you. They might still believe you're a nice man because of my… duplicity… Sylvie.'

'You know I hate it when you call me that.' Sylvester made to hit Al but Helmut tightly gripped his wrists until he winced.

Now Al was like a hound with its jaws in the neck of a fox. 'No come on Sylvie. Just tell me what I've done that's so wrong. There's not a single noble thought in your head, you unpleasant little hypocrite.'

Helmut let go and Sylvester gurned away, ineffectually, mumbling as his dirty linen was exposed to the community.

I had the distinct impression Al believed he had silenced them after his confrontation with Sylvester. But Edith voice pierced into the vacuum.

'So you're evicting your wife?'

It crossed my mind for a second he legally couldn't but the room was now dangerously volatile and that thought plummeted away.

Al paused. His reply was hesitant. 'No… do you want to stay with me, Edith?'

'And watch all these people leave with nowhere to go. No, I'll stick with them. I got to know you in that office of yours, listening to you creeping around like some frightened animal. I actually started to feel sorry for you in there. You seemed so alone. But look at you. Look at how far you're ready to go. Go on, tell them how you cut off John's finger. Can you get even lower?'

'There is no simple explanation for what you've just revealed.'

Sardonic laughter erupted round the table. Sylvester's high-pitched giggle was now like an axle spinning out of control.

'I'm not going into that now.' But the laughter hit the edge of hysteria. 'Really Edith. So this is what *you've* become. I felt such pity for you. I wanted to give you a life you'd never remotely touched. But now—you ungrateful bitch.'

Edith rushed at Al. She was screaming, inches from his

face. Al's eyes were possessed. His clenched fist landed on the left side of her mouth. Edith's face crashed back against the table and she slid onto the floor. The room swallowed a collective breath. Edith's hands gripped the table edge and then her head emerged. She was gaping in groggy disbelief, her mouth sagging open. One side of her face was a raw glistening welt. I found I was crying.

There were glances and nods from the other women. Rosamond, took up the handle of the cast -iron saucepan. Kate lifted a thick aluminium stockpot with both hands. Stephanie and Esther took the largest of the copper-bottomed pans down from their hooks.

They surrounded Al. He was puzzled and uncomprehending, trying to mouth phrases that wouldn't surface.

Rosamond spat the words into his face, 'We'll see if I lack capacity.' She leant back and aimed a blow at his stomach. She continued to batter him, the pan pounding in and out with the motion of a piston. Al stood there teetering. His eyes glazed over. Then he buckled like an imploding factory chimney. A trickle of blood dripped from the side of his mouth as he disappeared beneath the women standing over him. A grey-faced Sharpe slowly edged backwards out of the kitchen, and then raced through the hall.

The thick kitchen pans were crashing in on Al. I heard him moaning, 'What have I done to you… What have I done to you?' Then there were only indistinct gurgling noises. These stopped and a persistent dull thudding echoed against the kitchen walls as the pots began landing on Al's head. Then the rest of the community surrounded Al, a baying mass. They howled at Al's body. Some kicked it fiercely and then kicked it again. Al couldn't surely still be alive. Then they slowly drew back.

Edith didn't seem able to take her eyes off her husband of four weeks—his head crushed, stretched. The memory came back to me of the museum in Dublin; the flattened leathery faces of bodies found in the peat bogs, the fingernails perfect, the faces wrung out and wrenched, executed for a forgotten crime, sacrificed by the tribe.

One of Al's legs jerked, trembled once, and then was still. After a few minutes, a weeping Helmut laid an Indian blanket over Al's sprawled corpse. One sandalled foot jutted out from the edge of the cover.

The community collapsed onto the benches, faces spent and drained. Nobody spoke.

I remembered Sharpe. I had to transcend the paralysis around me and waylay him before he drove away. Sharpe was trying to start his little car. His quivering fingers couldn't force the key into the ignition. With his other hand he was attempting to guide a burning cigarette into a mouth mumbling and trembling.

'I've never seen anyone killed…'

'Well Charlie, who knows who you've caused to be killed…'

'Nobody… nobody… I swear!'

I leant into the open window and hissed, 'Buzzeee.'

Sharpe dumbly rotated his head from side to side.

'Listen Charles. I want you to pay attention to me. Listen to me. Stop all this…' Sharpe threw the cigarette away. His body became rigid and tense, but his eyes manically swivelled from side to side.

'I will only say this once. If you breathe one word of

what you've just seen, you know you are finished. Your cute little car, your picture-book cottage on the edge of the village, your cats you love so much—all of that can disappear ever so easily. There's enough in Al's room to have you inside a prison for years. And even if the bench is lenient to a fallen colleague, you'll be finished as if you had never been. You'll end up sleeping in a box in some doorway in Leeds.'

Sharpe could barely respond now.

'We'll be gone in a few days. Then you'll find an empty house. You can do what you like with whatever we leave, but if anyone is taken up by the police on your evidence, I will have kept enough to see you go down. And I will love that Charles. Every moment of it. I don't think I'd mind going to prison myself to see you inside some scuzzy cell smelling someone else's shit all day.'

Sharpe's breath exhaled hot and vile. His body had the dark odour of muck sweat, with a faecal undertow that the fragrance he must have sprayed with such abandon only this morning, could not conceal. That moment must have seemed years ago when the canister hissed and the minuscule droplets landed on his bare unwashed skin, standing in his bathroom with the sun gently caressing the tiles.

I quietly walked away and left him murmuring something like a prayer to himself. When I looked out later the car had gone.

Aftermath

I looked round the table from the Jacobean chair that had always been Al's seat. The community sat in unfathomable silence, faces immobile and waxen, posing for some warped version of *The Last Supper*. The blood was still hardening on their robes. Rosamond wore the vestments of a priestess after a morning of sacrifices. Hugh sat mutely next to her. His friend's blood was splashed across his face and dungarees as if flicked randomly from a paintbrush. He had become part of the crowd that finally kicked Al to death. They'd all woken believing they were well-meaning people. Now they were murderers.

Two months ago I had arrived dishevelled and unshaven in a shabby corduroy jacket. Now my straggly beard flowed outwards and I wore a white robe—apart from Helmut, the only one in the room with no blood on their clothes. I spoke. The words emerged with a gravity I could never locate when I addressed the indolent audiences in the lecture theatre.

'Tomorrow we'll find it hard to believe we ever did this. The decent people we thought we were before today—we could have simply had Al arrested for what he did to Edith—and that alone. He turned into a monster in front of our eyes.'

They still stared vacantly at the table.

'Except you were accomplices to all of this. The fraud, his impersonation of all of you. And Al pretty well revealed everything to me. I was his unwilling confessor.

But I did nothing, I told no one. And I had my own—well—my own grubby personal reasons for not wanting to step in at that last moment. An outsider would say what happened here today was just an extension of what had already gone before—those burials—Al killing Asif—Buzzy… You all knew he had killed these people. None of us discussed anything then…'

'Hey hang on man,' shouted Cyrus, 'that guy Asif was in pain.'

'And Cyrus, what exactly did *you* do to help him? You, all of you, might as well have sat on that pillow with Al… or whatever he did *to shut Asif up*.'

'Hell you don't know shit. You weren't even here.'

'Look around at your friends, Cyrus. I don't see a crowd of people leaping to your defence… let alone their own defence…' Cyrus went sulky and nobody else spoke.

'Any ideas you had left about being reasonable civilised people might as well be consigned to the dustbin now. Look at you all. You're covered in Al's blood. You're going to have to conceal this murder, like everything else that went on here. You colluded in all those other things Al did. Now you're all murderers as well…

'Al didn't found this community out of malice or evil. I think he wanted to make amends for his past. I really believe it was his intention to share his life with people who would understand and appreciate what he had to give. It all went wrong. I think by the end he was disillusioned—he was sick of everyone. The whole project had lost its purpose—or the purpose itself was gradually forgotten. Perpetuation just took on its own momentum. And he slid back into a squalor he thought he'd left behind. You'll have to decide if it was doomed from the start. When it comes to a dictatorship, you always feel it could only end like this, with the dictator savaged and blood-soaked, killed by the people who idolised him, who were too scared to cross him. You can see it on film, as they brandish their weapons, now all self-righteous and triumphant after they've dragged the gaping victim out of the sewer—the man they used to fawn over.'

Helmut began speaking with disbelief in his voice. 'Al was my friend—*mein Freund*—but I felt he no longer cared about me. He takes me for granted. I was angry with him. I did not stop him being killed. I could have stopped it. But he was ready to eject us, forget about us. I have killed him by watching—*ich kann es nicht glauben…*'

Rosamond spoke in empty tones. 'This morning I didn't wake up a killer but I am now—never expected that. You know I loved him. I adored Al. Then something died. It had died before today—and I end up like this possessed fury.'

The silence lengthened. Hugh's voice emerged from a deep dark place. People round the table couldn't believe it was him speaking. 'Al would have wanted to be buried here. It is the only thing left that we can do for him.'

And Edith walked over and raised the blanket from Al's feet and slowly took it up until she was looking at his caved-in head. One side of her face was swollen, the other soaked with tears. They placed a thin blanket under the head. Colin had found the gauze Al used to wrap John, only two weeks ago. They had to lift the face and wind it round several times. They were now in another world where they habituated themselves to soggy grey matter and slivers of red seeping from the back of Al's cranium. But once the head was covered it felt easier to wrap the body.

Edith continued to work with them until Al was a mummified shape. They wrapped layers around the head until the seepage was contained in the bandage. My mind wandered momentarily to the anonymous metal figures immersed in the sea at Morecambe. Al was now the shape of any man; a bandaged husk.

Helmut had left the house a few minutes ago. We could see him at the hill brow digging feverishly, the earth flying up onto a pile at one side of a gaping hole.

Twenty minutes later the community formed a cortege. Edith held a small bunch of dried flowers she kept from her wedding, and walked ahead of the body as they took the short winding path up to the grove where Helmut was quietly choking behind a tree.

Esther didn't sing and nobody asked her to. The burial was in virtual silence. Edith threw in the dry bouquet. I murmured to myself, 'Cut is the bough that might have grown full straight.' The thick clods landed on the white bandaged form. It looked so much more transgressive than the earth echoing hollowly on a coffin lid. The community straggled back down to the house in silence. Only the river could be heard roaring in the ravine and the small metal figures tinkled lightly in the breeze.

After we had returned, there were other tasks ahead. 'People we need to break open that room and strip it of everything that links us to Gritstone. Papers, devices, everything. Take what is yours and disappear. The bailiffs will come for Al. In time Sharpe will have some difficult questions to deal with. That may be weeks but we need to be well away from here.'

Helmut's axe splintered the frame and the door lock. But after that violence we entered tentatively.

The alarm howled and Helmut tore the entire box and wires from the wall. I was the only one apart from Edith to have ever entered the room before. They quickly realised it was as prosaic as any workplace. The room still seemed occupied, a functioning office. Al had just left, expecting to return to his everyday domestic surroundings—after evicting us. The PC and other screens were still on, waiting for him. The air was fuggy with a dense electric heat.

There was something that looked like a small television. On the screen they could see the empty kitchen with a stain on the floor by the range, where the kettle lids still rattled. They worked out where the camera was hidden—behind a carving of the river god that looked down from the wall.

Edith opened the desk and took out the phones, the tablets and the laptops.

She distributed them calling out the names on the neatly written post-it notes. Then she gave each a bundle of letters with their names. But this exercise quickly descended into chaos as they began reading and then passing them onto each other. There were deaths, divorces and unpaid fines. There were many letters replying to Al's impersonations from families, solicitors, ex-lovers. I could only watch as this imploded community slowly realised that they could not return to their former lives. They had no homes to return to, no money to rebuild a life back in the past.

Some were enraged. Kate was hysterically weeping after discovering her mother was dead. Esther found the invitation to her son's wedding. But Sylvester said, 'What did you think was happening here, man? You gave Al your permission to protect you from the outside world and then you complain. I heard what he said to Rosamond. *You asked me to manage this and now I've done it you get angry.* Come on. You knew what was written on the tin when you came here.'

Rosamond began shouting at Sylvester that Al was inhuman and sadistic. How could anyone not tell her that her husband was dying? 'I think he enjoyed sending those letters. He really got some twisted thrill.'

Sylvester forced the catch and pushed open the windows. 'But Rosamond, baby, maybe he didn't enjoy it. Perhaps he just got sucked in.' Then he looked at her with an expression that could freeze. 'You're shovelling all your guilt onto him. You knew you were leaving your beloved husband forever. You can't pretend to me even if you want to pretend to yourself—and Hughie boy here.'

Rosamond was choking with sobs. Hugh drew her into his arms and murmured to Sylvester, 'Nothing is simple…'

'Very gallant, Hughie boy. No, nothing ain't simple. Especially for hypocrites…'

I had to intervene. 'Sylvester, if you're starting to feel bad about what has happened…'

'I do feel bad man. But it's too late and we were all there.'

'I'm starting to think that it all got to him…' I said and told them about Al's secret smoking habit, which now seemed trivial but felt like the just the first fissure appearing in Al's façade.

'More secrets from Al!' Rosamond screamed at

Sylvester.

'What did he say to you about the smoking, Mike?' Esther vacantly asked. Meanwhile Hugh was cooing into Rosamond's ear. It looked insipid. It was insipid, but Hugh was inhabiting some kind of transfigured world.

'He said he needed something—that the strain was too great—but if I revealed it to you, that was the end of the community. That you had burnt your bridges. Many of you have nothing to go back to.'

'Well that's true enough.' Kate didn't so much speak as intone, staring blankly at the picture on the screen of an empty kitchen with the copper-bottomed pans strewn across the floor.

I thought we should leave the office. The letters would have to wait. They were draining momentum. I asked them to come in the kitchen for a final meeting.

'We need to be clear that there is a compact between everyone in this room. We will not reveal what has happened here and not just in the past few days but the whole story, the burials, the drugs... I don't think you should even talk among yourselves or when you leave here, to anyone you're intimate with, however much you may feel you can trust them.'

'I can assure you that if I hear you have spoken to the *Polizei* you will regret it,' Helmut said solemnly.

'Well you heard him.' I looked slowly round the table. 'But it's a heavy responsibility we are bound into now. I want to hear you all commit yourselves.'

And they went around the table making monosyllabic noises of agreement. Esther began saying 'I never like to be committed... to anything,' Helmut's stick began to tap the floor. Sylvester hissed 'Stop fucking dithering.'

Esther mutely nodded.

I urged the community to think of changing their appearance. As an example, I asked Alex for a haircut. I'd previously had my hair trimmed by him once it began to curl, but I had not interfered with the length. Now I went for as near to a buzz cut as was possible with scissors. I kept the beard but trimmed it close to the skin. I began to assume a new existence, walking around in my freshly cleaned chinos. Some people didn't recognise me at all until I opened my mouth.

Helmut found a community in the Highlands and messaged them on his restored laptop. They wanted a strong person for drystone walling. He also found emails from the Bavarian State police confirming they had concluded any possible investigations into his parents' death. Al had written to them in Helmut's persona a few weeks ago, thanking them in a short email written in passable German. Perhaps Al had valued Helmut more than anyone suspected, and as a result didn't want him to feel he could leave.

But Helmut disappeared before the others. A lorry turned up from Scotland and took him and the goats. Hercules the cat went with him in a carrying box. Others decided to set up together. There were houses going for virtually nothing in the North East. It turned out Esther had a secret account she had just left alone while she was in the community. She bought a place for £40,000 in cash. It would be in a dour part of Sunderland. She invited five of them to share with her. It was a gritty and cramped return to the world they had come here to avoid. But maybe they have brought something to that community.

Sylvester had overcome his qualms and was excited. '2020s going to be my year man. I'm gonna travel the globe. It's gonna be great... been in one place too long man.'

Hugh and Rosamond left a note.

Dear Mike,

Sorry we can't wait. Rosamond and I are going to stay in my boat. We'll help each other forget everything.

Hugh

Hugh had sold the car for scrap and they went back on the train.

Napoli

26th October 2019

So now I'm lying here on a lounger by this café, waiting for a last beer. I left Edith at the hotel and came out in a cab. The sun is still warming the sand. There is none of the underlying chill of an Indian summer in England. The driver will collect me in another hour.

We didn't have much of a plan when we left Gritstone. We needed a place where we could disappear. Edith's passport was still in her single name but we needed a new identity for her, the person most likely to be pursued about her husband's disappearance.

I suppose that's why we chose to come here. Naples seemed a place to live outside the law. When you walk the streets where the Camorra quietly run most of the city, you will pass by people for whom violence is a commodity as much as the euro. The mark of Cain is among them, and we share it with these men who have killed.

We moved into a cheap hotel in the narrow streets near the port where the smell of shallow drains drifted up to our balcony. For the first nights I woke at 4am with a recurring dream. Al's face pounded and flattened, the women landing the pans on Al's head in a mimed performance. The blows were silent, as if a sound mixer edited them out, so that beneath that layer of metallic echo, I could clearly hear the soft crunching of the imploding skull, and a subterranean moan. I tried not to wake Edith, but lay in the dark, knowing the dream would return.

We have enjoyed our time together, but a different Edith has slowly emerged. She wears jeans and plain t-shirts without logos, and seems to have transcended the past she left behind in that town in the midlands. She walks with a new confidence in a city that now seems her home. She also found a clinic to replace her teeth on the outskirts of Napoli. She smiles easily at everyone as we sip expressos standing in the small packed bars with the locals.

We often visit Caravaggio's picture, *The Seven Acts of Mercy,* above the altar in a small church near the hotel. Edith looks in rapt silence at the people performing these acts of charity in brooding semi-darkness. There is something furtive in their actions. Something that makes the acts murky—with no clear-cut motives.

And one evening she talked about Al for the first time since we'd left Yorkshire.

We were in a café in a narrow alley by the port. The air was thick, a windless heat, becoming heavy with exhaust fumes when a few scooters tore through. Edith told me she'd been thinking more and more about Al. She couldn't face the killing. She couldn't really remember it; as if it had been edited out. 'The brain can only take so much.' But she did try to rationalise it. 'Those last moments at the end of his life. I suppose if I can live through those few minutes, I can live through most things. Most ends are nasty even when people die *peacefully…*'

I thought that, yes, before those last murky weeks, there had been a huge canvas Al had filled for years, with ambitious schemes, sagas of power, wealth and desire. But Edith was the only person he'd actually asked to marry him.

And she couldn't unpick it. 'Mike I'd feel this shudder —this inner detonation when I knew he desired me. I mean I feel I can tell you this. And we used to laugh a lot on our own. I mean—he told me he had hoped to meet someone new through the community, someone he wouldn't meet any other way. He was surrounded by all these rich privileged types, doors automatically opening for him—it didn't feel like a real life. I know he hid things from me. I suppose he saw me as no different from anyone else in that way. I'm not sure if he felt it was natural to keep his secrets—even that he felt it was for my good— like he knew best.'

'Like how he never spoke about Maddie, I suppose.'

'Well exactly. Like how he contained the explosive knowledge about Maddie. How could he have kept that inside for so long? Only if you're so used to concealment, kind of pathological.'

'Still it was really for Siobhan to tell me—and to tell Maddie—and she never did. Well now Maddie needn't know at all.'

'So if you ever see her again, you'd carry on pretending you're her dad? Doesn't that start to feel odd? Won't that be as devious as Al?'

Edith made me feel uneasy, because I honestly couldn't imagine being able to tell the truth—to the person who used to be my daughter.

'The truth would hurt Maddie.'

'You sound just like Al—how the hell do you know?'

'I'd have to tell her that everyone killed him.'

'That's two different issues, Mike. She needn't know that he was killed. But if she had a blood test she'd find out you're not her dad. Bet she'd be thrilled with Siobhan and you then.'

'We're both going to have to get used to that kind of life now. Deception, lying, economy with the truth. Everyone who was at Gritstone has to.'

'But when it comes to Maddie, you're not hiding from a decision you *might* make, you're hiding from an obligation to her and her kids. You'd better think it through rather than all these—I'm sorry Mike—but these are mealy-mouthed excuses you're coming up with.'

One afternoon on Capri, she was tanned and smiling in a yellow summer dress. Her hair flowed down straight and long with a fine wispiness. The lines on her face were softened. She'd taken to wearing a pair of spherical glasses I'd seen Janis Joplin wearing. She got them on the NHS in the sixties, and now she'd had the lenses changed. She had brought the frames with her when she came to Gritstone, but never left the house to find an optician.

That evening we stayed on the island. We were sitting at a terrace bar, looking across to Amalfi, when Edith spoke to me with a loving gravity.

'Mike, darling, we're old enough to know this thing can end. I just want you to know that I care for you. Wherever you are, if you're in trouble, or you've got a plan I can help with, I'll come to you. Even if that's trying to get Siobhan back.' And Edith had struck a rich multi-noted chord on an instrument inside me and it echoed through me.

Edith believes she has a completely new existence in front of her and I can't begrudge that future. Like her I have embraced the chance of new life. We've agreed to part. But her words tore off the bandage over a still open wound. I'll always feel bereft of Siobhan. I sometimes finger the phone Edith handed me on her wedding day. Someone is paying the monthly rental. and it must be Siobhan. But to even phone her is dangerous. We don't know who may be pursuing us. I can't phone yet…

I lie back on the lounger. The temperature slowly falls. The golden sun disappears into the Mediterranean.

The first man would have wondered if it could ever return.

It's getting late. The cab will soon be back.

Acknowledgments

First, real gratitude to Jan Fortune, Rowan Fortune and Adam Craig at Cinnamon for choosing to publish *Gritstone* and making it happen so quickly.

To members of the Curtis Brown *Edit and Pitch* course who gave such a morale—boost to me and my then unfinished book. But also for the advice to dive under the metaphorical bonnet and get the story to Gritstone House asap. Two other members of that course are being published - something of a record.

To Alice Speirs who as a trusted reader commented on the whole book as a work in progress, giving invaluable week by week feedback. Alice has also helped me with medical advice in the quest for fact-based *grand guignol* for two incidents in the book—I'm profoundly grateful. Any errors are my own…

To the excellent Writing Room who put me in contact with Alison Chandler. Alison's deep-dive critique refocussed the writing, transformed the narrative voice and led me into the final full rewrite. I feel *Gritstone* ended a much stronger book through Alison's involvement.

Which brings me to a cat's cradle of coincidence. I discovered that one of the novelists Alison mentors is Mish Cromer. Mish was the first writer who I showed my work to, and her encouragement and advice was a real shot in the arm to my confidence at that time. When Mish subsequently had two novels published by *Leaf by Leaf*, I felt that this might be a safe and trustworthy home for my own book.

Finally to Cathy who always gave me the emotional support to continue with the solitary task of writing a novel. I'm relieved she likes it.

Milton Keynes UK
Ingram Content Group UK Ltd.
UKHW012329260624
444761UK00004B/51

9 781788 648905